Dying to Read

A Novel

Lorena McCourtney

Revell

a division of Baker Publishing Group
Grand Rapids, Michigan

MYS
F
mcc

© 2012 by Lorena McCourtney

Published by Revell
a division of Baker Publishing Group
P.O. Box 6287, Grand Rapids, MI 49516-6287
www.revellbooks.com

Printed in the United States of America

Library of Congress Cataloging-in-Publication Data
McCourtney, Lorena.
    Dying to read : a novel / Lorena McCourtney.
        p.   cm. — (The Cate Kinkaid files ; bk. 1)
    ISBN 978-0-8007-2158-9 (pbk.)
    1. Women private investigators—Fiction. I. Title.
PS3563.C3449D95 2012
813′.54—dc23   2012009174

12   13   14   15   16   17   18   7   6   5   4   3   2   1

1

Cate glanced at the identification card her Uncle Joe had printed out just before she left his office. Cate Kinkaid, Assistant Private Investigator. Complete with the photo he'd snapped, which showed a spike of red hair growing out of her left ear, and the address and phone number of Belmont Investigations.

An identification card that made her—what? An overage Nancy Drew? An underage Jessica Fletcher? A clueless Stephanie Plum?

Whatever, she was getting desperate, and the job was only temporary, not a lifetime commitment. She was, as Uncle Joe had put it, just dipping her toe into the world of private investigation. Just until one of the many résumés she had floating around brought results. All she had to do today was check on a woman named Willow Bishop living at an address on Meisman Street here in Eugene, Oregon, and then write up a brief report for the files.

Although Cate hadn't expected the house to look as if it had jumped off the cover of some old Gothic novel. She parked at the bottom of the steep driveway and stared up at the unlikely old place sitting on an oversized parcel among a subdivision of modest homes. Not dilapidated, but weathered and brooding, with oddly shaped windows tucked into unlikely nooks and several upper windows painted over. A witch, or maybe a vampire or vulture, wouldn't look out of place peeking over the peaked roof of a corner turret.

No witches, vampires, or vultures lurking today, Cate decided as she walked up the driveway. Not unless they'd taken to using Lincolns or Buicks as transportation. A handful of older women milled around the front porch. One woman was punching the doorbell with open-up-or-else ferocity. Another had her hands pressed to the sides of her face as she peered in a window.

A plump blonde woman in pink spotted Cate and immediately charged out to meet her. "Willow, thank goodness you're here! We've been waiting twenty minutes and—" She stopped and peered at Cate with disapproval. "Oh, you're not Willow, are you?"

"Actually, I'm looking for Willow myself. Willow Bishop?"

"I don't know that I've ever heard her last name. Are you her sister?"

"Does she have a sister?"

"I don't know. You look like a sister."

Cate had realized the description Uncle Joe had given her for Willow Bishop, age 26, 5'4", 120 pounds, red hair, blue eyes, came close to fitting Cate too, but apparently the similarity was even closer than the numbers suggested. Although she was nearer the dreaded 30 than 26.

"No, I'm no relation. It's a business matter." Uncle Joe had emphasized that the work Belmont Investigations did was strictly confidential. "And you are?"

"Fiona Maxwell."

Another woman, tall and gaunt and clothed in more purple

than Cate had ever seen on one person, said, "We're the Whodunit Book Club. We read a mystery and meet every other week to discuss it. Today we're meeting here at Amelia's house."

"She's our club president this year," a short woman with a squeaky voice added.

"Someone named Amelia, not Willow, lives here?" Cate asked.

"Willow lives here, but she works for Amelia," Fiona said. "We're supposed to have lunch here at 12:00, and it's already—"

Purple Woman filled in a time. "Almost 12:15." The broad brim of her purple hat flopped with indignation as she spoke.

"Amelia can be so *rude*. Making us wait out here like this." This woman, in a long, suede skirt, cowboy boots, and spur earrings, waved the book in her hand. "And insisting we read *Wuthering Heights* was ridiculous. It's no whodunit."

"It wasn't any worse than that awful spy thing you suggested last month, Texie," Fiona snapped.

"At least I had lunch on time," Texie snapped back.

Cate decided a prudent retreat was advisable before she found herself in the cross fire of a book war. Cowgirl-garbed Texie, more toned and tanned than the other women, looked as if she could be a tough adversary. Maybe she had a six-shooter tucked away in that outfit.

"Could Amelia be ill, and that's why she isn't answering the door?" Cate asked.

The women exchanged glances. What seemed a logical thought to Cate apparently hadn't occurred to them.

"I suppose it's possible," the woman in purple said, although the agreement sounded reluctant. "She's never sick, but she's always complaining about her fluttering heartbeat."

"It's her eyelashes that flutter. Whenever any good-looking male comes within flutter distance. And it doesn't matter who the male belongs to." Texie planted her fists on her hips. The venom in her voice suggested personal experience.

What Cate couldn't figure out was why this group bothered to meet, given the hostility billowing around them. Not her concern, however. She turned to go. She could come back tomorrow. It did seem odd, however, that neither Amelia nor Willow was around to feed what was apparently an expected horde of hungry mystery readers.

"Is there someone you could call who would have a key so you could go in and see if everything's okay?" Cate asked.

"Actually," Fiona said slowly, with a wary glance at the others, "I have a key. I didn't want to mention it because when Amelia gave it to me she said not to let anyone else know I had it."

"But she gave me one and said the same thing!" Purple Woman dug in an oversized purple purse and whipped out a key on a metal ring.

Almost instantly, five identical keys on five identical metal rings dangled from five not-so-identical fingers. Purple nails on the gaunt woman. Short, bitten-to-the-quick nails on Texie. Elegant, silvery-pink on another woman who now said, "Well, isn't that just like Amelia?"

"Why is that like Amelia?" Cate asked.

Texie took a step forward to answer. "Because she's under-handed and sneaky, that's why." Texie sounded triumphant, as if this were something she'd wanted to proclaim for a long time.

Purple Woman tilted her head thoughtfully. "It's a psychological thing. A power play. She wants to make you feel special, so you'll be indebted to her."

"I was in a garden club that broke up because of one awful woman," Texie said. "So then we got together and reorganized without her." She glanced around as if looking for support for a reorganization.

"Amelia'd find out," Fiona said, her uneasy tone suggesting the consequences could be dire.

In spite of the dangling keys, the women didn't seem inclined to make use of them. When Cate suggested someone unlock the door, a discussion followed, the consensus being that Amelia would be outraged if she unexpectedly found them all inside her house.

Cate impatiently grabbed a key. "Tell her to blame me then." She marched up the front steps and stuck the key in the lock.

With the door open, the Whodunit ladies swarmed inside. They headed for the dining room, apparently hoping lunch would materialize there, but Cate took a moment to glance around the living room.

Unlike the Gothic-gloom exterior of the old house, the interior held sleek, Danish modern furniture, an oversized flat-panel TV, and recessed lighting. Bookcases winged out on either side of a white marble fireplace. A curtain of wooden beads hung over the entrance to the turret room. A curved staircase, more Southern plantation than Gothic, swept to the second floor. A flamboyant painting of three green eyes immersed in what looked like a cauldron of boiling beans hung over the fireplace. Cate wasn't knowledgeable enough about art to identify what style the painting represented, but this was definitely a house with a split personality.

"The table isn't even set for lunch!" the squeaky-voiced person squeaked from the dining room.

Another voice suggested they move the meeting to a nice tearoom near the university.

"But it's Amelia's turn to provide lunch! She shouldn't get to just wiggle out of it. Sometimes she can be so cheap," Fiona said. "Remember that time she said she was serving lobster, but it turned out to be that imitation kind?"

"She's not cheap when she's buying shoes. Have you ever priced those Jimmy Choos she likes?"

"Hey, wait." This voice came from farther back in the kitchen. "This is odd."

Everything about the split-personality house, the missing Amelia and Willow, and the squabbling Whodunit ladies struck Cate as odd. But she was curious about what one of them might consider odd. She cut through the dark cave of the dining room, where heavy drapes closed off view of the backyard. The woman in purple stood at an open door on the far side of the kitchen. Cate stepped up beside her to peer inside.

The room was scantily furnished with a single bed, a night-stand with a lamp lying on its side, a mirrored dresser, and a swivel rocker. An open door led to an adjoining bathroom. Candy wrappers, dust balls, lint, and paper clips trailed across the floor. One white sock lay in the doorway. All suggested the room had just been hastily vacated.

"Willow's room?" Cate guessed.

From behind her, Texie said, "She must have had enough of Amelia."

"Not the first employee to walk out on her," Fiona said. "But Amelia might have fired her. You know how worked up she can get over some little thing."

"I don't suppose anyone would know where Willow may have gone?" Cate asked.

Negative murmurs from the group now clustered behind Cate in the doorway.

"How about where she came from, or where she has family?"
More negative murmurs.

A real private investigator would no doubt know what further questions to ask or what to do next to obtain information for the great-uncle client in Texas, but Cate didn't. She'd have to ask Uncle Joe if he had more ideas.

But at the door between kitchen and dining room, she reluctantly paused. She tried to reject the unwanted feeling that had suddenly kicked in, but it wouldn't retreat. Something did not feel right here. Something felt, in fact, very *wrong*. Then she scoffed at herself. When had her intuition ever been of any great value? Not in the job market. Not in her relationships with men. Not even when she'd chosen Hair Delights for a haircut last week. She fingered that odd spike sticking out behind her ear.

Had something changed now that she was a fledgling private investigator? She'd heard about people connecting with their "inner child." Had she connected with her inner PI? Because something definitely felt off. And a spider of apprehension skittered up her spine.

"Maybe we should look around upstairs," she suggested reluctantly. "Make sure everything's okay."

Fiona shook her head. "Amelia wouldn't like it."

Behind her, one of the women opened the refrigerator door. "Hey, there's food in here. Look at this! Salad and sandwiches . . . and cream puffs!"

Like a flock of hungry birds, all but the tall woman in purple descended on the refrigerator. She stepped toward Cate. "I'll go with you." She stuck out a hand, as bony as the rest of her. "I'm Doris McClelland."

Cate shook the gaunt hand. "Cate Kinkaid."

They crossed the living room and climbed the stairs. A fat

white cat sitting on the top step regarded them with regal blue eyes.

"That's Octavia. I think the name's from *Antony and Cleopatra*." Doris waved a hand back toward the bookshelves. "Amelia has all these literary pretensions."

The cat jumped up and scampered down the hallway with surprising agility, considering her weight, and disappeared through an open door.

"Would that be Amelia's room?" Cate asked.

"I don't know. I've never been up here." The woman tapped the carpet with a long, narrow purple pump, and Cate suspected she had come upstairs more out of curiosity than helpfulness. "I could buy a new car with what Amelia spent carpeting this house."

They walked down the hallway and peered into the bedroom together. A pale peach chiffon canopy draped the king-sized bed, beside it an identical canopy in miniature over a cat bed. An array of bottles with prescription labels surrounded a crystal lamp on a nightstand. A mirrored dressing table held an assortment of cosmetics and lotions. Octavia jumped on the unmade bed and kneaded a satin pillow. She stared at Cate and Doris as if challenging them to object. An oil portrait hung on one wall, a regal-looking woman with jet black hair and a red ballroom gown.

"Amelia?"

"They must have used a stand-in for the body. Amelia's never had that kind of figure. At least not since I've known her." Doris patted her own chest. "Oh my. I'm cattier than Octavia today, aren't I?"

A walk-in closet had been built into a corner so that it extended out into the room. Cate opened the door. Amelia's taste ranged from furs and glitter to designer jeans and cashmere sweaters. And if an army ever needed to march on high heels, there were enough here to outfit them. Amelia apparently liked scarves too, because designs from geometric to flowery, wool to silk, handkerchief-sized squares to toe length, draped a dozen hangers. A scent of some perfume that Cate suspected was too pricey for her to recognize hung in the air.

Doris circled the bed and studied the labels on the prescription bottles.

"What are they for?" Cate asked, curious in spite of a feeling this was getting a bit too nosy.

"Blood pressure. Heart. Cholesterol. Insomnia. I think she takes a sleeping pill almost every night. There's no point even trying to talk to her before she has her morning caffeine to unfuzz her head." She opened the drawer of the nightstand. "Of course it's no wonder she can't sleep. I wouldn't be able to either, if I were her."

"Why is that?"

Doris had already moved on to the bathroom and didn't answer. Cate followed and peered into the room with her. Double sinks, fancy gold faucets, garden-style tub with Jacuzzi jets, separate shower large enough to shower the Whodunit ladies en masse.

What neither bedroom, closet, nor bathroom contained was Amelia herself.

Back in the hallway, they cautiously opened other doors. Two were guest rooms, a bit musty smelling. The third held a four-drawer, wooden file cabinet, an old electric typewriter, and an expensive copy machine. At the end of the hall another narrower stairway led upward.

Cate and Doris exchanged glances, and then, in a conspiratorial tone, Doris said, "Why not? I've always wondered what's up there."

Cate paused midway up the stairs. "We probably should have checked the garage first to see if her car is here."

"Amelia hates to drive. She uses a taxi a lot of the time. So the Mercedes might be here, and she could still have gone somewhere."

"But surely she wouldn't leave knowing the Whodunit ladies would be here at noon. Unless she forgot, I suppose."

"Or got a better invitation from Radford." Doris gave the name an inflection that was not complimentary. "She'd dump us in a minute for Radford."

"Radford?"

"The current man in Amelia's life."

Cate had to admit she was surprised Amelia had a "current man," but then she chided herself for being ageist.

The third floor hadn't benefited from the remodeling and updating that had taken place on the floors below. Faded wallpaper in an old-fashioned cabbage-rose pattern covered the walls of small rooms stuffed with furniture and racks of old clothes. The last room held a jumble of golf clubs, fishing rods, a stuffed owl, and an accordion. Octavia raised a cloud of dust when she jumped up beside the owl.

"A memento room for old husbands," Doris observed. "Amelia had four of them, and the last one played the accordion, as I recall."

"You've all been friends for a long time?"

"Define friends."

"You've all been in the Whodunit Club together for a long time?"

"That's how we met. It used to be a larger group, but some people find Amelia's personality a bit . . . overpowering." Doris's smile unexpectedly changed her bony face. "And the rest of us have our peculiarities too."

The third-floor hallway ended in a door to the outside. Cate was surprised to see that it stood partway open. "Maybe she leaves this open for the cat to go in and out?"

"Not Octavia. That cat may have been a stray at one time, but she thinks she's queen of the universe now. She's also deaf, so Amelia keeps her inside."

Cate felt an unexpected flicker of kindliness toward Amelia. She hadn't heard much good about the woman so far, but anyone who'd take in a deaf stray must have some redeeming qualities.

Cate stepped onto a small square of weathered boards outside the open door, Doris right behind her. The steep stairway below them looked dangerously flimsy, the old boards dark and cracked. And at the bottom . . .

Cate's breath snagged in her throat. Uncle Joe had assured her this assignment was strictly routine. No murder, mayhem, or mystery, not like what those detectives on TV always encountered. No dead bodies.

Wrong.

◆ 2 ◆

"Oh no," Doris breathed. "Amelia."

Cate grabbed the rough handrail, rammed a splinter in her palm, but ignored it as she dashed down the stairs. Even with the handicap of high heels, Doris was only a few steps behind. At the concrete landing at the bottom, they both knelt by the crumpled figure. Cate awkwardly fumbled with the wrist for a pulse. Doris touched the woman's throat.

"I don't feel anything," Doris whispered.

Amelia's eyes were neither open nor closed. Slitted, as if she looked into some eternity beyond this world. Blood matted the dark mass of her hair and oozed onto the concrete. Her skin felt cold beneath Cate's hand.

Still on her knees, Cate dug the phone out of her purse and punched in 911 with fingers that felt peculiarly numb. A brisk lady took the information and said help would arrive within a few minutes. After Cate put the phone away, she and Doris just looked at Amelia. Cate felt as if she should *do* something, but she had no idea what.

"She likes black," Doris said. "Liked," she added with a catch in her voice. "She said it made a woman look sophisticated."

Amelia was in black now, but she didn't look sophisticated. The slacks were ordinary, a bit snug, and a swirl of Octavia's white hair decorated the front of the sweatshirt. Amelia was a large woman, her body matronly, her personality apparently formidable, but she also seemed so vulnerable, so exposed and defenseless lying there. One fuzzy pink slipper lay near her foot, the other upside down in the grass. The little-old-lady slippers seemed at odds with all those spike heels in her closet.

Which meant . . . what? That, at the time of her fall, the arrival of the book club was not imminent, so she hadn't yet dressed for the lunch? Uneasily, Cate looked up the stairs again. A dangerous stairway, obviously. But falls weren't always accidental, and the Whodunit ladies, including Doris here, were so hostile toward Amelia.

No. Ridiculous. The women obviously had their squabbles and hard feelings, but surely that wasn't enough to motivate a fatal shove. None of them could have done it anyway. They were all clustered on the front porch when Cate arrived, all puzzled about Amelia's absence.

But one or two or more of them could have come earlier, done the deed and departed, then returned at the lunch hour to play innocent. And they each had a key . . .

Get off it. This was just an accidental fall, not a conspiracy of little old ladies.

But what about the missing Willow Bishop, who had apparently disappeared in haste?

Doris's gaze followed Cate's up the stairs. "I can't imagine what Amelia was doing out here. I didn't think she ever used these old stairs." After a moment, she added, "I guess I'd better go tell the others."

Cate wanted to jump up and follow Doris, but leaving Amelia lying there alone didn't seem right. "I'll wait here."

Cate, stiffening in her uncomfortable kneeling posture on the concrete, scooted over to the bottom step. Someone had made a rock garden beneath the stairway at one time, but now it was a neglected jumble of weeds and rocks and a broken metal statue of an antlered deer. Maybe the rickety stairs and weeds were the reason Amelia kept those dining room drapes closed.

Cate didn't want to stare at the body, but she couldn't not look, either. The almost-black hair had to be a dye job. It did not go well with Amelia's aged skin. Overly taut skin. One too many face-lifts? Trying so hard to hang on to a long-lost youth . . .

Then Cate felt guilty for such unkind thoughts. She jumped back to speculation about time of death.

No makeup, which further suggested the fall may have happened several hours ago, before time to get ready for the lunch group. She remembered hearing somewhere that rigor mortis set in at some predictable number of hours after death, but she had no idea how many hours that was. Hey, she could ask Uncle Joe. He'd know. Or he had all those reference books in his office—

She dumped the thought. Rigor mortis had nothing to do with anything beyond this awful moment in her life. No need to learn anything about it. Her toe, much less any larger part of her anatomy, did not belong in the PI business.

Cate was digging at the sliver in her palm when the Whodunit ladies swarmed out the back door and surrounded Amelia's crumpled figure. One woman knelt and touched Amelia's throat with an authoritative gesture.

"Krystal works with a volunteer group at the hospital," pink-clad Fiona said, the information apparently aimed at Cate since everyone else undoubtedly knew it.

The elegantly white-haired Krystal, with fashionable wedge shoes, shook her head and confirmed what already seemed inescapable fact. "Dead." She looked up the stairs. "And no wonder, if she fell all that way and hit her head on this concrete."

"How horrible," Fiona said. "How truly, terribly, incredibly horrible. Dying out here all alone." She lifted her glasses and swabbed her right eye with a tissue. "I feel so awful. Saying what I did about her being . . ."

Fiona didn't repeat the word, but Cate remembered. Cheap. And someone else had called Amelia rude.

"And I didn't really mean it when I suggested we disband the club and cut her out." Texie swallowed hard and added virtuously, "We'd never have done it, of course. She had a wonderful lunch waiting in the refrigerator for us."

Krystal stood up. "She really held our group together all this time."

"Deep down, she was a wonderful person." Fiona hesitated, as if trying to think of examples of that, but apparently came up blank and instead murmured, "One we all cared deeply about."

More murmurs echoed that thought. Death had apparently upgraded Amelia's character considerably.

Cate looked at the stairs again. Octavia stood at the edge of the landing now, tail twitching. Amelia might have stumbled over the cat. Yes, that was probably it. A tragic stumble.

Octavia cautiously descended the stairs, as if she suspected they might be booby-trapped. At the concrete landing, she eyed the group of women warily, then headed straight for Amelia's body. Cate could almost see the cat's confusion as she prodded the hand with her nose and got no reaction. She circled the body twice, then curled up in the bent crook of Amelia's arm.

"What will happen to the cat now?" Cate asked.

"There's a niece," Doris said. "Maybe she'll take it."

"Shouldn't somebody call the niece?" Cate asked. When no one offered to do so, she added, "Does anyone know the niece?"

"Her name's Cheryl Calhoun," Fiona said. "She and Amelia never seemed very close. Although Amelia thought Cheryl's husband was a financial genius."

Exchanged glances in the group seemed to give that statement some special meaning that Cate couldn't interpret.

"They live over in Springfield," Doris added. "Cheryl has an interior decorating business, but I don't remember the name. The number might be in Amelia's little red book, on the stand there by the phone."

"Then maybe—" Cate didn't get to finish the suggestion about calling the niece before a siren screamed to a stop on the far side of the house.

"I'll go tell them Amelia is out here," Doris said.

She disappeared through the open back door. Everyone else, by some unspoken agreement, backed away from the body. Another siren screamed up, then went silent at the same time as two white-clad EMTs ran out the back door. Octavia skittered to hide among the rocks under the stairs. Cate expected the EMTs to load Amelia up and instantly take her away, or maybe try to revive her with shock equipment. But, after a quick check, the men in white also stepped back. A moment later two police officers burst through the door.

"Don't anyone leave," one of them barked. "We'll need to talk to all of you."

The Whodunit ladies gravitated into a silent huddle. Cate stood off to one side.

The officers also checked the body briefly. They asked if

anyone knew her identity, and Doris volunteered the information. Amelia Robinson, age seventy-four. Widowed, no children. The only relative known to those present was the niece in Springfield. While the older officer was writing down the information, the other officer got on his cell phone.

"Was anyone here when this happened?" the stocky older officer asked.

Doris explained about the Whodunit Book Club and the lunch, and then how she and Cate had discovered the body. "Could she have had a heart attack?" Doris asked. "She had heart trouble and high blood pressure."

"That will be for the medical examiner to determine. Officer Detrick is on the phone with the ME's office now."

"But isn't the medical examiner the one who looks at a body when there's a crime?" Fiona's voice rose in alarm.

"The medical examiner is called in any situation such as this. Someone from that office will be here shortly."

Any situation such as this. Did they have a lot of elderly ladies tumbling down stairs?

The EMTs left, but the younger officer repeated the earlier instructions to the women that they were not to leave. Cate doubted anyone planned to leave. They were obviously horrified by what had happened here but also morbidly mesmerized by it.

One officer went back to the police car and returned with both digital and video cameras to photograph the body and stairs from all angles. Both officers climbed the stairs and took more photos. Octavia dashed out from under the stairs and disappeared around the corner of the house. The officers closed the upstairs door. They came back to the body and made sketches and took measurements.

"There's someone else you might want to talk to," Doris

suggested. "An employee who also lived here, Willow Bishop. But her room is empty. She seems to have moved out."

"Quite suddenly," Fiona added.

Mention of Willow immediately brought questions from the officers about the departed employee. Cate expected answers from the club women, but, except for Doris's comment that Willow drove a red Toyota and Fiona's statement that she looked a lot like Cate, no one seemed to know anything.

"Anyone know the year of her vehicle?" an officer asked. "Or the license number?"

Cate hesitated. Along with Willow's physical description, Uncle Joe had given her information he'd obtained from DMV records about Willow's car. Confidential client data. Yet she surely couldn't withhold from the officers what might be important information. She told them the car was a 2009 Toyota Corolla and gave the older officer the scrap of paper on which she'd scribbled the license number.

"You have this information because . . . ?"

"I'm working with a private detective agency." Cate handed the officer the ID card Uncle Joe had made for her. She heard a whispery hum of excitement among the ladies at the announcement about her employment. "A client has a family message for her. That's why I'm here. Because I'm looking for her."

The officer inspected the card. "I know Joe Belmont, but . . . ?" He looked at her again.

"I'm his new assistant."

Cate halfway expected some expression of doubt, but the officer merely nodded and handed the card back. "Good man."

The officer wrote something more in his little notebook, but if he thought Willow's hasty departure had any connection to Amelia's fall, he wasn't saying so. But now there were more questions about Willow. The only information anyone had to add was Texie's statement that Willow was a real fanatic about trees.

"Amelia said a couple of times that Willow asked for a day off so she could go join some protest about logging. She was a, you know, one of those tree-hugger people."

After that, they were each interviewed individually. Someone from the medical examiner's office was just arriving as they were finally allowed to leave.

"All this questioning for an accidental fall?" Cate whispered to Doris as they all trooped around the house. They'd been told not to enter the house again.

"You're suggesting . . . ?"

"Nothing!" Cate said hastily. She lined up mental support for that statement. Amelia wasn't young. Heart attack. Stroke. All those pills in the bedroom. Maybe a momentary attack of dizziness there at the top of the stairs. A stumble over the cat. Lots of innocent explanations for the fall.

"There are peculiarities, though, aren't there?" Doris added thoughtfully. She itemized the oddities that also clung like white cat hair on black velvet in Cate's mind. "What she was doing out there on the stairs. Willow disappearing so suddenly."

The entire Whodunit bunch, with more hostilities than the Mafia toward an informer.

"I didn't notice, but now I wonder, was Amelia wearing any jewelry?" Doris asked.

Cate tried to remember. The slacks and sweatshirt weren't the kind of outfit you'd worry about accessorizing. "I don't know. I don't remember seeing any." But she hadn't been thinking about jewelry then. "Why?"

"Amelia has a lot of jewelry, expensive stuff. You know,

23

push someone down the stairs. Grab the jewelry off the body. Run." Doris smiled ruefully and waved a hand in front of her face as if to dispel such thoughts. "I've been reading too many mysteries."

Out in the driveway, Cate exchanged good-byes with the Whodunit ladies. She handed out business cards and asked them to call if they heard anything more about Willow. Doris headed for an older-model compact Ford parked farther down the street, well away from the more expensive vehicles in the driveway.

Cate headed home to where she'd been living with Uncle Joe and Rebecca since just before Christmas. The sunny spring day had turned to a gloomy drizzle, and Cate found doom-and-gloom settling around her like a soggy blanket. The terrible image of Amelia's body lying on the cold concrete. Suspicions tumbling around inside her head that someone may have deliberately done this to her. A disappointing sense of failure about today for herself. Her report to Uncle Joe would be short and uninformative.

Went to address on Meisman Street.
Subject no longer living there.
Don't know where she went.
End of report.

By the time Cate turned onto the street where Uncle Joe and Rebecca had lived for the past fifteen years, the sense of gloom had advanced into an all-too-familiar feeling that she was drifting in life. Or, to put it more accurately, floundering. Floundering from failure to failure. Here she was, twenty-nine years old, and what did she have to show for it? She'd graduated from college with a degree in education and failed as a teacher. Two years as marketing manager with a bath and spa products company, until the company merged with a larger company and she wasn't one of the employees retained after the merger. A collapsed engagement. Two years in the office of a construction company that was downsized when the California housing market crumbled. Nine months of looking for a job and finding nothing.

Oh, there'd been a few jobs since she'd come to Eugene. She'd grabbed anything that offered a paycheck. Christmas elf at the mall. Stuffing flyers under windshield wipers. Wearing a bunny costume and waving a sign directing people to Top-Time Tax Service. But she hadn't been noticeably successful even at those endeavors. At the mall, she'd tripped over her pointy elf slippers and fallen into a buxom woman who whopped her with a purse. The flyers job ended when she accidentally dropped her entire stack of flyers in a Noah-sized puddle in the mall parking lot. The tax people had let her go because her sign waving lacked "exuberance."

If God had a plan for her life, it was as invisible to her as the calories in a plate of brownies.

By now the embedded sliver throbbing in her palm felt as if it went all the way to her elbow, but she forgot pain at the sight of an ambulance pulling out of Uncle Joe's driveway. Next-door neighbors and people across the street stood outside their homes watching.

Cate screeched her car to the curb and jumped out. "What's wrong?" she called frantically to the next-door couple leaning on their rail fence. "What happened?"

"It's Joe," the woman said. "They took him in the ambulance."

"Was he conscious?"

"We couldn't tell," the man said.

"Rebecca went with him?"

"She practically jumped in the ambulance."

"Where would they take him?"

"They took my sister to RiverBend when she had a heart attack."

Heart attack. All too possible, given Uncle Joe's cholesterol and blood-pressure numbers.

Cate was marginally familiar with Eugene area hospitals. She'd been turned down for an office job at the RiverBend hospital. She jumped back in the car. At the emergency room, she gave Uncle Joe's name at the desk, and the woman told her to wait while she checked on whether he'd been brought there.

Cate perched on a sofa in the waiting room, but she couldn't sit. She paced. She sniffed that faintly antiseptic/medicinal scent of all hospitals, a scent that seemed more a message of doom than vigilant cleanliness. She prayed. She drank coffee from a machine in the corner. Prayed and paced some more. Wondered if she should call the other hospital. Flipped through a magazine. Prayed again. *Take care of Uncle Joe. Please, please, please, Lord. And Rebecca too.*

She finally got the meager bit of information that yes, Joseph Belmont had been brought to the emergency room. Privacy regulations prevented them from giving out information about his condition, but the person who'd come with him would be notified that Cate was out here.

After an hour and a half Rebecca emerged through the swinging doors. Her usually crisp gray hair drooped into a wispy halo around her tired face. Her shoulders also sagged wearily. She and Cate met and silently wrapped their arms around each other.

Cate didn't know what to ask because she feared the worst. "Is he . . . ?"

"They're taking him into surgery."

Not the worst—*Thank you, Lord!*—but . . . "Heart attack?"

"No. Can you believe it? He was cleaning gutters on the garage. I heard a thud—" Rebecca shook her head, her brow scrunched, and Cate suspected exasperation was how she was dealing with the fear. "Can you imagine? Up on a ladder. With that bad leg of his."

"He fell?"

"And broke his hip. The surgery is to put it back together."

"He'll be okay?"

"He's probably too stubborn not to be okay." Rebecca pressed her lips together, then the fear burst through, and her face crumpled. "Oh, Cate, I'm so scared! I know of two people our age with broken hips. Neither of them lived more than a year."

"We'll pray."

Which they did, arms around each other there in the waiting room, asking for skill and wisdom for the doctor and healing for Uncle Joe, and Cate added a prayer for strength for Rebecca. The hospital staff let Cate accompany Rebecca to a smaller, more intimate waiting area nearer the operating room.

"All this time I've been fussing and worrying about his cholesterol and his heart. All that tofu! Tofu burgers. Tofu turkey. Grabbing the salt shaker away from him. And what I should have been doing was following him around with a mattress so he wouldn't get hurt if he fell. Serve him right if he limps on both legs now." Then Rebecca broke into another torrent of tears that contradicted her grumpy words. "I feel so helpless. I know God is in control, and he listens to prayers, but sometimes . . ."

Cate patted her shoulder, feeling helpless too. Because bad things happened to good people. Rebecca and Uncle Joe had been married some fifteen years now. Both had gone through several years of aloneness after their mates passed away, before square-dance lessons . . . and God . . . had brought them together. *Please, Lord, don't separate them now.*

It was evening by the time the doctor came out to talk to Rebecca. He explained how he'd inserted screws and a metal plate to hold the bone together, and Uncle Joe had come through the surgery satisfactorily. He also said, in a very offhand way that Cate suspected was designed to be honest but also to keep from alarming Rebecca, there could still be complications, and Uncle Joe would require physical therapy. Rebecca didn't want to leave the hospital, but Cate finally persuaded her.

The phone was ringing when they walked in the door at the house. And it kept ringing. Concerned neighbors and friends from church who had somehow already heard the news, wanting information or offering help. Rebecca gave out information while Cate opened a can of chili because they'd missed dinner. She tried to dig the sliver out of her hand, her ineffectual efforts reminding her that the world was probably fortunate she hadn't aimed for a medical career. She finally had to ask for help.

Rebecca swabbed the spot with alcohol. "How did you manage to do this anyway?" she scolded. "I thought you went to confirm some woman's address, not tear into the woodwork."

Cate decided not to tell her the full story. After the worries Rebecca already had about Uncle Joe, she didn't need to hear about someone else's fatal plunge. "Just an old stair railing I happened to grab at the house."

◆◆◆

Next morning, the phone rang continuously with people calling to ask about Uncle Joe. Cate and Rebecca finally let the answering machine take care of the calls. At the hospital, a nurse let Rebecca in to see Uncle Joe for a few minutes, but he was nauseated, perhaps an aftereffect from the anesthetic, so no other visitors were allowed.

They had come in Cate's car. Rebecca didn't want to leave the hospital, even if all she could do was sit and wait. They agreed that she'd call Cate's cell phone if she needed Cate to come get her during the day, otherwise Cate would return that evening.

On the way back to the house, Cate made a determined decision. She was not going to have another failure on her record. Because, even if she didn't have to put it on a written résumé, it would be on a mental one. She *was* going to find Willow Bishop. Uncle Joe's accident, terrible as it was, gave her a little more time.

At the house, she ignored the ringing phone. She cautiously opened the door to Uncle Joe's office. Maybe she'd absorb something PI-ish in there.

Uncle Joe had kept an office in a professional building back when he was a full-time PI, but he'd worked out of a home office the last couple of years. Clients seldom came to the house, but there was a separate entrance to the office if they did. The no-nonsense room held a glass-topped oak desk, a computer and printer setup, filing cabinets, a copy machine, two hard-backed chairs for clients, and Uncle Joe's framed PI license on the wall. Under the glass covering the desk was an oversized map of Oregon.

Cate retrieved the key from where Uncle Joe kept it under a lamp and unlocked the desk drawer containing his files on current cases. He'd shown her all this before she'd gone to locate Willow. But this time she saw something she hadn't earlier. A gun! Tucked in the back of the drawer, small, but sinister as a hooded figure in a dark alley. Which somehow suggested that not all Uncle Joe's work had been routine and unexciting. Cate pulled out the folder on Willow, shut the drawer on the gun, and studied the contents of the file.

Uncle Joe had skipped over some of the information. Willow's real name was Winona. She seldom used it, but she'd had to provide a birth certificate to get an Oregon driver's license. The great-uncle who was trying to locate Willow was Jeremiah Thompson, and he'd said his grand-niece might be using a different name than Willow, possibly something tree connected. Holly or Laurel or Aspen.

The phone on the desk rang. Belmont Investigations was on a different line than the home phone. She checked the caller ID. An out-of-area number. She intended to let the call go to the answering machine, but a raspy-sounding voice identified himself as Jeremiah Thompson. Willow's great-uncle! Cate grabbed the phone.

"Mr. Thompson? This is Cate Kinkaid, Mr. Belmont's assistant. I'm afraid he's incapacitated at the moment but—"

"Incapacerated?" In spite of the rasp in the older man's voice, the mispronounced word came out with a hint of Southern drawl.

"He's had a bad fall and broken a bone—"

"But I gotta find Willow! The family's chargin' around like a herd of hungry sharks, and I don't want 'em cheatin' Willow out of what she's got comin' from her grandma's estate."

"Actually . . ." Cate swallowed and tried to inject efficiency and competence into her voice, though that was a lot like trying to make a steel rod out of a noodle. "I'm working on your case myself. In fact, just yesterday I went to Willow's most recent address. She's no longer there, but I'm, um, hopeful that I can locate her for you within a very short time."

"You sound awful young to be a private investergator, missy. Everywhere I go, some young whippersnapper's runnin' things now," he muttered darkly, the Southern accent even more noticeable, along with a hint of hillbilly twang.

"Yes, I know," Cate soothed. "But I have the file right here, and I'm wondering if there's anything more you could tell me about Willow that might be helpful."

"I ain't had no contact with Willow for nigh on to . . . well, I dunno. The years go by faster'n I can grab 'em with a pitchfork. But, lemme see. She's got that sweet smile, and all that red hair, purtier than a red heifer, as my mama, bless her heart, used to say. When she was little I used to tease her 'bout her hair lookin' like she fell into a bucket of barn paint."

Cate pulled a spike of her own hair forward and peered sideways at it. Red barn paint it was. "I was thinking more along the lines of occupational abilities. It appears she may have recently been employed as a helper for an older woman."

"Well, I remember she was a waitress, but she'd be right good at helpin' people, you betcha. A real carin' type gal she is, always one to bring home stray critters. Might be she'd go to work for a vetinary guy."

Jeremiah's ramblings weren't going anywhere, Cate realized with a certain frustration. "Well, if you think of anything more or if you hear from her, you let me know, okay? I'll call you as soon as I locate her."

"Call me how?"

"The number's here on the caller ID."

"Well, don't do that. I'd have about as much chance of gettin' the call here as I have of growing more hair on this bald head. They're always messin' up stuff like that here at

Millview Acres. Miserly Acres, we call it. Too cheap to hire enough help. But they always got somebody comin' in to tell me to take a pill or haul me off to some fool doctor," he added sourly. "I'm a-figurin' on moving to another place in the next few days. I'll have to call you agin."

"Fine, but give me a few days to get the case wrapped up, okay?"

"Okay, and you tell Mr. Belmont to get well quick, hear? Though I'm sure you're an A-OK investergater too," he added.

"I'll tell him you called. And he's supervising the case, of course."

"Okay. You take care. Don't take no wooden nickels."

Cate put the phone down, pleased with herself. At least Jeremiah Thompson hadn't fired her from the case. However, she wasn't any further along on how to proceed with finding Willow Bishop. Now what?

Cate grilled a tuna and cheese sandwich for lunch and contemplated her problem further. Basically, she had only one connection with Willow. The house. So that was where she had to start.

Rain still drizzled from low clouds, and the big old house looked more like vulture or vampire territory than ever. But no detectives swarmed it, and no crime scene tape circled it. That must mean the authorities had concluded the fall was accidental. Good. She could put her nagging suspicions about both the Whodunit ladies and Willow to rest.

No cars stood in the driveway, but she parked out on the street anyway, and rang the doorbell. No answer. She punched the bell again. Again, no response. Apparently Willow hadn't returned. She jumped when something brushed her legs.

Octavia, looking more bedraggled than regal today, meowed forlornly. She obviously hadn't spent last night in her canopied cat bed. Cate leaned over and rubbed the cat's wet fur.

"Hungry?"

Another plaintive meow. Cate felt in her pockets, but she wasn't carrying anything edible. But she was carrying . . . She pulled the metal object out of her pocket. A key! In the flurry of what had happened yesterday, she'd never returned the key she'd grabbed to unlock the door. If she went inside, she could feed the cat. She could also look around Willow's room and perhaps peek in a few other places and find something to suggest where Willow had gone.

Would that be an illegal entry? But it wasn't as if she'd *do* anything illegal inside. It was just that poor Octavia was hungry.

With that righteous motive in mind, Cate unlocked the door and dropped the key in her purse. Octavia scooted inside, raced through the dark dining room, and skidded to a stop at a kitchen cabinet. Cate opened the cabinet door and found both dry and canned cat food, some brand she'd never heard of, plus a dish decorated with a grinning Garfield. She filled the dish, and while Octavia ate and purred approval, she went back to the phone in the living room where Doris had said Amelia kept a "little red book" of numbers. Another righteous thought was that she needed to get names and numbers so she could find out whose key she had and return it. She wasn't just snooping.

Numbers for the Whodunit ladies were conveniently listed on the first page. More than had been at yesterday's meeting, although some were crossed out. She copied everything on a scratch pad from her purse. She was skimming the other unalphabetized names in the notebook when a noise at the front door stopped her. Someone trying the door? No, someone unlocking the door. Someone opening the door! The niece? The police?

Somehow she doubted a do-gooder explanation about entering the house to feed the cat would carry much weight with either niece or police. She groaned. All Uncle Joe needed on top of his broken-hip disaster was the police interrogating him about an employee making an unauthorized entry into a private home.

A vision of the door on the third floor torpedoed into her mind. Escape! She took the stairs two at a time. At the second floor hallway, safely out of sight, curiosity stopped her. Who was down there? Maybe just a quick peek around the corner . . .

No. She reminded herself about what happened to curious cats, which probably also applied to curious assistant PIs. On the third floor, she congratulated herself. A quick sneak down those outside stairs, a dash to her car, and she'd be home free.

Except here came Octavia thundering down the hall, stalking her like a were-beast from some horror story.

"Go away!" Cate whispered as she frantically flapped her fingers at the cat. "Shoo!"

The cat sat on her plump rump and eyed Cate reproachfully.

"Look, I'm sorry," Cate whispered. "But you belong here and I don't."

Octavia didn't understand the words, of course. She was a cat, and deaf besides. But she certainly knew how to lay on the guilt with those blue eyes. Cate muttered another apology, got the now-locked door open, and squeezed outside. A quick dash down the stairs, then another around the house through the rain. This was going to work!

Until a voice stopped her in her tracks.

Reluctantly, she turned. A woman stood under a red umbrella beside the open door of a silver BMW in the driveway.

"Willow?" The woman was slim and blonde, stylish in a fur-trimmed leather jacket and heels. Late fortyish. Very put-together. "I thought you'd moved out."

Cate reluctantly approached the car. "Amelia told you that?"

"The officers who came out to tell me about her fall said the house appeared to be empty, and I came over to—" Then Cate saw an emergence of the puzzled expression that was almost familiar. "But you're not Willow. Who are you? What are you doing here?"

Cate hastily produced her identification card and an explanation about how and why she'd been here the day before. "And then I found the body out there at the foot of the stairs. A terrible tragedy."

"Yes, a terrible tragedy," Cheryl echoed, although it was a preoccupied-sounding statement as she stared up at the house.

"I came back today because I'm still looking for Willow. A family member is trying to locate her."

"And you were snooping around back of the house because . . . ?"

With sudden inspiration Cate said, "I was worried about the cat. She got out during all the confusion yesterday, and I wondered if she was okay. She was around back of the house when I last saw her yesterday."

"Did you find her?"

"Not out back, no." Perhaps not a spandex-cling to the truth, but no actual lies there. Preferring to get away from that subject, she added, "Someone said yesterday that Amelia had a niece?"

"Yes, I'm Cheryl Calhoun. Amelia was my aunt."

"I'm so sorry for your loss."

The woman stared up at the house again as she elbowed the car door shut. Finally, as if jerking back from some private thoughts, she nodded. "A tragic loss, yes. Thank you."

The words and tone were appropriately solemn, but if

Cheryl was in deep mourning over her aunt's death, Cate didn't see any real sign of it. The thought occurred to her that if Cheryl was Amelia's only heir, this property was now hers. Was that also what Cheryl was thinking as she stared up at the weathered hulk? Was it valuable? The house was old, but prices for vintage places were sometimes quite amazing. And the top-of-the-hill, end-of-the-street parcel was huge, probably dividable into several lots.

"I don't suppose you'd know where Willow might have gone when she left here?" Cate asked. "Her great-uncle in Texas is really anxious to locate her."

"No idea." Cheryl paused and tapped a glossy fingernail on the handle of the umbrella. "It just seems very peculiar that she took off right after Aunt Amelia's fall down the stairs, don't you think? Maybe something a private investigator would want to look into," she added with a meaningful lift of well-groomed eyebrows.

"We're not that kind of agency," Cate said, even though she wasn't certain what kind of agency they were. Uncle Joe had assured her that most of his current work was mundane: finding a deadbeat husband, running background checks, serving a subpoena. Not the thrilling car chases and gun-fights that occurred regularly on TV crime shows. But there was more than routine work in his past, Cate was certain. He didn't talk about how he'd gotten his limp, but she doubted it was while running a background check on his computer.

"Well, what I need to do is go in and check on Amelia's jewelry."

"Check on her jewelry?"

"If Willow saw Amelia fall down the steps, maybe she decided it was a good time to grab the goodies and run. Willow had worked here only a few months, and I have no idea who she is or where she came from. In the business you're in, I'm sure you run into unsavory people all the time."

Cate decided not to offer the information that her experience with private investigation hadn't been much longer than a bad date.

Cheryl raised a hand, palm outward. "I'm not making accusations, of course. At least not yet. I do wish Scott were here," she fretted.

"Scott?"

"My husband. He's up in Seattle at a conference. He was very disturbed about all this when I called him last night. He's going to rush home as soon as he can." Cheryl started toward the house steps, but a gust of wind almost tore the umbrella out of her hands. For the first time she apparently noticed that Cate was wet and cold. "Would you like to come inside and warm up? Although it's not all that warm inside. Amelia always did keep the place cold as an igloo. That's why I came back out to get a heavier jacket."

"I'd appreciate a chance to warm up."

"To tell the truth, this is such a creepy old place that I hate to be alone in it, especially with Aunt Amelia dying here only yesterday. Who better for company in a creepy old house than a private investigator?"

Again Cate held back on listing her shortcomings in that area. Inside, Octavia met them at the door. Thankfully, cats couldn't ask incriminating questions, such as, *Oh, you're back again?*

"There's the cat now," Cheryl said. "Spoiled rotten monster that she is. You wouldn't believe how much that cat food Amelia feeds her costs. And white hair! It's all over the place. Shoo!" She flapped the umbrella at the cat.

"Did the police say anything about how your aunt happened to fall?" Cate asked.

"All the officers said last night was that Amelia had fallen on the steps and was dead. They did ask a lot of questions about her health and medications. She took all those pills, but I always suspected she was more of a hypochondriac than actually ill. But it's a wonder something ghastly hadn't happened here long before now." Cheryl waved a hand around the living room. "Just look at this."

Cate wasn't certain what she was supposed to look at. The sleek furniture? The garish but probably expensive painting over the fireplace? Nothing dangerous so far as she could see. "The inside of the house isn't nearly as gloomy as the outside," she offered tentatively.

"But it's all so *wrong*." Cheryl waved her arms with a fervency that Cate thought a bit overdone considering that they were talking furniture, not worldwide injustice. "My interior decorating business specializes in feng shui . . ." She whipped out a card and handed it to Cate.

Interiors by Cheryl. Feng Shui to improve your environment and your life. Cheery rays streaming from a golden sun decorated the card, apparently the cheerful life you'd have if you got your environment properly feng-shuied.

"Proper alignment makes all the difference in our lives."

Is that what she needed? Her own life was not exactly well-aligned. Dead-end job situation. Fizzled romantic relationships. Bad haircut. Bank balance that looked like a ten-year-old's piggy-bank savings. Lack of success with the easy assignment Uncle Joe had given her. But she doubted any of that was because her bed wasn't properly aligned with the door or wall. "Do you plan to live here?"

"Live here?" Cheryl almost shuddered. "No way. We have

a lovely home over in Springfield. My husband is with a prestigious stock brokerage firm here in Eugene. I don't know what I'll do with this place. This is a terrible time to sell, with prices so low, but renting is such a hassle. But Scott will know what to do."

"That's good," Cate murmured.

"Now I'm going upstairs to see what that woman made off with. I know there's a valuable squash blossom necklace, possibly an antique. Amelia and one of her husbands traveled the southwest extensively. I remember emerald earrings and a rather spectacular necklace to match. Oh, and that fabulous ruby tiara and earrings."

It sounded as if Cheryl had already decided Willow had stolen the jewelry. She tapped her chin with a manicured finger, and Cate suspected, given a little time, she could come up with an itemized list of every piece of jewelry Amelia owned. All of which, plus the house and whatever assets the apparently wealthy Amelia owned, now belonged to her. Cheryl didn't look like a push-auntie-down-the-stairs type, and a dead body would surely do terrible things to the feng shui of a place, but if the stakes were high enough . . .

Oh, c'mon, Cate, she mentally muttered to herself. *You're seeing suspects like termites marching out of the woodwork. The Whodunit ladies, Willow, now the niece.*

It was none of her business anyway. Her job was just to find Willow, give her the message about an inheritance from her grandmother, and provide the great-uncle with an address. Which gave her a sudden idea.

"I don't suppose you'd know where Willow worked before she came here? The information might help me locate her for our client."

The woman stopped the chin tapping. "That's an excellent

idea. Aunt Amelia must have asked for character or employer references before she hired the woman. Perhaps the information will aid the police too. If you have time, we can go upstairs to her office and take a look right now."

Cate almost clapped her hands. Maybe she wasn't totally hopeless at this PI stuff after all.

She already knew where Amelia's office was located, but she didn't let Cheryl know that. She just followed Cheryl up the stairs, then down the second floor hallway.

In the small office, Cheryl opened a middle drawer of the wooden file cabinet. The numerous manila folders were neatly labeled, although their order seemed to be based on some unique interpretation of the alphabet. Appliances and warranties. Property taxes. House insurance. Bank accounts. Income tax returns.

Cheryl's hand hovered over the bank accounts file, as if she'd like to take a look, but apparently she decided to wait until later. Probably, Cate guessed, until her own curious eyes weren't present. Cheryl had just pulled out a file labeled Employees when Cate felt a brush against her legs. Cheryl spotted the cat at the same time and instantly flapped the folder at the cat.

"Shoo! She leaves cat hair on everything. Shoo!"

"Will you take her now?" Cate asked as the cat skidded out of the room.

"I have two burgundy velvet chairs. Need I say more? She's going to the animal shelter."

"The animal shelter?" Cate repeated, appalled. "But your aunt must have cared a great deal for her."

"I'm sure they'll find her a good home."

"But she's deaf."

Cheryl's flutter of fingers dismissed that as not her concern.

41

Cate *was* concerned. She kept remembering how the cat had curled so forlornly by Amelia's arm. How, in spite of all the good efforts by the shelters, so many pets, even young, healthy, hearing ones, didn't find homes because there were just too many of them.

"Maybe one of the women from the book club would take her," Cate suggested.

"If I have time maybe I'll call them." The careless comment suggested that the possibility of enough time to do that was remote. "Oh, look! I think I've found something."

She had indeed. It wasn't a formal employment application, but it had Willow's name at the top of the page. Listed below were a few lines about each of several jobs she'd held. Stapled to the page were three references from former employers.

"It looks as if she's worked for several older women," Cate said. "Do you mind if I use the copy machine to make copies of these?"

"Help yourself. The police will probably want them too."

The copy machine hummed efficiently and quickly turned out clear copies. "I met the women from your aunt's book club yesterday," Cate said as she turned the machine off.

"Oh yes. The Whodunit Club."

"Do you know them?"

"I've probably met most of them at one time or another. There's a Fiona somebody. And a woman who looked as if she'd just come in from feeding the cows. I remember her telling me, 'You can take the girl out of Texas, but you can't take Texas out of the girl.'" Cheryl wrinkled her nose. Cate wasn't sure if the distaste came from a reaction to Texie's cowgirl outfit or the "girl" reference Texie had made to herself.

"An interesting group," Cate murmured.

"And there's a Doris. Tall and skinny, with a face like a hungry hawk. A real nosy busybody. I remember Aunt Amelia saying how the woman always wanted to know how much her shoes cost."

"They all seemed quite nice," Cate said in a neutral tone.

"Oh yes, of course. Although I think they took advantage of Aunt Amelia's generosity."

"Really? In what way?"

"Oh, you know. She was always taking them to lunches or movies or little outings of some kind. Things like that."

A rather different view than the Whodunit ladies had given of Amelia's tightfisted ways. But, again, not her business. Her assignment was to find Willow.

"I certainly do appreciate your helpfulness." Cate folded the photocopies and stuck them in her purse. "Is the funeral service scheduled yet?"

"Scott and I will have to discuss that. It also depends on when they release the body, of course. I don't think Amelia would want a big fuss, so we'll probably have something small and private at the cemetery where a couple of her husbands are buried."

Cate hadn't known Amelia, but she suspected a big fuss was exactly what a woman who owned a tiara would want. "Maybe you could talk to her friends in the book club. They seemed to know her well and thought so highly of her." Maybe a smidgen of white lie there, even though the women had spoken well of Amelia after she was dead.

"You think so?" The niece sounded skeptical. "They struck me as a bunch of piranhas who'd happily turn on Amelia or each other over a good quiche."

That seemed a little harsh to Cate. But maybe not totally untrue.

"Can you see yourself out? I want to get started on Amelia's jewelry so I can get word to the police about what's missing."

Cate started to say sure, then had second thoughts. Could this be a smoke screen? A sly proclamation of "Look how innocent I am!" to throw suspicion toward Willow and away from some involvement of her own in her aunt's fall?

"Could I be of any assistance?" Cate asked, all innocence herself.

"I don't know that I need any help. But, like I said, this place is so creepy. Like all those old husbands might still be lurking around watching." Cheryl glanced at a ceiling corner as if expecting to find one hovering there. "So sure, c'mon. We'll see what we can find."

They started down the hallway to Amelia's bedroom, but Cheryl paused when her cell phone chirped. Cate continued on down the hall and spotted the cat hiding behind a drapery in Amelia's bedroom. The pill bottles on the nightstand were gone now. The police must have taken them. A ceramic hand on a mirrored dressing table held several rings. They all looked like costume jewelry to Cate, but then, she had no great familiarity with real jewels. One ceramic finger was empty. Was that a place for some ring Amelia had been wearing, a ring someone had snatched off her finger? Or had someone with familiarity with real jewels snatched the only valuable one?

Cheryl joined her a few minutes later. "Sorry for the interruption. That was Scott. He's trying to get away from the conference as soon as he can. Even though we've been married for four years now, he just has to call several times a day whenever he's out of town."

Cheryl rolled her eyes, and Cate interpreted the movement as Cheryl wanting to imply she was exasperated with such solicitous husbandly attention but actually being quite proud of it.

Cheryl opened several drawers and found an old-fashioned cedar jewelry box in one. She set it on the dressing table and pushed the contents around with her forefinger.

"The squash blossom necklace is here." Cheryl dangled the heavy necklace of silver, turquoise, and coral from a finger. "It looks like sterling silver, but I have no idea of its value."

Monetary value was obviously the big factor in Cheryl's judgment of worth, not the fact that her aunt had owned and probably treasured the necklace.

Cheryl set the necklace beside the cedar box and rummaged further, finally grabbing a handful of jewelry and holding it up as if it were a fistful of spaghetti. "The rest of this is junk! All the good jewelry is gone. There should be emeralds. And the tiara. And I remember diamond-stud earrings too, at least a carat each."

"Maybe she has a home safe?"

Cheryl, suddenly energized, dashed around the bedroom, shoving aside mirrors and paintings, pushing one so hard it crashed to the floor and shattered the frame. None of which revealed anything more than empty wall space.

Cheryl finally paused and planted her hands on her hips. "Well, Willow definitely got herself enough here to finance an escape to Mexico or the Bahamas or somewhere. And I'm wondering now if she didn't do more than take advantage of Aunt Amelia's fall to steal the jewelry. Maybe she pushed her!"

"What about a safe-deposit box?"

Cheryl took a deep breath, sliding one hand from her throat down her chest as if to calm herself. "Amelia liked to flash her glitter. I don't think she'd hide anything in a safe-deposit box. But I'll check. You'll let me know if you have any luck finding Willow?"

Cate wondered about the client/PI ethics of that, but Cheryl was too absorbed in her loss to notice that Cate's murmur was noncommittal. Octavia was peeking out from behind a drape now.

"You're definitely taking the cat to the animal shelter?" Cate asked.

"I mentioned my burgundy velvet chairs, didn't I? And royal blue carpeting as well."

Cate hesitated, feeling as if she were skidding down a path she didn't want to take. "Maybe I could take her . . ."

Shut up, mouth, she commanded. What she did not need was an oversized, spoiled feline with epicurean tastes.

But maybe she could find a good home for the cat among Uncle Joe and Rebecca's neighbors. Yes, that would work! She'd find a home for the cat and then come back and get her. But Cheryl jumped on Cate's cautious words as if they were an offer she couldn't refuse.

"You can take her? What a wonderful idea! I'm sure there's a cat carrier out in the garage."

So not more than five minutes later, feeling rather like a piece of flotsam carried along by an irresistible tide, Cate found herself back in her car. With Cheryl at the car window saying, "I'm sure she'll make you a wonderful companion."

"But I didn't intend—"

"It's been lovely meeting you. And do let me know if you locate Willow, if the police don't beat you to it. I'll make up a list of the missing jewelry and give it to them. Although it's probably a lost cause if she's already left the country."

Cheryl waved as she headed back to the house. Cate drove down Meisman Street feeling a little dazed. She'd come here hoping to gather information that would help her locate Willow. Instead, what she had was a backseat full of canopied cat bed, two cases of some gourmet brand of cat food, a padded scratching pole, and an enclosed litter box with the name Octavia written in gold script over an arched doorway. Plus a pet carrier full of spitting, clawing, yowling cat.

❖ 4 ❖

Cate managed to get the cat to the house without major damage to anything except her eardrums. She installed a still-yowling Octavia in her own bedroom, where the cat's bed was considerably grander than her own. She wanted to get started on contacting Willow's former employers, but she decided that a home for the cat took priority at the moment.

She went around the neighborhood and enthusiastically extolled Octavia's virtues to several people. Such beautiful blue eyes and classic white fur! Free bed, food, and litter box! Honesty made her add that the cat was deaf, but she also assured potential cat owners that this didn't appear to be a problem. She didn't mention that it certainly didn't seem to hamper Octavia's own vocal abilities. But everyone was either disinclined to enter cat ownership, already had a lone cat diva in residence, or had a feline or two they tried to pawn off on her.

Back in her bedroom, she discovered Octavia had calmed down and made herself at home, preferring Cate's pillow to her own canopied cat bed. The cat had obviously explored her new surroundings. White cat hair decorated everything from Cate's black sneakers in the closet to the top of the drapery rod at her window.

"This isn't home," Cate warned the cat. "So don't make yourself too comfortable." Then Octavia's blue-eyed stare punched her with guilt. The cat had just lost both home and owner. She had to feel confused and traumatized. Cate amended the statement. "But I'm not going to toss you out on the street to fend for yourself, so don't worry about that, okay?"

The cat condescended to offer a purr as she tucked her white paws under her body. *Who me, worry?*

Cate took the photocopies of Willow's employment references into Uncle Joe's office. She reread the letters. None of the jobs had apparently lasted very long, but the letters glowed with praise. Cate wished she had such enthusiastic references. She picked up the phone to call the name on the top letter.

Which was when she discovered something peculiar. The letter had a name and address, but no phone number. She flipped through the other references, and the peculiarity expanded. No phone number on any of them.

A thud, a skid, and papers flew like oversized confetti. And then there was Octavia sitting on the desk with a smug expression, her plump rump anchoring a lone letter remaining on the desk.

"Octavia! How did you get out of the bedroom?"

She must not have closed the bedroom door tightly. Cats couldn't open doors.

She tried to snatch up the cat, but Octavia eluded her grasp and dashed out to the living room. Cate followed. The cat was faster and more agile than her weight suggested, a Wonder Cat taking sofa and chairs in single bounds, then racing back to the office. She finally thunked down on the desk again, the skid flipping the letter remaining there into Cate's hands.

This was a reference from a Mrs. Beverly Easton, with

an address on Westernview Avenue. It looked as if it had been written on an old typewriter, a haphazard mixture of lighter and darker letters, the *e* slightly off-kilter. The woman praised Willow's "commendable and caring work ethic" and her "cheerful good nature and impressive cooking skills."

Cate studied the letter, then the cat, who was now industriously tongue-cleaning her left hind leg. Twice now the cat had targeted this particular letter.

"Are you trying to tell me something?" Cate inquired. "You think this is the one I should contact first?"

Nah. What did a cat know? Octavia was an oversized feline, not a PI.

But neither was Cate a real PI, so maybe this was as good a place as any to start. She found a phone book in a desk drawer and turned to the E's. No Beverly Easton. Okay, she'd do this in person. Uncle Joe had more faith in old-fashioned legwork than high-tech investigative techniques anyway. He used the internet frequently, but he tended to yell at the TV when he watched crime shows. He said most of the technology they showed, if it even existed, wasn't available to the average police department and definitely not available to him.

Cate retrieved the scattered papers, carried the cat back to the bedroom, and opened a can of "wild salmon in a delicate seafood sauce." She called Rebecca's cell phone to ask about Uncle Joe, but Rebecca wasn't responding. She googled Westernview Avenue to pinpoint its location and headed out.

The drizzle had lifted, and sunshine peeked through the clouds. Much of Eugene was flat, but Westernview Avenue snaked up a ravine—older fifties houses on the left, steep hillside of blackberry vines tangled with manzanita and fir and shiny-leaved madrone on the right.

The one-story house had a hint of sag to the roof. A picket fence, recently mended with new pickets in several places, enclosed a small yard. No evidence of a "western view," as the street name suggested. No view of any kind. This hardly looked like a residence for people who could afford household help. The house needed painting, and roots had humped the sidewalk into continent-shaped sections. In contrast to the modest house, however, a new-looking blue SUV stood at the curb.

There was no doorbell, so she knocked. No response. Another harder knock. Still no response. She tilted her head toward the door. Was that a clunk from inside the house or around back?

She followed the cracked and bulging sidewalk around the house. An empty wheelchair stood near the back door. And a woman in faded jeans, heavy jacket, and stocking cap lay on the sidewalk with her head in a flowerbed of pansies.

Another body? No, no, no!

Cate ran to the prone figure, crouched over her, and tried to loosen the zipper at the woman's throat. A gurgle and slight movement told her the woman wasn't dead. At least not yet. Frantically she tried to remember what she knew about CPR. Clear the airway. Tilt the head back. She stuck two fingers in the woman's mouth to clear it.

Something rammed her in the shin, throwing her back to the sidewalk. She blinked, her bottom stinging from contact with the hard concrete.

An elbow. The woman had whacked Cate in the shin with an elbow! And now, definitely not dead, she was glaring over her shoulder. Bewildered, Cate scrambled to her feet, only to find an arm clamped around her throat, her body skewered against a solid wall of muscle.

She clawed at the arm. But even as panic roared through her and she kicked backward into whoever . . . whatever . . . was behind her, a sour thought slammed into her head.

What can you expect, when you take advice from a cat?

"She tried to choke me!" the woman on the ground yelled. "Stuck her fist in my mouth!"

"I did not!" That's what Cate tried to say, but with the arm cranked around her throat, it came out in glug-glub gurgles.

"The wedding ring wasn't enough? You came back to see what else you could grab?" a male voice close to her ear accused.

Cate glubbed more protests, but the arm didn't loosen. The figure on the ground twisted to a sitting position. Her sharp brown eyes peered at Cate.

"Hey, wait a minute. I don't think she's the girl I told you about."

"She isn't?" The arm loosened slightly.

"Let go of me! I thought she was dead!" Cate slammed her heel into his instep, but sneakers pitted against male boots had all the effect of a bicycle in a demolition derby.

"So if I'm dead, why're you sticking your fist in my mouth?" the woman challenged.

Cate put both hands on the encircling arm and yanked. The arm still didn't let go, but she got a little more breathing space.

"You were lying there. I thought you'd fallen out of the wheelchair! I put my fingers in your mouth to clear your airway so I could give you CPR."

"Who are you?" the woman demanded with a fraction less hostility.

"Isn't she the woman who worked for you?" the male voice asked. "The one who stole your ring?"

This time Cate used her own elbow to wham him in the ribs, although she was the one who oofed when the blow hit the solid rib cage. She suspected it was confusion more than effectiveness of the jab that made him finally release her.

She turned to look at him. Tall, brown-haired, wide-shouldered, paint-blobbed. He returned the glare, the hostility only marginally marred by a dribble of paint on his nose.

"She looks like your description of the woman who worked for you and stole your ring," he said.

"She looks some like her, all right," the woman conceded. "Red hair, same size, pretty and all. But not her."

"Her, meaning Willow Bishop?" Cate asked.

"You know her?"

"Kind of."

"She worked for me after I fell on the sidewalk and messed up my back and got my legs like this. Useless as a couple of noodles. Then she took off, and so did the wedding ring I usually kept in my bureau drawer."

Cate didn't like the sound of this. Amelia Robinson tumbles down stairs, jewelry and Willow go missing. Here, a ring and Willow disappear. Was Willow Bishop something other than the sweet grand-niece Jeremiah Thompson wanted to find?

"Okay," Cate said cautiously. "So, you just fell out of the wheelchair?"

Cate now noted that the woman wasn't lying on bare sidewalk. Her forearms were in the flower garden, but she had a square of black plastic spread out under her.

"No, I didn't 'fall out of the wheelchair,'" the woman mimicked. "You try weeding a flower bed from a wheelchair and see how well it works."

"Beverly says her pansies are special because they keep blooming all winter, so she likes to treat them special. I helped her get down on the ground so she could weed them from a lying-down position," the man explained in an if-it's-any-of-your-business tone.

"Mitch is here painting my bedroom," the woman said. "He's going to do the outside of the house too."

"Mitch Berenski," the man said. He didn't offer to shake hands, although Cate didn't know if that was because he didn't want further contact with her or because his own hands were paint smeared. "And you are?"

She yanked a card out of her purse and slammed it into his hand. "I'm here on official business."

He inspected the card but gave her a skeptical look. "You don't look like a Joe."

"I work for him. I'm Cate Kinkaid, an . . . uh . . . assistant PI. I have my own identification card."

"Let's see it."

After several awkward minutes, Cate finally found her own card where she'd stuffed it in a side pocket of her purse when the police officer had returned it. The guy examined the card critically, then glanced back at her. Perhaps checking to see if she really did have hair growing out of her left ear? Finally, without comment, he handed the card back.

"Maybe we should all go inside to figure this out, then," he said. "I don't want Beverly getting chilled there on the ground."

He didn't sound convinced that Cate had any business being here, but his concern for the woman somewhat lessened Cate's annoyance with his treatment of her. He scooped Beverly up in his arms and settled her into the wheelchair. Beverly took off the stocking cap and shook out curly gray hair. Mitch opened the back door, and she wheeled herself inside.

The door opened into a sunshine-yellow kitchen that also looked recently painted. Pansy decals decorated the cabinets. Mitch Berenski's work? Nice, though Cate made the admission to herself grudgingly.

Beverly kept going, leading the way into a living room with an old brown plaid sofa, a modest-sized TV, pansies in a vase, and a lineup of teddy bears on a shelf. A metal wind chime of dolphins hung over the front door to signal when it opened.

Cate perched on the sofa. Mitch remained standing. Cate deliberately ignored him as she explained to Beverly that Belmont Investigations had been hired to find Willow because of an important family matter. She pulled the copy of the reference letter out of her jacket pocket.

"I had an address on Meisman Street where she's been employed most recently, but she's no longer there. I thought I'd check back with former employers to see if they knew anything helpful. This is the copy of your reference letter for Willow." To forestall questions from either of them, she added, "The similarity in our appearance is purely coincidental. We aren't related or anything."

Cate glanced between Mitch Berenski and Beverly. He looked the more hostile of the two, the one who most needed convincing. She handed the copy of the reference letter to him.

"I was going to call, but there was no listing in the phone book."

"That's because this is all I use now." Beverly indicated a cell phone tucked into an embroidered holder on the wheelchair.

Mitch read the letter, frown lines cutting between his dark brows, then handed it to Beverly. "Did you write this?"

Beverly read the letter more slowly than he had. "It was written on my old typewriter, that's for sure." She traced a fingertip across a line of irregular print. "It always makes those funny *e*'s. And Willow was a really good worker, just like this says. She made the best ever meat loaf. But then she left so suddenly, and my ring was gone too . . ."

"So you didn't write the letter?" Mitch asked.

"I don't actually remember writing it, but maybe I did. Sometimes it seems like my brain doesn't work any better than my legs anymore." She snapped the paper with a forefinger. "But that's definitely my signature."

Mitch took the paper back. "She could have typed the letter on your typewriter, then got you to sign it in with something else."

"That's not fair," Cate accused. "You didn't actually know her. If you did, you wouldn't have mistaken me for her and attacked me."

"I didn't attack you! I merely . . . restrained you. I thought you were trying to harm Beverly."

"I gather from this that neither of you has any idea where Willow might be now?" Cate asked.

"No. But if you find her, get her meat loaf recipe for me, will you?" Beverly sounded wistful, as if she really missed that meat loaf. "Great spaghetti too."

"I'll take you out for meat loaf or spaghetti anytime you want," Mitch offered. "I know a great Italian place over near the mall."

Beverly reached over and patted his arm. "You do enough for me already. How's the bedroom coming?"

"One more wall. I can finish it tomorrow. Then I'll get the furniture in the other bedroom pulled away from the walls and covered so I can do that room."

"You're going to church in the morning, aren't you?" Beverly asked him.

"Well, uh . . ."

Obviously not an enthusiastic yes.

"I need a ride. Marcie can't take me tomorrow."

"Oh, well, sure. I'll pick you up and take you then."

Cate saw a satisfied smile, close to a smirk, on Beverly's face, and she realized what the woman had just done. Sweetly coerced a foot-dragging Mitch into going to church. Cate stood up to leave, then thought of an additional question.

"How did you acquire Willow as an employee?"

"After I got hurt, I was in a nursing home for physical therapy for a couple months. When I came home I still needed help, so my son came up from LA to get me settled. I think he saw an ad she ran in that little free paper that comes out every week."

"So you don't know if she had references from previous jobs to show him?"

"It's not easy to find someone for a job like this when you can't pay a lot, so he may have figured he was lucky to get her and not even asked." She held up a forefinger. "Wait, I remember now. She said she didn't have a reference from her most recent employer because the woman was dead."

Cate felt a cold trickle of uneasiness. "Dead?" she repeated.

"A fall off a balcony or deck, something like that."

A fall. The uneasiness increased from a trickle to a stream.

"Then, by the time she picked up and left," Beverly continued, "my son had got laid off from his job and couldn't afford to hire someone else for me. But the church has this Helping Hands thing going, and they send someone to do house cleaning and other stuff. I appreciate everything they do. But no one makes meat loaf like Willow."

"How long did she work for you?"

"Couple of months, I guess."

"Why did she leave?"

"I don't know. One day she just said she had to leave, and she went. That very day."

"And you really think she stole your wedding ring?"

"She's gone and the ring's gone," Mitch cut in.

"Circumstantial evidence," Cate muttered. Then she blinked at her own unfamiliar words. She'd read or heard them somewhere, sure, but they'd certainly never come out of her mouth before. That inner PI surfacing again?

Cate was at the door before she had one last question. "Did you report the theft to the police?"

"I guess I should have, but I never did. I kept thinking, oh, maybe the ring just accidentally got in with her things, and when she realized it, she'd bring it back."

Roll of eyes from paint-blobbed Mitch. "Beverly is the kind of person who always sees the best in people."

"Unlike you." Cate's neck still felt kinked where he'd put a mugger's hold on it.

"Well, not always me either," Beverly said. "I was kind of hasty thinking you were sticking your fist in my mouth. I'm sorry about that. If you find Willow, maybe you could ask her about the ring?"

"I'll do that." Cate headed out the front door, wind chime tinkling. "Thanks for your help. Give me a call if you think of anything. The number's on the card."

"Oh, wait," Beverly said. "I want to give you something." She wheeled to the shelf, grabbed a teddy bear, and handed it to Cate. "That's Rowdy."

"I couldn't—"

"That's what I do with my time. Make teddy bears. I'd like you to have him. Helping Hands gives them out to kids in families they help sometimes."

"Well . . . thank you very much then."

Mitch followed her outside, hands in the pockets of his paint-daubed khaki coveralls. Apparently the painting was a fairly lucrative occupation. Cate noted now that the SUV was a Cadillac Escalade. They didn't come cheap.

"What will you do now?" he asked.

"Check out some of Willow's other former employers." Cate glanced at her watch. Time to get out to the hospital to see how Uncle Joe was doing and pick up Rebecca. "But not today."

"Got to rush home to the husband?"

For a moment she thought he was fishing for personal information. Another look at his scowl and she decided he was simply still skeptical about her. Did he think she had some scam going? Convincing little old ladies she was a private investigator so she could make off with their teddy bears?

When she didn't respond, he added, "Look, I'm sorry. I probably shouldn't have grabbed you like that. But you have to be suspicious of almost everyone these days."

"Right," Cate muttered as she opened her car door. She slid into the car and set Rowdy on the passenger's seat. After a moment's thought, she buckled him in.

"Maybe he's a suspicious type person because he's a person to be suspicious of," she suggested to the teddy bear as Mitch returned to the house. "What do you think?"

◆ 5 ◆

Cate went directly to the hospital. She found Uncle Joe had been transferred to a regular room. He appeared to be asleep when Cate tiptoed in. Rebecca sat by his bedside.

"He's doing okay," Rebecca whispered. "They had him up walking earlier, but he's on heavy pain pills now."

Cate certainly wasn't glad Uncle Joe needed pain pills, but it meant she didn't yet have to tell him her efforts to find Willow had stalled. Or that she'd stumbled into various awkward complications. A dead body. An overweight deaf cat now spreading cat hair around his house. An encounter with a strong-armed painter.

Although on the way home she had to tell Rebecca about one of those situations. She couldn't hide the creature in her bedroom indefinitely. Rebecca took the news well, a cat newcomer apparently low on her worry list. Cate was especially glad she'd told Rebecca about Octavia when the cat greeted them at the back door with a yowl that plainly said, "Finally!" as if Cate, as her personal servant, had been derelict in her duties.

"Octavia! How'd you get out here? I left you in my room." She looked at Rebecca. "Cats can't open doors, can they?"

"I've heard about some that can flush toilets, so who knows?" Rebecca patted her arm a bit absentmindedly. "You don't need to lock her away. It's okay if she has the run of the house."

"She's only temporary," Cate assured her.

Somehow, the cat, now perched on the windowsill like a furry queen surveying her domain, didn't look all that temporary.

◆◆◆

Cate and Rebecca went to the early service at church the next morning. Uncle Joe was already on the weekly prayer sheet, and numerous people asked about him. Afterward Cate took Rebecca to the hospital again.

"Give Uncle Joe my love, and if he's feeling up to it I'll see him tonight," Cate said when she dropped Rebecca off.

She briefly wondered what church Beverly had trapped Mitch Berenski into attending this morning. Of course, she had to admit, it was a small point in his favor that he *could* be trapped into going. Most guys she'd met could slither out of such a trap faster than a snake slithering over hot rocks.

Back at the house she found Octavia had adopted the teddy bear as a buddy and was curled up with him on the bed. Cate decided to use the phone numbers she'd collected from Amelia's little red book and call the Whodunit ladies. She could use as an excuse that she needed to find out who owned the house key she had, although a stronger motive was to see what information she could pry out of them. They were still high on her list of murder suspects. But a little inner voice asked, *What are you doing making a list of suspects? Not your business. Finding Willow is your one and only job as a toe-dipping PI.*

It turned out to be an unproductive effort anyway. Not a single Whodunit lady was home answering the phone. So much for senior citizens sitting around stagnating, with nothing to do.

Okay, back to the missing Willow. She again examined Uncle Joe's file on Willow. She didn't find anything new. She wandered over to his bookshelves. Maybe he had a *Finding Missing People for Dummies* book. No, nothing like that, but she did see one on death and autopsies.

She sat at Uncle Joe's desk and skimmed through the book until she came to a section on rigor mortis. About two to three hours after death, the muscles of the face and neck start going rigid, with stiffness moving on down the body until rigor mortis is complete in about twelve hours. Then the process begins reversal, with all signs of rigor mortis usually gone after thirty-six hours. Cate glanced up from the book. That meant, in regard to Amelia's body—

She slammed the book shut. She was not interested in this. A real PI might need to know this stuff, but she was no PI. Even if that unfamiliar "inner PI" did seem to surface every once in a while, and even if right now it wanted to keep on reading about something called livor mortis.

No, no, no.

She went for a short but fast run. Uncle Joe's office phone was ringing when she unlocked the front door at just past 5:00. She picked it up.

"Belmont Investigations. Cate Kinkaid speaking." She tried not to sound breathless.

"Hi. This is Mitch Berenski. We met yesterday?" He said it as if the meeting had been a social occasion and he wasn't certain she'd remember him. He was mistaken. She never forgot a man who clamped his arm around her throat as if she were Public Enemy #1. She was mildly annoyed that she'd been thinking of him only a moment earlier, as if her very thoughts had yanked him out of some paint-splattered cyberspace.

"Yes?" she said, deliberately giving no hint whether she remembered him.

"Are you okay? You sound—"

"I'm fine."

"You asked that we call if we remembered anything helpful about Willow?"

"I asked Beverly to call," Cate corrected. "Since you never knew Willow, I don't know what you could remember."

"That's true," he conceded. "But when I was moving furniture away from the walls in Beverly's second bedroom this afternoon, the bedroom that was Willow's when she worked for Beverly, I found something."

"The missing wedding ring?"

If he noted the snideness of both tone and question, he ignored it. "It's an envelope addressed to Willow. There's no name, but there is a return address here in Eugene."

"Okay, what is it?" Cate grabbed a pen.

"It's kind of blurry. I was thinking we might get together and see if we can figure out what it is. Maybe have dinner tonight, if you have time?"

Cate drew back to look at the telephone, momentarily astonished. He was suggesting a dinner date? Then he added an explanation.

"I'd really like to help Beverly get her ring back. If you can find this Willow woman, maybe, even if she pawned or sold the ring, I could find out where. It would mean a lot to Beverly."

No, not a dinner date. Just a joint effort to find Willow.

Okay, she could go for that. On second thought, however, dinner sounded a little too intimate. "How about a sandwich somewhere?" Cate suggested. "Arby's on Silver Lane? That's not far off Beltline."

"I know the place. They make great curly fries. Meet you there in, say, forty-five minutes?"

"Okay."

Cate recognized the blue SUV when she turned into the parking lot. Mitch was sitting at a booth by the window when she walked in. Jeans and a blue turtleneck, suede jacket. He stood up as she approached. Blue eyes, which she hadn't noticed yesterday. A dazzling sea blue, if you wanted to be romance-novelish about it.

Cate slipped into the booth. "It's nice of you to be so helpful to Beverly. Does she know you're here?"

"No. Maybe I can surprise her by getting the ring back. What would you like to eat?"

"Plain roast beef sandwich. Curly fries. Jamocha milk shake."

She thought about saying she'd pay for her own, but he was already striding up to the order counter. Okay, maybe he owed her a sandwich and fries for trying to choke her yesterday. He was back with a tray in a few minutes. Cate didn't waste time when he slid into the other side of the booth.

"Let's see the envelope."

He pulled the envelope out of a pocket and set it on the table. Cate couldn't make out the postmark date, but the return address was plain enough.

"That isn't hard to decipher," she said. "2782 Lexter Drive."

"I couldn't tell for sure if that was a seven. Maybe it's a nine." He pointed to the address with a solid forefinger, now paintless. "See, there's kind of a loop at the top, so it could be a nine. And it might be Hexler Drive. Or maybe Laxton or Lester."

She studied the envelope again. No, not Hexler, Laxton, or Lester. Not even close. Definitely Lexter. And definitely 2782, not 2982. She couldn't see how he could possibly have thought either street name or number was different. "Okay, I'll check it out tomorrow." She looked at her watch. "I have some other business to take care of this evening."

"Private investigator business?"

"Kind of." She saw no reason to tell him about Uncle Joe's broken hip, or that Joe was in the hospital. What did she know about Mitch Berenski anyway, except that he had a strong right arm and a suspicious nature? Well, so did she. The suspicious nature anyway. She unwrapped her sandwich.

"Horseradish sauce?" He held up a packet of sauce.

"Sure." She opened the sandwich and doused the roast beef liberally. He did the same. "Have you been a painter long?" she asked, mostly to make polite small talk.

He, apparently feeling no need for tactful tiptoeing, said bluntly, "Longer than you've been an assistant private investigator."

She rejected an impulse to aim the packet of horseradish sauce at him and squirt. "What makes you think that?"

"You didn't ask for a description of the missing ring. Someone with experience would have done that."

And she hadn't. And a description of the ring was something she should know, wasn't it? Groan. Reluctantly, somehow already knowing the answer, she asked, "Do you know what it looks like?"

"I asked Beverly." Smug.

He pulled another scrap of paper out of his pocket. A sketch showed a wedding band with two rows of diamonds, four stones in each row. "She said the stones aren't large, but they add up to about one carat total weight. Enough to make it worth something in a pawn shop. There's nothing strikingly individual about the design, but she says the inside of the ring is engraved with 'Love you always, G.' Which should make it easily identifiable."

"G was her husband?"

"Right. Gerald. He died of a heart attack about ten years ago. They'd been married forty-two years."

Cate forgot her annoyance with Mitch in a rush of sympathy for Beverly. "No wonder the ring means so much to her." *And you'd better not have taken it, Willow Bishop*, she thought with sudden vehemence. "I appreciate your, um, thoroughness. Getting a sketch of the ring was very clever." Right at the head of the one-upmanship parade.

"I read some detective novels."

Which meant he probably knew more about PI work than she did, Cate had to admit. She changed the subject. "Did you take Beverly to church this morning?"

"Yes. Then out for spaghetti afterward."

"But you don't usually go to church?"

"I go sometimes." He sounded defensive. "That's how I got the painting job for Beverly."

"So basically, when you go to church, it's so you can pick up painting jobs?" she suggested.

"I do other stuff besides painting. Yard work. Minor repair jobs."

He'd answered a question she hadn't asked, and skipped the one she had asked, but she let it go. "A general handyman, then."

"I guess you could say that."

She thought about Uncle Joe and the uncleaned gutters and

his broken hip. "My uncle may be needing some handyman help before long, if you're available."

He blinked in mild surprise. "I don't usually do outside jobs, but . . . yeah, sure, if he needs something done, I could do it."

"You have references?"

"References? You saw my work at Beverly's. I did her kitchen. And you want references saying . . . what? That I can tell white paint from green, or I won't paint the family dog by mistake?"

"It wasn't necessarily your painting expertise I was concerned about. It's best to be careful about letting strangers into your home." She realized that sounded prim and huffy, but being careful about strangers was something her dad had drilled into her when she left small-town Gold Hill in southern Oregon. "You didn't answer my question about how long you've been painting."

"When I was a teenager back in Tennessee, my uncle had a construction business. I was dangerous with a hammer or saw, and a major menace with a jackhammer, but I did learn to paint. And I picked up a few skills with plumbing and roofing eventually."

How old was he now? Thirty, thirty-one, somewhere in there, she guessed. So he'd been painting quite awhile. What she'd seen in Beverly's kitchen showed he did good work. "Do you have a business card I can give my uncle?"

"No. But I'll give you my phone number." He tore a scrap off the flap of the envelope, wrote a number on it, and slid it across the table to her.

"So why didn't you go to work for the uncle in Tennessee? Why come out here to Oregon?"

"Look, I think it's my turn to ask questions. And I have a big one." He leaned forward, arms on the table, blue eyes intent. "Your employer, this Joe Belmont, he sends you out to these strange places by yourself? Where you don't know what kind of situation or what kind of people you might run into?"

"Actually, Uncle Joe doesn't know I'm doing this," she admitted. "All I was supposed to do was go to a certain place and find out if that was Willow's current address. But she wasn't there anymore, and I didn't want to tell him I hadn't found her, especially when he has . . . other problems."

She also didn't want to admit failure. Failure as a PI might not be something she'd have to add to her written résumé, but it would go on her mental list. "So I've kind of expanded the search on my own."

"A search that might well be dangerous."

"So far, the biggest danger I've run into has been you," she pointed out.

"Yeah, but there could be a lot worse guys than me out there. Maybe that's why I don't like to see you chasing around alone and running into them. And women can be dangerous too. What do you know about this Willow? Maybe she doesn't want to be found. Maybe she'll strongly object to being found. She left Beverly in a suspicious hurry, if you ask me. I'm not even convinced Beverly wrote that reference letter. Maybe Willow Bishop is a forger and a thief and who knows what else."

"Actually, she left the other employer rather abruptly too," Cate admitted. With a dead body in her wake. And more missing jewelry.

"I could go with you to find Lexter Drive tonight. Unless there's that husband or boyfriend you have to get home to."

Cate glanced up. That definitely sounded like fishing. But with Mitch Berenski she wasn't sure. "I live with my uncle and his wife. He's Joe Belmont. Belmont Investigations. But you were right when you said I haven't been a PI long," she admitted. "I haven't been able to find a steady job here, so Uncle Joe hired me temporarily."

"Then let's go to this address together tonight. I just don't think you should be chasing around to strange places where you don't know what you'll run into. I mean, what if I'd been a serial killer yesterday? And you had just wandered into my clutches? Anything could have happened."

"Why do you care?" she asked, bewildered by what seemed an unexpected concern about her welfare.

"I don't know." He leaned back, took a bite of sandwich, and chewed as if he were angry at it. "Maybe I have some kind of knight-on-a-white-horse complex. Subconscious need to save beautiful damsel in distress."

"You make a habit of damsel saving?"

"No. It's brand-new."

Mitch connecting with his inner knight-on-a-white-horse, the same as she was connecting with her inner PI? And not a connection he wanted to make, if his grumpy stab of curly fry into ketchup was any indication.

Still, it might not be a bad idea to have a male with a strong arm along when she visited a strange address. He'd made a good point about Willow perhaps not wanting to be found.

"I'll have to make a phone call first."

She left the table and pulled out her cell phone. Rebecca answered immediately. She said Joe was awake now, cranky as a bear with a thorn in his paw, but he'd like to talk to her.

When he came on the phone she asked how he was doing, but Uncle Joe was not interested in giving a medical report and immediately asked about the Willow Bishop case. Cate gave him a highly condensed and edited version of her progress in finding Willow, leaving out dead body, unauthorized entry into Amelia's house, missing jewelry, suspicions about Willow, a strong-armed painter, and a missing wedding ring. That didn't leave much, but she firmly repeated to herself that there was no need to worry Uncle Joe with those details now.

"Anyway," she ended brightly, "I'm on my way now to talk to a friend of Willow's. But what I'm wondering is about Rebecca getting home. May I talk to her again?" Which got Uncle Joe off the phone before he could entangle her in incriminating questions.

Rebecca said she wasn't sure how much longer she'd stay, but she'd just catch a taxi home. Cate dropped the phone back in her purse. It clunked against Amelia's house key. She still had to see about returning that. When she returned to the table, Mitch had the address located on his smart phone.

"It's not an area I'm familiar with," he said, "but it shouldn't be hard to find."

She side-eyed him warily, weighing what she knew about him against the advisability of letting a strange guy into her car or getting into his vehicle. She didn't see any knight uniform or accompanying white horse. "I'm taking my car," she said.

"I'll follow in mine."

She guessed he knew what she was thinking. She gave him points for not trying to convince her of his noble intentions.

The plan went fine until they reached the street that was supposed to connect with Lexter Drive. It was blocked off, various hunks of yellow heavy equipment looming behind a lineup of sawhorses. She pulled up beside the barrier. Behind her, Mitch turned on the blinkers on his SUV and got out. She opened her window when he walked up.

"Looks as if they're tearing up the street to widen it and put in a new sewer line," he said.

It was an area of large, older houses that had seen better days but still maintained a genteel dignity in spite of a ripped-up section of sidewalk. A line of stately old trees stood between the remaining section of sidewalk and street. The trees were apparently destined to come down because two already lay on the ground. Down the street several people and a big yellow dog were clustered around the largest tree in the row. The people were looking up into the tree. The dog was doing something else.

"What's going on down there?" Cate asked.

"Looks like neighbors standing around grumbling about their torn-up street. Maybe one of the kids climbed a tree."

They looked at his smart phone again and decided that by going on for three more blocks they could circle around the closed-off street and still get to Lexter.

In those blocks, the ambiance changed to a rather shoddy commercial area. 2782 Lexter was a narrow, two-story white house sandwiched between an auto-repair shop and a tavern with a neon sign that read "icky's Tavern." The name looked appropriate, but Cate assumed there was supposed to be another letter up front to make it something else. She was suddenly not sorry she had a guy with a strong arm accompanying her.

They got out of their vehicles and walked to the door. No red Toyota parked in the driveway or at the curb, but there was a garage where it might be stashed. Lights shone dimly inside the house, but no amount of knocking or doorbell ringing brought any response.

"I guess that's it for tonight, then." Mitch sounded disappointed, which was also how Cate felt. "I'll call you tomorrow, and we can figure out what to do next."

"You have another painting job tomorrow?"

"I just paint on evenings and weekends. But I can take time off so we can come back tomorrow evening."

Cate didn't recall agreeing to an extended "we" situation, so all she said was a noncommittal, "Well, I'll see."

Just before she reached her car, he touched her arm. "I suppose I should tell you. I didn't have any trouble reading that return address. Anyone could see it was 2782 Lexter Drive. I was trying to think of an excuse to see you again. I figured if I just called and asked you out, you'd tell me to go stick my head in a bucket of paint."

Quite possible, she had to admit.

"Anyway, I thought you should know. I don't like operating under false pretenses. But if your uncle needs some handyman help, I'll be glad to do it."

"I'll keep that in mind."

Back in their separate vehicles, she turned left at the corner and he turned right. She was relieved. Given his knight-on-a-white-horse attitude, she'd been afraid he might feel some obligation to see her safely home. Or would she really object to that?

She'd gone perhaps a mile before a thought interrupted her musings about Mitch Berenski. It just slammed into her head like a laser beam out of nowhere. A fantastic, totally improbable leap of imagination, which should probably be rejected like a Nigerian email offering fabulous riches.

Or perhaps it was an unexpectedly insightful intuition, that inner PI surfacing again?

She whipped into a U-turn right there in front of "Kelly's Dog Grooming and Boutique," where a pink neon poodle in the window wagged a blue neon tail.

◆ 6 ◆

Cate edged her Honda out of the lane of traffic and as close to the sawhorse barrier as she could get. There were no evening strollers on the blocked-off street now. Which wasn't as Norman Rockwell serene as it had looked earlier.

Now the hulks of equipment loomed like yellow dinosaurs with metal teeth. Maybe the kind of dinosaurs that snacked on assistant PIs. Long lengths of black pipe, apparently destined for burial in the open ditch, stretched out like bloated snakes. Dark pockets of shadow could conceal anything from muggers to creepies released from some underground depths. A damp, earthy scent lingered in the air.

Cate skirted around the end of the blockade and determinedly picked her way past the downed trees and lengths of pipe. She wasn't certain now which tree the people had been clustered around. Not the first one in the row. She waited until she got to the second tree, then looked up and called softly, "Willow?"

No answer. No answer at the next tree either. But at the one after that, branches rustled when she repeated the call. She craned her head backward trying to see up into the tree, but the shadows lurking among the branches were only unidentifiable blotches.

She felt a little foolish, as if she might merely be talking to a tree, but she tried again, louder. "Willow, are you up there?"

"Who wants to know?"

The voice was so close that Cate jumped. So did her goose bumps.

"My name's Cate Kinkaid. I've been looking for you. Could you come down so we could talk? It's hard to talk with my head all bent back like this."

"Tough. If the construction company sent you to sweet-talk me out of here, forget it. This tree isn't coming down, and neither am I. It's criminal even to think of cutting down big, beautiful old trees like this."

"How long have you been up there?"

"Awhile. I'd like to climb higher, but I'm kind of . . . nervous about heights."

Not a good trait for a tree-sitting rebel. But admirable that Willow was doing this in spite of her fears.

"There's no one here cutting anything down right now. Don't you have to eat or go to the bathroom or something?"

"Are you a reporter?"

"No. Don't you like reporters?"

"I've seen newspaper photos and TV videos of people sitting in trees or chaining themselves to tree trunks or logging equipment."

"Does that accomplish anything?"

"Sometimes." Then Willow stubbornly repeated her first statement. "I'm not coming down. I brought sandwiches. Though I spilled my bottle of water."

"I have a bottle in the car. I'll go get it."

Cate picked her way back through the jumble of downed trees, mountains of asphalt and concrete, and yellow dinosaurs. She got a fresh bottle of water and took it back to the tree. She stretched on tiptoe to hold it up, and a hand reached down out of the branches to grab it.

"Do you really think you can keep them from cutting the tree down?" Cate asked.

"I have to try. People here on the street are upset about what's going on. But the bathroom thing is a real problem."

"Where would you have to go to take care of that?"

"Over on Lexter. Next to Nicky's Tavern."

"That's where you live?"

"I'm staying with a friend for a while."

Cate gave a mental fist pump of satisfaction. She had it, a current address for the client! Maybe she wasn't such a failure as a PI after all. Now she could go home with a successful report for both Uncle Joe and client Jeremiah Thompson.

Yet she didn't like walking off and leaving Willow here in her tree. Needing to use a bathroom. There was also the matter of Beverly's wedding ring. Plus Amelia's jewelry. And her death.

"If you want to come down, I could, you know, kind of watch the tree for you if you want to run home for a minute."

"Maybe this is just a trick to get me out of the tree."

A face appeared in the branches overhead. In the shadowy light, Cate could make out only an oval face, rather pale, but Willow could apparently see more.

"Hey, you look like me!" she said.

"That's what I keep hearing."

"You do. You really do."

"I'm not from the construction company or the city. Or the police," Cate added, after a moment's reflection on Willow's possible past activities. "I look honest, don't I?" she said, trying to take advantage of their similar looks.

The face disappeared, but a moment later a slim figure shimmied down the tree trunk and dropped to the ground. They appraised each other through streetlight trickling through the branches. Willow dusted her hands on her jeans.

"You're older," she said.

And this vulnerable-looking woman, with twigs in her red hair and scratches on her hands, did not look to Cate like an Amelia-shoving, jewelry-stealing criminal. She was bundled in old jeans, ratty sneakers, and a gray hoodie. She was also cold, Cate guessed, from the way she danced from foot to foot and wrapped her arms around herself.

After a glance around the empty street, Willow said, "I guess the tree will be okay if I leave it for a while. You want to come over to my place and have a cup of tea or something? I need to get a heavier jacket too."

"We can go in my car."

◆◆◆

At the narrow white house, Willow said her friend was at work. She waved Cate to the kitchen and headed down the hall to the bathroom. When she came back she yanked off the hoodie and, apparently not a tea purist even if she did make awesome meat loaf, stuck two cups of water in the microwave. She offered Cate her choice from a box of mixed tea bags. Cate selected an orange-cinnamon bag and dangled it from a finger as they waited for the water to heat.

Here, under the fluorescent kitchen light, she had a better chance to study her look-alike. A generic description indeed fit them both. Red hair. But Willow's hair was more the "mane" of a romance heroine, Cate's the picture in a shampoo ad recommending a remedy if your hair looked like this. Similar weight and height. But the pounds weren't homesteaded around Willow's hips, like Cate's were.

Willow didn't seem to be examining differences and similarities, but the bond of being look-alikes had apparently deteriorated, because she suddenly sounded less friendly when she said, "You said you were looking for me. Why?"

"I have some, um, news for you."

"Good news or bad?" Willow asked in a wary tone.

"Both, kind of. I'm an assistant investigator with Belmont Investigations, and your great-uncle in Texas contacted my employer. Your grandmother recently passed away. I know that's sad, but the good news is that she left you an inheritance. Your great-uncle is trying to locate you about it."

Willow rubbed the back of her neck, as if tree climbing had stiffened the muscles. She did not seem excited by this news. "I see. And this great-uncle's name is?"

"Jeremiah Thompson." Did Willow have a lot of great-uncles?

"And I'm supposed to contact him?"

"No, there was something about his moving from one assisted-living home to another, so he's going to call back later so I can give him your address."

The microwave dinged. Willow handed one cup to Cate and dunked a peppermint tea bag in the other. "Good ol' great-uncle Jeremiah," she muttered. No sadness about the grandmother, no curiosity about the inheritance. "How'd you find me?"

"I've been hearing about how concerned you are about preserving trees, and I saw these trees being taken down, so it was just a hunch." She handed Willow her identification card.

"A private investigation agency." Willow shook her head. "He really sicced a detective on me?"

Mitch's warnings about Willow ricocheted into the danger zone. Willow definitely did not sound happy about being

77

found. Cate took a step backward. Cautiously she said, "Joe found an address where you were working for a woman named Amelia Robinson, but when I went there you'd already moved out."

"Amelia told you about my interest in trees?"

"Well, uh, no. I met some women from a book club she belonged to. Also her niece and another woman you'd worked for," Cate said, careful to keep her comments vague. She didn't want Willow retaliating on anyone for giving out information.

"So one of them told you I'd been fired?"

"Fired?" Cate repeated blankly.

"You didn't know I'd been fired?" Willow sounded surprised.

"No. I didn't know why you'd left Amelia's. No one else knew either. They thought it odd you'd left so abruptly."

"Amelia's idea, not mine." Willow tasted the tea and dumped in two teaspoons of sugar. "She was in an awful mood that last morning I was there. I think she'd had a fight with her boyfriend or something. She asked if I had lunch ready for her book club, and I said I didn't even know the book club women were coming for lunch. Then she called me forgetful and incompetent and fired me on the spot. It was so unfair!" Willow grabbed a dishcloth and wiped furiously at a stray spill of water on the counter, as if she were trying to eradicate some deadly germ, but Cate saw that she was also blinking back tears. "So I went and got stuff for the lunch, and then I just picked up and left. She was really hard to work for anyway."

Cate broke the news gently. "Amelia's dead."

Willow choked on a swallow of tea. "Dead!"

"The police haven't talked to you about the death, then?"

"I didn't know anything about it. I can't believe it! Dead?

What happened?" She paused reflectively. "Though she did take all those pills, and sometimes she was a real zombie in the morning. If one sleeping pill didn't work fast enough to suit her, she'd take some other kind. I always wondered if some morning I'd find her fallen headfirst in the bathtub or toilet."

"Actually, she did fall. Down those stairs going from the third floor to the backyard. She hit her head on the concrete at the bottom. One of the Whodunit Book Club women and I found her."

"How awful." Willow paused, her expression going from horrified to puzzled. "I don't remember her ever using those stairs. They looked like they might collapse under a toe tap."

Cate nodded without saying anything.

Willow gave her a sharp look. "Is there something you're not telling me?"

"No! Certainly not."

"Why did you ask if the police had talked to me about her death?"

"There seems to be some . . . uncertainty about how she happened to fall." At least there was uncertainty in Cate's mind.

Willow's eyes widened as the meaning of that sank in. "You're saying maybe she didn't just fall? Maybe she was pushed." She stepped backward, eyes blazing. "And you think I did it! That's why you're really here!"

"No! My job with Belmont Investigations is just to find you for your great-uncle," Cate said.

"Really?"

"Really." Cate lifted her hands, palms up, in a gesture of innocence.

After giving Cate a long, hard look, Willow's tense body

relaxed, and she seemed less like a runaway horse about to bolt. She sounded reflective when she said, "I guess it's possible someone could've pushed her. Not me, but someone. She wasn't the nicest person in the world."

"Anyone in particular you think could have done it? Not that I'm investigating," Cate said hastily. "Just curious."

Willow turned, picked up her cup of tea again, and took a sip. Her gaze slipped out of focus as she looked off into space. "She had those book club friends. Although they're the kind of 'friends' who do a shark attack on anyone who leaves the room. There's a niece who lives over in Springfield, some kind of snobby interior decorator who thinks where you put your sofa will change your life. Though her husband's a little nicer than she is. I never found any of them very likeable, but I don't know that any of them would push Amelia down the stairs." Another pause. "But then, I don't know that they wouldn't do it, either."

"I understand she had a male friend."

"Oh yeah. Radford. A real sleaze, if you ask me. He might have pushed her."

"A sleaze in what way?"

"Oh, you know." Willow lifted her shoulders, as if "sleaze" was self-explanatory. "Dark hair. Sprayed hard as a turtle shell. Sunglasses. Expensive clothes. Younger than Amelia. He looked like he had money, but sometimes I wondered if it wasn't all a big show and he really had in mind marrying her for her money."

"It wouldn't make much sense for him to push her down the steps, then, before he married her and got it," Cate said. "Even though some of Amelia's jewelry is missing."

"He could have pushed her down the stairs and taken it. Not as big a payoff as marrying her, but it would be a lot faster, wouldn't it? She had some really valuable stuff. And she usually left it all just lying around on her dresser."

Where Willow could have grabbed the jewelry just as easily as sleazy Radford. Cate didn't want to think that. From what she'd seen so far, she rather liked Willow. There was also the odd bond of looking so much alike. But there were trouble points.

Cate tackled the problem head-on. "There's also jewelry missing at another place you worked. A wedding ring, to be exact."

Willow didn't miss the implication. "So now you think I'm some kind of serial jewel thief as well as a killer?"

"No, but there's a . . . troubling similarity in the situations."

"Similarity between who and what?"

"Between Beverly Easton's missing wedding ring and Amelia's missing jewelry."

Willow grabbed Cate's arm, her eyes alarmed. "Beverly isn't dead too, is she?"

If Willow was faking concern, she deserved a reality show of her own for her expertise.

"She's okay. Still in the wheelchair, of course. She was weeding her pansies when I was there."

"I'm glad she's okay." Willow let go of Cate's arm. "She's such a sweetie. A bit of a flake sometimes, but still a sweetie."

Cate's impression exactly. Proof that she and Willow were alike on the inside as well as the outside? "She said she missed your meat loaf. She also wondered why you picked up and left in such a hurry."

Willow sighed. "Okay, this is going to be a complicated story. The kind that needs chocolate. Want a brownie to go with the tea?"

"That sounds good."

Cate expected Willow to pull a bag of brownies out of the cupboard or freezer, but instead she grabbed a bowl and started measuring flour and sugar.

"You're going to *make* brownies? And from scratch, not a mix?"

"Sure. You aren't in a big hurry, are you?"

"I guess not. What about your tree?"

"It'll be okay if I get there really early in the morning, before the construction crew shows up. Maybe you could join me in another tree?"

"Well, um, no, I don't think so. But I'm sure it's a good cause," Cate said hastily.

Willow collected cocoa powder, eggs, and oil. She talked as she mixed.

"Okay, about Amelia. I did leave in a hurry—" She broke off abruptly. "What about Octavia? Oh, I hope nothing happened to her too."

"She's okay."

"I'd have brought her along when I left, but I couldn't find her. She's such a fat, sweet thing. Would you believe she figured out how to open the door to my bedroom if I didn't shut it tight enough?"

Yes, Cate could believe that, but her attention zoomed in on what Willow said just before that. "You'd have just walked off with Amelia's cat when she fired you?"

"I was worried that—" Willow broke off, waved a hand, and went back to her mixing. "I was just so upset, being fired and all. Not thinking too straight, I guess."

Cate had the feeling Willow had started to say something entirely different but had caught herself and reverted to her distress about being fired. "Actually, I have Octavia. Cheryl was going to dump her at an animal shelter, so I took her."

"Sounds like something Cheryl would do." Willow turned and appraised Cate again, this time apparently on her qualifications for cat ownership. Cate must have passed, because she said, "Good." Then she changed the subject again and demanded, "How'd you know about Beverly?"

"Cheryl gave me copies of your reference letters. I wanted to find you and make sure you got your inheritance."

"Okay, thanks. I appreciate that. I had a good reason for leaving Beverly's so suddenly. But it had nothing to do with a wedding ring." She grimaced. "What it had to do with was dear ol' great-uncle Jeremiah Thompson. Anyway, I do remember the ring. Beverly was always afraid somebody was going to steal it, so she kept hiding it in different places around the house. Sometimes in a kitchen canister of rice or sugar. Sometimes in a bureau drawer or a box under her bed. Once in the toilet tank. Then she'd forget where she'd put it and go into panic mode until we found it."

"Why didn't she just wear it?" Cate asked.

"She said she'd lost weight since her husband died, and it just falls off her finger now."

"So maybe it isn't really missing?"

"Oh, I imagine it's 'missing,' all right, in that she can't find it. But I'll bet it's right there in the house somewhere. I feel bad that she thinks I could have taken it. I thought she liked me. I know I liked her."

"Oh, she does like you! She'd like to have your recipe for meat loaf."

"I don't have a recipe. It's like these brownies. I just put in what seems right." She tasted the mixture in the bowl and cocked her head to one side. "This needs vanilla."

She pulled a bottle out of the cupboard, read the label, and grimaced. "Ugh. Imitation, not the real stuff."

After an unmeasured dribble of the imitation vanilla, she added a handful of chopped nuts, and a minute later the brownies were in the oven. She set the timer to buzz. By now Cate was sitting at the kitchen table with her tea. Willow plunked into the chair across from her. Lines creased her forehead.

"Beverly mentioned that someone you worked for before her was also killed in a fall."

"Yeah. Margaret Addison. Maggie. That was awful. I tried to get rid of her liquor, but she always seemed to have a stash of it hidden somewhere I didn't know about. That night . . ." She shook her head. "If you ever take up drinking, here's my advice: don't try dancing on a balcony railing when you've had half a bottle of vodka."

Two employers, two falls, two deaths. The coincidence was a bit worrisome. But Cate reasoned that a lot of elderly people fall, drinkers or not. Look at Uncle Joe.

"Are you going to tell the police where I am?" Willow asked.

"I think it would be better if you went to them yourself."

Willow's shoulders slumped, but she nodded. "I suppose I'll have to do that." In an abrupt change of subject she said, "So, you like being a private investigator?"

"Finding you for your great-uncle is my first assignment," Cate admitted.

"Oh yes. Great-uncle Jeremiah. I'm sure he's eager to find me."

"He sounded very nice on the phone. Very concerned about you."

"The thing is . . ." Willow paused to take a long sip of tea. "There is no great-uncle Jeremiah."

Cate straightened in the chair. "There isn't?"

"No. No Jeremiah Thompson. No great-uncles of any variety. No grandmother in Texas who left me an inheritance. There's probably a Texas, but if this guy is saying it, I wouldn't be too sure of even that."

"I don't understand."

"What did he sound like on the phone? Other than 'nice.'"

"Old. A little shaky, with kind of a hillbilly-southern drawl. Very fond of you."

"Have you ever been in love?"

Cate blinked at the out-of-the-blue question. "I was engaged once."

"Were you in love?"

"Of course I was! I wouldn't have been engaged if I weren't."

"So what happened?"

"We just had a big meltdown. He's engaged to someone else now."

"Were you heartbroken?"

Cate considered the question, not sure herself. "I was . . . stunned. I'd thought God meant us to be together for a lifetime."

"But there's never been anyone else since this guy?"

"I haven't been a hermit. I've had a few . . . relationships."

The hunk who, at thirty-one, turned out to be addicted to video games. The charmer who declared he'd love her forever—and moved to Australia the next week. The guy who embezzled a hundred thousand dollars from the company where they both worked. A friend had once asked, "Where do you find these guys? Creeps-R-Us?"

"But you think God's going to bring the guy you were in love with back to you?" Willow asked. "Because that's your destiny or something?"

Cate didn't believe in "destiny," but she did believe in God's will, and what God could do. And she had thought, even after Kyle accepted a sudden transfer to the Georgia head-quarters of the company he worked for, that they would get back together. All they needed was a little time, a little space. Hearing he was engaged to someone else rattled that thought like the tremor of an earthquake, but she rational-ized that engagements didn't necessarily end with a walk down the aisle.

Now all she said was a flip, "God's going to send me a package by UPS or FedEx, maybe Pony Express, and Kyle will jump out and surprise me?"

"Doesn't God work in mysterious ways?"

The often-repeated quotation coming from Willow startled Cate. "Where'd you hear that?"

"I don't know. But sometimes I think about it, because most stuff that happens in my life doesn't make much sense. Maybe it's God working in some mysterious way."

"God working in mysterious ways isn't actually a biblical quotation, but—"

Willow cut her off with a some-other-time wave of hand.

"I was in love too. His name's Cooper Langston. Coop. Tall and blond and rugged. Too handsome for his own good. Remember the Marlboro Man? That's Coop." She paused, her fingers threading together as if to form a protective shield. "Everything was great when we first got together, but then he got all moody and possessive. We were living in this little cabin out near the river, and he wanted to know where I was every minute. He wanted to *control* where I was every minute. He didn't want me to have any friends. He just turned . . . weird."

An appalling suspicion leaped into Cate's mind. "Did he mistreat you?"

"He slapped me. I should have left right then, but he was so sweet and apologetic, and he felt so awful about it. I thought maybe it was my fault anyway, that I must have driven him to it."

A classic abuser. Abuse, apologize, repeat. And make the victim feel it was her fault. "But it did happen again?"

"A couple more slaps. A punch. A really bad punch." Willow didn't elaborate, but she rubbed her ribs as if in painful memory. "That was when I knew I had to get out."

"Before it escalated to something even worse."

Willow nodded. "But I couldn't just walk away. I was scared of what he'd do if I tried. But sneaking away was hard too. He worked from home, a phone-sales thing, and he was always there. But finally he had to attend a sales conference at the main office up in Portland, so I threw what I could grab in my car and sneaked away. He'd taken my car keys, of course, but he didn't know I had another set."

"Good for you."

"Anyway, I thought once I'd gotten away, that would be the end of it. I wasn't hiding at first, just trying to get my life back together. I got a job taking care of a sweet old lady. But after a while I realized he was watching me. I sneaked away again, and that time I did hide. But he found me. It was almost like he had some sixth sense about where I was."

"He stalked you."

"I guess that's what you'd call it, yeah. Then he caught me on the street there by Beverly's, grabbed me by the throat, and said if he couldn't have me, nobody could. Which I took as a threat."

"I think so."

"I felt bad, leaving Beverly like that, but I was scared. I'm thinking now I should have gotten out of Eugene, probably clear out of the state. But I didn't know where to go, and I didn't have any money either."

Cate's heart went out to her. Willow, broke, alone, scared. Then a startling thought occurred to her. "What if he found out you were living at Amelia's? And when he showed up, she wouldn't tell him anything about you, so he got angry and—"

"I don't know how he could have gotten out there on the stairs with her. But maybe he did. And after he pushed her, he figured he might as well steal something." Willow's hand went to her throat. "I know he stole a car once, a long time ago. But to kill someone . . ."

They looked at each other over the kitchen table, the tantalizing scent of baking brownies an unlikely background for a conversation about possible murder.

"He threatened to kill you, didn't he?" Cate said softly.

Willow nodded as if the movement were painful.

Cate was having a difficult time rearranging her own thinking. Both the great-uncle "Jeremiah Thompson" and the story he'd told about an inheritance for Willow were just a wild fiction invented by Coop Langston. "He's not in Texas, is he? He's right here in Eugene."

"Right here in Eugene," Willow echoed. She shivered and rubbed her arms.

"But he was calling from out of state." Oregon had only two area codes, and the code Cate had seen wasn't one of them. "I saw it on the caller ID."

"Spoof."

"Spoof?"

"You know, you get a spoof card and you can use it to make any number you want show up on someone's caller ID. You can get 'em on the internet."

Cate had heard of that, though she'd never known anyone who'd actually done it. "Is anything he told Uncle Joe and me true? What about the Southern drawl?"

"He always had fun doing impersonations." Willow smiled, as if the memory were an unexpectedly fond one. "He could do a great John Wayne, and an amazing Jed Clampett, from that old *Beverly Hillbillies* show."

Now that she thought about it, Cate realized that Jeremiah Thompson's accent did have a touch of *Beverly Hillbillies* reruns. With a little Andy Griffith and Mayberry thrown in.

"How'd you get connected with him to begin with?"

"I had an untypical upbringing, I guess. My folks were part of a carnival, and we were on the move all the time. My mom told fortunes. She was Karma, the Princess of Prophecy, and my dad managed the rides. The only time I went to school was when we stayed in Texas for the winter. By the time I was fourteen, I could tell a pretty good fortune myself." She grabbed Cate's hand and studied her palm. "I see a long life . . . and look at this! Three kids. And some years living in a foreign country."

Cate felt a brief flare of excitement. A long time ago, she'd thought about doing missionary work in Africa. Was that still in her future?

She squelched the unwarranted excitement as quickly as it flared. All her palm showed was wrinkles, plus a scar from the time she'd tried to do a flip with her bicycle like the motorcyclists did on TV. No prophecies about the future there. Though the scar suggested she should stay away from daredevil activities.

"So where did Cooper Langston come into this?"

"I got married when I was eighteen. Biker guy. It lasted a couple of years while we chased around the country. After we were divorced, all I wanted to do was settle down in one place and live a nice, ordinary life. Then Coop started coming into the coffee shop where I was waitressing at this little burg in Texas. One day he said let's move on . . . and I picked up and left with him."

"Just like that?"

"Just like that. Definitely not the brightest thing I ever did, but I was in love with him. You fall in love and you make mistakes." There was something both forlorn and bitter in Willow's assessment about love.

"So nothing this Coop guy told Uncle Joe or me was true?"

"It sounds as if he threw in a few tidbits of truth. I do have some family in Texas. No great-uncles, but there are some not-so-great cousins. The only grandma I have used to live in Texas, where I lived with her for a while, but she's in Florida now."

"You're sure she isn't dead?"

"I talked to her a while back, to let her know I wasn't with Coop anymore. She said she'd pray for me." Willow sighed in a put-upon way, as if being prayed for was a heavy burden to bear. "But she can be a lot of fun, even if she is a little strong on the God stuff. She's the one who taught me to cook. Coop can be fun too. When he isn't being such a jerk."

"You wouldn't go back to him, would you?" Cate asked, alarmed at the hint of nostalgia she heard in Willow's voice.

"No. Of course not. I was in love with him, but I'm cured now." Willow wrinkled her nose. Love was some unpleasant disease. "Are you going to tell him where I am when he calls again?"

"No! But I'll have to explain all this to Uncle Joe. Maybe, when you go to the police to tell them about your connection with Amelia, you should talk to them about getting a restraining order against Coop."

"Like that would do any good. What do you do, wave it at him while he's choking you?" Willow put one hand to her throat and gagged as she waved the other hand in the air.

Good point. "Does he know this friend you're staying with here?"

"He knows Nicole, but she and Coop don't like each other, so I let him think I never saw her anymore. She's moved a couple times, so I don't think he can find me here."

"I found you."

"Yeah, that's true." Willow peered toward the unlit living room as if afraid Coop might storm through the front door at any moment. "But I don't want to do anything about him with the police. I'm hoping he'll think I left town, and a restraining order would let him know I'm still here, wouldn't it? Mostly I just want to get on with my life."

The buzzer on the stove dinged, so Cate didn't have to answer the question. Willow opened the oven door, tested the doneness of the brownie batter with a toothpick, then set the pan on a hot pad on the counter. "These'll be cool in a minute. Then I'll make some frosting."

"Actually, I should be getting on home." Cate looked at the clock in the shape of a fat owl on the wall. "Are you going back to the tree now?"

"Maybe I'll get a few hours of sleep first. I could be up there for several days. Providing I can work out the bathroom problem."

"I'll tell Beverly to look around the house for her wedding ring."

"Tell her to look under her mattress," Willow advised. "And in the freezer. She froze it in a carton of ice cubes once. And when Coop calls, maybe you could tell him I left town?"

"I'll think of something," Cate agreed. "Be careful up in the tree, okay? Don't climb too high and fall out."

"And you, you be careful too. This whole thing with Amelia sounds, you know, kind of scary."

"I'm not really involved."

Willow turned and studied Cate. "Aren't you?"

❖ 8 ❖

Cate drove home still in shock about what Willow had told her about Jeremiah Thompson/Cooper Langston. It was disconcerting how easily he'd deceived both Uncle Joe and her, scary how she could have put Willow's life in danger if she'd given "Jeremiah Thompson" Willow's address.

But she had fulfilled her assignment as a PI now. She'd tell Uncle Joe and write a report for the files. She'd get rid of Cooper Langston when he called and get back to looking for a real job.

If she could just blast that vision of Amelia lying dead on the concrete out of her head. And get rid of a feeling she couldn't quite pin down, like when a name or word hid just out of reach somewhere in your subconscious.

When Cate got home, she found Rebecca in a bathrobe, surrounded by a gardenia scent of shampoo, with a towel around her head. She was watching the news on TV, a sacked-out Octavia overflowing her lap. She said they'd been planning to move Joe to a nursing home the following day for a few weeks of physical therapy, but he'd run a fever this evening and would be in the hospital a little longer. She sounded weary and discouraged, and new lines of worry cut between her eyes.

Rebecca turned off the TV and they joined hands to pray for Uncle Joe. Willow had sent brownies home with Cate and they shared them, soft but chewy, crunchy with nuts, and altogether delectable. When Cate went to her room for the night, Octavia followed. Cate snuggled the cat into her canopied bed, but two minutes after Cate was in her own bed, she felt the cat cuddle up beside her.

"Snuggling is okay," she told the cat. "Just don't give me any more advice."

◆◆◆

In the morning, Rebecca drove her own car to the hospital. Cate returned two calls that were on Belmont Investigations' answering machine and made notes to pass along to Joe. She'd barely set the phone down when it rang again. Her intuition kicked in with a name. Mitch! She was surprised when her heart gave a non-PI-ish flutter. Then she looked at the caller ID. Not an Oregon number. This was more normal. Her intuition had reverted to its usual not-a-clue status.

"Belmont Investigations. Cate Kinkaid speaking."

"Well, howdy there, little missy. Is Joe handy?"

Jeremiah Thompson. Spoofing again.

"I'm sorry, he's still unavailable." Her mind did a spin and loop as she tried to decide how to handle the call.

"So, do you have that little redhead's address for me now?"

"Is this Mr. Thompson?" she inquired as if she didn't already know, stalling for time while she decided what to do.

"Yes, missy, it sure is. You got Willow's address for me?"

"I'm, um, working on it. Are you sure you can't give me any more information about her?" she added. Knowing whatever he knew about Willow might help her escape him. "Oregon's a big state."

"Well, like I tole you, she's a real fanatic about the tree stuff. Hey, did I mention she might be using some other name? Holly or Aspen or Laurel. Some tree thing. I don't like saying this, but Willow's kind of a flighty little gal, not too reliable. Always jumpin' up and movin' around, busier'n a squirrel packin' nuts."

Willow, flighty, always "movin' around"? Of course she was always moving around! Because she was afraid of him. With good reason.

"Mr. Thompson, I think it would be best if you gave up this search for Willow," Cate said. "In fact, I must inform you that the agency cannot continue working for you at this time." Under the circumstances, Uncle Joe would surely approve of that decision.

Silence. "You found her, didn't you?" The accent hadn't totally disappeared, but it had definitely moved north. "I already sent Belmont a deposit, you know. Cash on the barrel-head."

Stalking Willow, and now demanding his money's worth! "I don't know anything about that, Mr. Thompson, but I'll see that you get your deposit back." Sweetly she added, "If you'll just give me an address there in Texas to send it to?"

"I'm a-thinkin' you Oregon folks are a buncha shysters, that's what you are," he growled. Southern style, of course.

"And I'm a-thinkin', Coop, that you'd better back off and leave Willow alone!"

Uh-oh. Not a smart move. But his blatant deception fired her temper into the red zone. She expected him to sputter and ask what in tarnation she was talkin' about, but instead total silence translated into a peculiar ringing in her ears. She squelched a nervous impulse to jump into the silence.

"You have found Willow, haven't you? And she's told you

some off-the-wall story about me." No trace of accent now, and no longer the voice of a shaky old man.

"I know now that Willow has no great-uncle named Jeremiah Thompson and no dead grandmother in Texas. But that there is a man named Cooper Langston right here in Eugene looking for her, and he's certainly not someone she wants to find her."

"Of course she doesn't want me to find her! Look, there's a whole lot more to this situation than you know, and it sure isn't whatever wild story Willow told you. The fact is—"

"We've heard enough of your 'facts.' And the next episode of this story is that Willow is going to the police to get a restraining order against you."

To her surprise, he laughed, a deep, all-male chuckle. "Don't hold your breath on that one," he advised.

The comment made Cate both curious and uneasy, especially since Willow *had* seemed reluctant to go to the police about Coop. But no way was she going to let him suck her in with more wild stories. "Okay, this conversation is over," she said. "If you won't give me an address, you won't get your deposit back. But thank you for using Belmont Investigations."

She hung up the phone. Good-bye, Jeremiah Thompson/ Cooper Langston. She'd get busy on a new internet site for job hunting that she'd recently heard about.

But there were a couple of loose ends to tie up first.

◆◆◆

Cate drove around by the construction area. One yellow dinosaur was loading chunks of asphalt and concrete on a dump truck, another was digging more ditch. Another tree had been felled, and the raw stump and crushed branches gave Cate a pang. Couldn't they have done this a different way? Willow's tree was still standing, and Cate couldn't tell if Willow was in it. No one seemed to be paying attention if she was.

Cate obviously couldn't go wandering through the construction zone with the machinery running full blast, so she went to the house on Lexter. She hoped to find that Willow had decided to take time off from tree-sitting to contact the police about both Amelia and Coop, but no one answered her pounding on the door. She decided to drive on to Beverly's, since that was the second item on her to-do list. She'd come back to the tree later.

At the little house on Westernview, Cate knocked and Beverly yelled, "C'mon in."

Cate pushed the door open under the tinkle of the wind chimes and caught a whiff of fresh paint. "You really shouldn't holler for just anyone to come in," she scolded. "What if it were a burglar or home invader at the door?"

"You think my yelling 'Go away, I'm not home' would be more effective?"

"It wouldn't hurt to keep the door locked. And then take a peek through the window first."

"I'll think about that. So, now that we have that settled, I'm glad to see you again." Beverly pointed the remote at the TV and flicked off a game show.

Impulsively, Cate reached into the wheelchair and hugged her. "I wanted to come and tell you I located Willow. She feels really bad that you think she may have taken your ring. She mentioned that you sometimes hide it and then can't recall where."

"Well, yes, I guess I've done that."

"She said you might have put it under the mattress or in the freezer. I'll help you look, if you'd like."

Beverly touched a finger to her cheek. "Oh, my. I did make some Kool-Aid cubes a while back. They're really good to suck on, you know? And sometimes the neighborhood kids come around for them. Maybe I did put the ring in there."

Cate inspected a half dozen trays of rainbow-colored cubes from the freezer section of the old refrigerator. No ring. At Beverly's suggestion, she also defrosted several frozen containers of chili and stew in the microwave, enough so she could poke around in them with a spoon. No ring. But Beverly said they may as well completely thaw one of the containers of chili and some cornbread too, if Cate could stay for lunch. Cate said she could. Before they ate, Beverly took Cate's hand and offered a blessing.

"Awesome chili," Cate said when she spooned up a second helping.

"Willow made it. The cornbread too. She always made extra so we could freeze some. But I'm going to run out pretty soon. I do miss that girl."

"She told me why she picked up and left so suddenly. It had to do with a man."

"A man. I shoulda known." Beverly nodded, a frown puckering her forehead. "I hope she didn't get involved with some guy who'll do her wrong. There's a lot of 'em around, you know." Apropos of nothing, or so it seemed to Cate, she added, "Mitch has a lot of good qualities, as a man. A real handy kind of guy. I think he's interested in you. You could call him up and tell him about finding Willow to kind of get things going."

"I haven't had much luck with relationships."

"Finding a good man isn't *luck*. It's you and God, seeing what's right for you," Beverly chided. "Did Mitch tell you about himself?"

"A little."

"You do like him, don't you? He's a great guy. He can do all kinds of things. He's going to paint the outside of the house in a few weeks. He has to fix Roberta Elly's fence first."

"I like him okay. But it seems a little, oh, self-serving to go to church occasionally just to pick up painting and handyman jobs."

"That's what he told you?"

"He didn't exactly tell me that, but you had to trick him into going to church this past Sunday."

"That's true," Beverly conceded. "But . . ."

"But?"

"I don't know if Mitch would want me to tell you or not." Beverly buttered a square of cornbread while she thought. "Well, phooey, I'll tell you if I want. Painting isn't a job with Mitch. He and a partner have a business doing individualized computer setups for small businesses. The Computer Solutions Dudes. They write some of the . . . what do you call it? . . . software themselves. He says they aren't running Bill Gates any big competition, but they do okay. That's his real job."

The information surprised Cate, but she gave it a second inspection. "Apparently the Dudes aren't doing too great, if Mitch has to work nights and weekends for extra money."

"He isn't painting for money." Beverly waved her spoon in exasperation with Cate's denseness. "He's doing it with the Helping Hands volunteers from church. His grandparents back in Tennessee are dead now, but they'd told him how the church helped them when they were in need. He wanted to help repay what the church did for them by helping someone else's grandparents now. He doesn't meet needy people much in his regular life, so he started coming to church so he could be a part of the Helping Hands group."

Another rethinking. A man helping people in need not because he was a Christian, but joining with a Christian group because he wanted to help people in need. A little backward, but there was that old line that even Willow knew: the Lord worked in mysterious ways.

After lunch, Cate wrestled with the heavy mattress. By the time sweat ran down her back and she'd found a parrot earring, which Beverly embraced with glee, plus toenail clippers and a page from a 2008 calendar, she was reasonably certain no ring was hidden between mattress and box springs. Beverly's other ideas had her down on her knees checking under a chest of drawers, rummaging through a box of Cheerios, and running her hand to the scummy bottom of the toilet tank. No ring.

Beverly thanked her profusely when she left. "And if you see Willow again, you tell her I'm sorry I thought she took my ring. I'm sure it's right here under my nose somewhere, and one of these days I'll find it."

"If you think of any more places to look, let me know and I'll come back and help you."

"Okay. And you think about what a great guy Mitch is."

◆◆◆

At the house, Cate parked in the driveway, leaving space for Rebecca to pull her car into the garage beside Uncle Joe's SUV. There wasn't room in the garage for a third car, of course, and she always parked in the driveway or at the curb. She was putting her key into the front door when her back suddenly prickled with the feeling someone was watching her.

She whirled and instantly knew who he was. Tall, blond, and rugged. Too handsome for his own good. Long-legged in jeans, broad-shouldered in a black leather jacket. Maybe he wasn't sneaking up on her, but that didn't make her feel any safer.

"You must be Cate," he said with a smile, as if they shared some secret joke. Then his head jerked back in a double take. "Hey, you didn't tell me you looked enough like Willow to be her sister."

Cate yanked the key out of the lock. Rebecca wouldn't be home yet, and no way was she giving him a chance to get inside the house with her alone. She didn't need video-at-eleven to know he was way more dangerous than that easy grin suggested.

With what she hoped was a professional edge to her voice, she said, "I don't believe we've met?"

"You know who I am. Willow surely gave you the full description." More easy smile. Coop Langston oozed male self-confidence. He draped his thumbs in the back pockets of his jeans as if he were posing for her inspection.

"Why are you here?" Finding the house hadn't been any problem for him, of course. Belmont Investigations was listed in the yellow pages, with an address.

"You wouldn't talk to me on the phone. What choice did I have?" He managed to sound both reasonable and reproachful.

"I told you, as far as Belmont Investigations is concerned, you are no longer our client. Not as Jeremiah Thompson, not as Coop Langston." Cate's gaze edged around him. The sidewalk was empty. The yards around the houses on both sides were empty. Where was a nosy neighbor when you needed one? "I can't at this moment return your deposit, but I'll discuss it with Joe and get the money back to you."

Big put-upon sigh. "I don't want my money back. I just want to know where Willow is."

"Stalking is against the law, in case you don't know."

"Stalking? Is that what Willow told you, that I'm stalking her?"

"If the shoe fits, wear it." *Oh, great originality, Cate. That ought to really intimidate him.* She tried to put more threat into it. "I think she will get that restraining order against you."

"Restraining me from what?"

"From stalking."

"How can I be stalking her?" he asked, his tone still reasonable. "I haven't seen her for, let's see, almost eight months now, which was when she picked up and left. I haven't known where she was. I kept thinking I'd run into her somewhere around town, but I never did. So I figured maybe she'd left town, and it would take a real investigator to find her. That's why I hired you."

"But you located her at Beverly's. And you tried to choke her!"

"Who's Beverly, and when and where was this?" Coop sat down on the step and patted the space beside him. He reverted to Southern drawl. "I think you 'n me better have a talk about all this, little missy, because that sweet-talkin' redhead has been tellin' you wilder stories than a tabloid expo."

Cate didn't sit. "What do you mean?" she asked warily.

"I don't suppose you're going to tell me what all she told you, but surely you can be fair enough to listen to my side of the story."

"Uncle Joe and I listened to your side of the story, about a dead grandmother and an inheritance. Oh yeah, and you being in an assisted-living home down in Texas. Miserly Acres, I believe it was."

He laughed as if delighted with her memory for details. "That may have been a, oh—"

"Lie?" Cate suggested.

"More like a tall tale. Although I have had to be rather miserly these last few months, considering what Willow did to me."

Cate didn't encourage him to continue, but neither, because she had to admit a reluctant curiosity, did she refuse to listen. She folded her arms across her chest.

"The thing is, Willow and I were living in a little log cabin over near the river. Belongs to a friend of mine." He lifted blond eyebrows, and Cate gave a slight nod to show she accepted this much as fact. "Willow, in case you don't know this about her, is . . . Well, some people might call her a free spirit. But when you get right down to it, she's like I said on the phone, flighty. She's fun, but you can't depend on her. Willow and truth have only a passing acquaintance. She likes making up stories. And she has a temper. Oh, hey, does she have a temper!"

"I didn't see any indication of that."

"She didn't throw any frying pans across the room at you? Didn't toss your socks in the trash because you forgot and left them on the bathroom floor? Didn't berate you for being insensitive, inconsiderate, stubborn, and cheap?" He sighed. "And forgetful about her birthday?"

"She said you slapped and punched her!"

He touched his chest. "Oh, that's a low blow. A really low, low blow. I've been in a barroom brawl or two, but I'm not a woman hitter." Both his gesture and injured tone struck Cate as melodramatic, but then he added reflectively, "Though I guess I did throw a dish towel at her once when she complained I didn't put the dishes away right."

Cate hesitated with another retort. He really sounded hurt about being accused of punching Willow. And how dangerous could a dish-drying guy be? Then her spine and resolve stiffened. What phony, good-guy role was he playing now that he'd given up the Jed Clampett drawl?

"The thing is, Willow got mad at me. Like I said, it was about eight months ago. She wanted a new car, and she somehow got it in her head that I was going to get her one for her birthday. But no way could we afford it, and . . . okay, I admit it, I actually did forget her birthday. But things were rough at work—"

"You worked at home. Willow had a hard time escaping from you because you practically kept her a prisoner."

Coop blinked, as if the statement amazed him. "I didn't work at home, except to call a potential customer in the evening once in a while. I worked at a shop called Ridley's Cycles. We sold and serviced motorcycles and ATVs. I don't work there anymore. Hard economic times, and the place closed down. Now I'm selling and installing car stereo systems. Though business is going down the tubes there too."

"Where is this place?"

"You interested in a stereo system?" He eyed her car. "I can get you one that'll blast your socks off. Place called Sound by Sammy."

"I don't think so." She needed her socks, thank you. "Okay, so you forgot Willow's birthday." She didn't necessarily believe any of this, but his quick and prolific imagination did make her reluctantly curious. "So what happened?"

"When I got home from work the day after her birthday, she was gone. Packed up and moved out. Without so much as a good-bye note. She took everything from the toaster to the bedroom TV. Probably would have taken the bedroom set too, if she could have gotten it in the car. But what was more important, she cleaned out our bank account, almost ten thousand there, and got a bunch more in cash advances out of our credit cards. Leaving me to pay that off, of course."

"If Willow'd had any money, she'd have left Oregon," Cate scoffed. "She's been trying to hide from you by taking live-in jobs around here."

"What Willow obviously didn't tell you is that she's always had this belief, and it's a real belief, not just a hope—she says she can see it in her palm—that she's going to hit it big in a lottery. The big Powerball one, or the Oregon lottery, or maybe some scam on the internet. Which is probably where all the bank account and credit card money went."

"Willow wouldn't waste all that money on a lottery. If you're even telling the truth about her taking it."

"Wouldn't she? Her grandmother sent us a thousand bucks once, and that's exactly what she did with it. Well, with about half of it," he amended. "The rest of it went to some screwball save-the-trees outfit."

Cate sat down on the step. "I don't believe you," she said, but the statement didn't hit bedrock level this time.

"Anyway, all I want is to find her and see if I can get my money back. Some of it anyway. Is she still driving the old Subaru?"

Cate almost said no, she has a Toyota Corolla now, but she caught herself in time. She wasn't telling Coop Langston anything. But now she had to wonder: How had Willow managed to get that car, broke as she claimed to be? *Had* she cleaned out bank accounts and credit cards and used the money to buy the car?

"And there's another thing," Coop added. "Maybe this hurts worse than the money. My dad was a rodeo cowboy. He's been dead a long time now, but the one thing I had left

105

of him was an engraved buckle he won in a bull riding over in Idaho. She took it when she left."

"It's valuable?"

"It's sterling silver, maybe worth something that way, but what it means to me has nothing to do with money. It was my dad's, something he won. Maybe she took it for the money value. Or maybe she took it because she was mad at me." He looked down at his foot, where his boot heel made half circles on the concrete step. "I'd really like to get it back."

"Willow doesn't seem like the kind of person who'd do something just to be mean." Cate didn't totally believe him, but the buckle story had a troubling ring of truth.

"Maybe Willow wasn't 100 percent honest with you. And sometimes she can be a real drama queen."

Cate rubbed her temple. Had Willow fed her an invented-on-the-spot story? Or was Coop Langston giving her a new story now, since the first one about grandma and an inheritance hadn't worked? The money thing sounded uncomfortably possible, especially since Willow now had that new car. But if she'd taken money when she left him, and she really was afraid of him, why hadn't she left Oregon?

"So I'd really like to find her," Coop said. "I don't figure I'll ever get any of the money back, but I'd sure like to have my dad's buckle."

Amelia's jewelry missing. Beverly's wedding ring. Now Coop's belt buckle. But there was that original pothole in Coop's story.

"So you couldn't find Willow, and you hired a private investigator to do it. Why pretend you were an old man from out of state if you weren't out to do her harm if you located her?"

"I guess I figured a detective might think I really was stalking her," he admitted.

"I'm not making any promises, but I'll see what I can do," Cate finally said warily. "Where can I reach you?"

He patted his pockets, then said, "You got something I can write on?"

Cate reached in her purse and handed him a pen and scratch pad. He scribbled a number on it.

"Cell phone. Call me anytime."

Reluctantly Cate asked, "Are you going to keep looking for Willow?"

"Do I look like a man who gives up easily?"

Cate watched Coop saunter down the sidewalk. At the corner, as if he knew she'd be watching, he turned and gave her a smile and wave. A few moments later a motorcycle roared from around the corner.

The fact that he'd deliberately parked the bike out of sight increased Cate's uneasiness. Had he figured Willow's description of him included a motorcycle, and Cate would be suspicious when she arrived at the house if she saw one? She doubted his determination to find Willow was solely because he wanted that belt buckle back; he had more than that in mind if he was willing to fake an identity and hire a private investigator.

A gust of wind hit her as she stood there waiting to make sure he was well gone before she unlocked the door. A storm was moving in fast. Dark clouds churned in from the west, bringing a raw scent of rain and early darkness. She shivered. Would a storm chase Willow out of her tree?

If Cate had to choose whom to believe, she'd go with Willow, she decided. She glanced at her watch. She wanted to rush over there now and warn Willow that Coop was still on her trail, but she wouldn't put it past him to lurk out of sight and follow her.

◆◆◆

Inside, the house was empty except for Octavia cuddled up to teddy bear Rowdy on the sofa. She'd taken to dragging him around by the ear. On sudden impulse Cate went to the house phone, looked up a number in the yellow pages, and dialed.

"Sound by Sammy. Ed here."

"I'm—" Cate broke off. She should have thought this through first. She rejected an impulse to come up with some over-the-top story, a la Coop Langston himself, and took a straightforward approach. "I need to corroborate some information about one of your employees. Nothing personal, I just need to know if he is employed there. Cooper Langston."

"Coop? Yeah, he works here. Not here today, but you can probably catch him tomorrow. Or I can take a message."

"No, that's all I need to know." So he had been telling the truth on one point at least; he did work at Sound by Sammy. "Thanks."

When Cate was off the phone, Octavia gave her a grumbly *mrrow*, as if the level of service here could definitely use improvement. Cate ruffled her fur. "That's all you have to say? No advice today?"

Octavia looked at the closed office door, and a moment later the phone in there rang. Cate considered the possible connection, then shook a finger at the cat. "No way," she said. "Pure coincidence."

She answered the office phone with her usual line. "Belmont Investigations. Cate Kinkaid speaking."

"Hi, Cate. This is Mitch. I was wondering if you'd like to go back to that house this evening and look for Willow again. Or try one of her other former employers."

"Actually, I went back and found Willow last night."

"Oh." He sounded disappointed, but he added, "How'd it go?"

"It's an odd situation, but I don't think she stole Beverly's ring." She almost told him about Coop Langston's visit, then remembered Uncle Joe's warning about confidential client information. Or did that apply now, since Coop was no longer a client and had been deceptive when he was a client? While she was still tangled in the PI ethics of all that, Mitch took the conversation in a different direction.

"You mentioned that your uncle might need some handyman help. I'll be glad to—"

"Mitch, I know you have a computer business, and you do painting and handyman work as part of a church project, not as a job."

"That doesn't mean I can't help your uncle."

"It's cleaning some gutters. Full of old leaves and gunky stuff."

"My favorite job."

"You don't have to do it for free. He can afford to pay you."

"We can talk about that later."

"Why are you doing this?" she asked.

"Because I want to see you again, and I'm afraid if I ask you out, you'll just turn me down. I got the impression that you were kind of . . . unavailable."

Unavailable? Because somewhere down deep in her subconscious she really did think, like Willow said, that God would send Kyle back to her? That God had some as-yet-invisible plan for them to be together? Did she *want* Kyle back? Could wanting him be why the only guys she'd had relationships with since the breakup were ones that same subconscious told her were basically unavailable themselves?

Or was her subconscious working overtime when it ought to be taking a coffee break?

"Okay, come do Uncle Joe's gutters," she said.

"When?"

"How about Sunday afternoon? We can barbecue something."

"I'll be there."

◆◆◆

She'd barely set the phone down when it rang again. She gave the response that was beginning to feel almost comfortable. "Belmont Investigations. Cate Kinkaid speaking."

"Miss Kinkaid, you don't know me, but this is Scott Calhoun . . . Cheryl Calhoun's husband?" An upswing at the end turned the statement into a question, as if he weren't certain she'd recognize Cheryl's name either. As further identity he added, "Amelia Robinson's niece?"

"Yes, Cheryl mentioned you. Actually, I was there with her at the house when you called from the conference. Can I do something for you?"

"I hope so. But first, there are a couple of things Cheryl wanted me to mention to you. You're probably wondering why I'm calling instead of Cheryl, right?"

Cate hadn't actually wondered anything yet, but she gave a noncommittal murmur.

"She's just too upset to do much of anything. Amelia's death, of course, is such a shock. It's really hit her hard, and then my being up in Seattle when it happened, and then this disturbing autopsy thing—"

"The autopsy showed something disturbing?"

"Oh no. Sorry, I didn't mean that. The autopsy simply showed that Amelia died from the head injuries when she fell, and that there were traces of her sleeping medication in her blood. She had the unfortunate habit of taking way too many of them. I didn't know it before, but Cheryl tells me Amelia occasionally walked in her sleep too."

"A dangerous combination."

"Exactly. So it isn't that the autopsy turned up anything disturbing about her death. It's just that Cheryl found the whole idea of an autopsy so upsetting. Knowing a loved one is being . . . well, you know what an autopsy is."

"Yes, I'm sure that would be disturbing."

"But it's a tremendous relief knowing no foul play was involved. I didn't mention it to Cheryl when she called me that night the police came to the house, because I didn't want to upset her further, but my first thought was that someone had deliberately pushed Amelia down the stairs."

"Why was that?"

"Amelia could be . . . abrasive. And then there's that boy-friend . . . Well, it doesn't matter now. I'm just relieved that the fall truly was an accident."

"Yes, that is a relief."

"The other thing is, Cheryl wanted you to know she was mistaken about the jewelry being missing. We found everything tucked away in Amelia's closet. Cheryl was quite shocked to find diamonds and emeralds and rubies just sitting there in an old shoe box. I'm not that surprised, I must admit. Amelia was a wonderful person, but she did have her . . . peculiarities."

Cate made an all-purpose murmur. Scott sounded as if he felt he had to do what the Whodunit ladies had done, upgrade Amelia's character and personality because she was dead now.

"Anyway, Cheryl feels really bad that she suspected the woman who was working for Amelia had stolen the jewelry."

"Has Cheryl mentioned to the police that she thought Willow took the jewels?"

"No, fortunately we found that old shoe box before saying anything to the police about anything being missing. But Cheryl said you were trying to locate Willow in connection with some other matter, so what we're wondering is, have you found her?"

"I spoke with her for a few minutes," Cate said, wary about where this was leading, although she wasn't certain why. "I recommended she talk to the police about having worked for Amelia. She said the reason she left the house so abruptly the morning of the accident was because Amelia fired her."

"Really? Actually, I'm not surprised. Amelia's done that before. She was probably sorry the minute Willow was out the door. Personally, I always thought Amelia was fortunate to have the woman. She seemed competent, and apparently didn't get excited when Amelia went off on one of her tangents. She couldn't have been the easiest person to work for. Anyway, the basic purpose of this call is that we'd like to talk to Willow, so we're hoping you can put us in touch with her."

"Talk to Willow about what?" Cate asked.

Scott Calhoun didn't sound offended by the blunt question. "We'd like to hire her to work and live here again. We live over in Springfield, and we need someone dependable here in the house until we can get the legalities with the will taken care of and sell the place, and she's the first person we thought of. It isn't good to have a house sitting empty, but we don't want to get involved with tenants. Without Amelia here, there wouldn't be much work for Willow to do. Basically, just house-sitting."

Cate hesitated. Probably she could safely give them Willow's current address. Her look-alike undoubtedly needed a job. But in spite of the autopsy findings, she couldn't quite squelch that earlier suspicion about the possibility of Cheryl's involvement in Amelia's death. There was also the thought that Willow ought to get out of town before Coop found her.

"I don't know if she'll be interested, but I'll try to pass the word along."

◆ 9 ◆

Cate glanced at the clock on Uncle Joe's office wall. It was too early yet to go to Willow's tree. She'd have to wait until the work crew finished for the day or she'd be dodging bulldozers and guys in hard hats. She'd just decided on a quick run when the office phone rang once more.

"Belmont Investigations," she responded. "Cate Kinkaid, assistant investigator speaking."

"Cate, this is Doris McClelland. I don't know if you'll remember me?"

"Yes, of course I remember you." She wasn't likely to forget the only person with whom she had ever shared discovery of a dead body. Doris's bony build and purple ensemble were also fairly memorable. "Is everything okay?"

"Well, I've been thinking about Amelia's fall."

"Cheryl's husband Scott just called me. The autopsy showed traces of sleeping medication in Amelia's blood. As you already know, she was in the habit of taking more sleeping pills than she should. It appears she simply wandered out to the stairs in a less-than-fully-aware state, and fell. Apparently no foul play is suspected."

"That's good to hear," Doris said. After a long hesitation, she said in a cautious tone, "Do you believe that?"

"You doubt the autopsy findings?"

"Oh no. I'm sure they know what they're doing. She used to sleepwalk once in a while. She told us a funny story once about waking up and finding herself in the kitchen eating pickled pigs feet." Cate thought Doris was simply going to say good-bye then, but after a moment she burst out, "But if Amelia's fall was just an accident, then I'm—I'm Oprah in disguise!"

An odd comparison, but the vehemence in Doris's voice was unmistakable. "Doris, if you know something, you should go to the police. Right away."

"Well, that's just it." Doris made a little clicking sound of frustration. "If I was sure I knew something, I *would* go to the police. It's just that I have these . . . suspicions. I have an inquisitive nature, I suppose. And finding Amelia's body out there like we did makes me curious. I also keep feeling a sense of . . . oh, I'm not sure what it is. Responsibility, maybe."

Responsibility. The word dropped on Cate like a brick out of nowhere, and the same word leaped up out of her subconscious to meet it. Because *responsibility* was what had been lurking in there, silently nagging at her. Telling her that because she'd found Amelia's body, and if the death was getting passed off as an accident and it wasn't an accident, she had the responsibility to *do* something about it.

"I feel as if Amelia is depending on me, and I don't want to let her down," Doris added.

"You aren't. This is a police responsibility, not yours," Cate assured Doris. And herself.

"And I feel guilty too."

"Guilty?"

115

"Oh, you know. Saying unkind things about Amelia, being petty and mean and gossipy. Amelia and I even exchanged some harsh words a time or two. As anyone in the club would probably be happy to tell you. Although there were lots of harsh words among all the Whodunit members."

"I'm sure it doesn't matter now." Cate hesitated, but curiosity wouldn't let her not ask, "Is there someone specific you're suspicious of?"

"Well, that's another thing. I have several suspicions. If I go to the police, I'll just look like some eccentric old lady with an overactive imagination. Especially if they've already decided it was just an accidental fall."

A strong possibility, Cate agreed. Both on how the police might react and on the overactivity of Doris's imagination. Except Cate's imagination kept ricocheting in that direction too.

Doris sighed. "Maybe I have read too many mysteries and seen too many crime shows on TV. And probably spent too much time thinking about this."

"Finding a body tends to make you think."

"Right." As if Cate's throwaway line had yanked the door open for her, Doris suddenly leaped into her suspicions. "I think about Cheryl inheriting everything from Amelia. The house and jewels and stock market account, and *cash*. Amelia got a big insurance payoff on her last husband. Then I think about Texie being so furious with Amelia for stealing that Radford guy from her, and pulling her disappearing act. And that woman who worked there, Willow, the one you were looking for, also disappearing right after Amelia's fall."

"Willow didn't actually disappear. I located her. Amelia had fired her that morning, which was why she left so abruptly. She didn't even know Amelia was dead until I told her."

"That's what she said?" Skepticism draped Doris's words like a heavy veil.

A skepticism that was perhaps warranted, Cate reluctantly had to admit. She liked Willow. There was something about their looking so much alike that made it difficult to think badly of her, as if exterior similarities meant interior similarities too. But if what Coop said was true, that Willow and truth weren't exactly good buddies . . .

Then Doris's earlier line grabbed her. "What do you mean about Texie and a 'disappearing act'?"

"Well, I'm not so suspicious of Texie now," Doris said. "It's that Radford guy who really gives me the willies."

"I'm getting confused," Cate said. "Texie disappeared, and you were suspicious of her, but now you're not, and it's really Radford you're suspicious of?"

"I tried to call Texie several times, and she was never home. Just disappeared and never returned my calls. But then she did call me earlier today. She said she knew I'd be worried, so she just wanted to let me know she was okay. She sounded really jumpy and hemmed and hawed around about staying with a friend out of town for a while because she wasn't feeling good. So right away I'm thinking maybe Texie is so jittery because she pushed Amelia down those stairs, and now she's hiding out from the police."

"She wouldn't have called you if she was really hiding out, would she?"

"That's what I decided too!" Doris sounded relieved to have that thought confirmed. "Anyway, I told her that as far as I knew, there wasn't any murder. Just a fall. Like you just now told me. But Texie practically jumped through the phone and said, 'Don't you believe it!'"

"Don't believe it because . . . ?"

"I'm getting to that. First off, the guy's full name is Radford Longstreet. Texie said that when she was dating Radford, her niece was suspicious of him. He'd told Texie he'd been married once, and his wife died of a heart attack years ago. But the niece works for a collection agency, and they do a lot of work chasing down people who skip out on paying bills. So she checked up on him. The niece wouldn't tell her exactly how she did it, because they're not supposed to use agency resources for private information, and she'd lose her job if they found out what she'd done. Radford had already dumped Texie for Amelia by then anyway, but the niece told Texie what she'd found out, just in case she had any ideas about wanting him back."

"And the niece found out . . . ?"

"Radford has been around here for the past few months, but he used a different name when he was down South. And he's had not one wife but *four*. The first marriage did end when the wife had a heart attack. The next wife died under rather peculiar circumstances, some kind of mysterious food poisoning, and he got property she had in Alabama. Wife number three disappeared. He said she'd run off with some rich guy from Mexico. No one seems to know if that's true, but he divorced her on the basis of desertion. Texie's niece thinks he murdered her and got away with it. He got the house. Wife number four died a couple years ago—get this— when she fell off the ship when they were on a cruise in the Caribbean. *Fell*," Doris emphasized.

Cate's stomach did a slow churn. She'd heard of guys like this. Going after vulnerable older women with money, marrying them . . . murdering them. And there'd been those rickety old stairs at Amelia's house practically inviting a rerun if a shove and fall had worked before.

118

"I figure he dumped Texie and jumped to Amelia because Amelia had more money, a *lot* more money, and was a better catch," Doris said. "Catch spelled v-i-c-t-i-m."

Cate was about to agree, but she immediately stumbled over a big flaw in this line of thinking. "But even if Radford planned to marry her and add her to his lineup of dead wives, he didn't have a chance to do it. Radford had no reason to murder her. He doesn't stand to gain anything from her death."

"Unless," Doris pointed out ominously, "she'd already changed her will to give him something. Or everything. Gullible women do that sometimes, you know."

From what she'd heard so far, Amelia hadn't struck Cate as "gullible," but love was blind, etc. Though surely such a provision in the will would wave a red flag for investigators.

"Do you know where Radford lives? Or what he does for a living?"

"Texie said he claimed to live off investments. I think Amelia was the current 'investment' he had in mind. I don't know where he lives."

"Do you know what name he used before he came here?" Cate asked.

"Texie didn't say. I don't know whether she knows or not."

But that niece who did the detective work at the collection agency knew. "What's the niece's name?"

"Jane or Carol or Betty, something ordinary like that. I never met her."

"How about the name of the collection agency where she works?"

"I don't know that either."

Cheryl had called Doris a "nosy busybody," but she didn't seem to be a particularly competent one. "Can you call Texie and ask?"

"I tried to call her back, but the cell phone number I have for her isn't working. I think she got a different cell phone because Radford has that other number, and she's really scared of him."

"Why would she be scared of him? He'd broken up with her."

"That's the scary part. Amelia was mad at Texie for telling her about Radford's past. She accused Texie of being jealous and vengeful and making up stuff about Radford because he'd dumped her. But apparently Amelia did say something to Radford, because he went to Texie and warned her if she messed up his relationship with Amelia, she'd be 'sorry.' So, when Amelia turned up dead, Texie was afraid she might be next and hotfooted it out of town."

Probably a good idea, if Radford was as dangerous as he sounded.

"I'm also thinking maybe Amelia had Radford investigated and found something even more incriminating about those wives' deaths and was going to the police. So he got rid of her."

"Texie needs to go to the police right away."

"That's what I told her. But she's too scared. She's afraid if it takes them awhile to investigate him that he'll nab her before they get him. I think she's figuring on getting a lot farther away than wherever she is now."

Which meant Radford might be long gone before Texie told the authorities what she knew.

"Where is Texie now?"

"Well, she was real cagey about that. I think she thought she wasn't telling me enough that I'd know where she is, but I'm pretty sure I do." Doris sounded pleased with herself. "She almost said the friend's name, but she caught herself after only a 'Lor' slipped out. But I remember a friend from over on the coast who came to visit Texie once, and her name was Lorilyn. I thought it was such a pretty name, even if the woman herself was boring as cold oatmeal. All she could talk about was herself. How great she was doing in her real estate business and how she'd tried skydiving and was into taking self-defense lessons with some unpronounceable name. Anyway, I wrote the name Lorilyn down so I could suggest it to my cousin's daughter for her baby. I really like the name, even though I didn't especially like her. But then Tammy went ahead and named the poor baby—"

"Lorilyn what?" Cate interrupted before Doris could ramble further into baby names. "What's her last name?"

"Well, I didn't write that down."

"And she sold real estate where?"

"Someplace over on the coast. That name that has to do with the funny law."

Big help there. A Lorilyn Somebody who sold real estate in a coastal town with a name connected with a funny law. Doris really did need lessons in busybodyness. Did the university offer Busybodies 101?

"But you're not really suspicious of Texie herself now, like you were at first?"

"We-l-l-l," Doris stretched the word into multiple syllables, then rushed on. "I do remember how Texie gave Amelia a shove one time when Amelia complained about the oysters Texie served at a lunch. Texie's in pretty good shape, a lot better than the rest of us. She has a weight machine and works out. It was a really hard shove."

"Which may have had more to do with Radford than oysters?" Cate speculated.

"Yes! Anyway, it occurs to me that the real reason Texie

called was to pump me for information, and the rest of it was just a creative pack of lies."

Yeah, there was a lot of that going around.

◆◆◆

Cate sat there tapping her fingers on Uncle Joe's desk. Octavia walked around on the desktop, batting at pens and sniffing at various spots on the glass.

"Any thoughts on all this, oh brilliant one?" Cate inquired.

The cat plopped down on the desktop and looked up at Cate expectantly. Reluctantly, Cate pushed the cat aside to see what was under her. There, in teensy-tiny words befitting what was apparently a teensy-tiny town, was a name. Murphy Bay. A law . . . Murphy's Law! If anything could go wrong, it would.

Which, in an irrelevant aside, sometimes seemed the story of Cate's life.

"That doesn't mean anything," Cate scoffed. "With the size of your rump, you covered fifty miles of coastline. With all kinds of town names under you. Florence. Reedsport. Your tail was up in Newport."

Octavia stood and stalked off with cat dignity in top form, as if to say, *You did ask me. And now all I'm getting is snarky remarks about my weight.*

"Hey, wait, you don't need to get all uppity," Cate called after her. But Octavia was apparently through dispensing PI advice for the day.

Cate studied the under-glass map. She could drive over to Murphy Bay and back in a day, but how would she find Texie even if she did that? On second thought, how many real estate offices could there be in a town the size of Murphy Bay, especially offices with an agent named Lorilyn? With her cowgirl flamboyancy, Texie might be fairly noticeable to the population there on her own.

A few minutes on the internet told Cate there was only one real estate office in Murphy Bay. She started to dial the number, then stopped. If she talked to Lorilyn, the woman would tell Texie, who might just pick up and run.

Cate left off that search and went after Radford Longstreet on the internet. Her search turned up nothing. No phone number, no address, no property ownership, nothing. She knew Uncle Joe had special databases that provided more information, but she didn't know how to access them.

The phone rang once more. Cate didn't look at the caller ID before she answered, this time with a simple "Hello," because she was still thinking about Radford.

"Hi, Cate, it's me again. Mitch."

"You can't make it on Sunday?"

"I just got to thinking. Sunday is a long way off. How about I do the gutters Saturday morning, and then we could have lunch? Maybe take a hike along the river in the afternoon?"

"I'd like to, but"—as she suddenly realized—"I have some plans for Saturday."

"Oh. Well, sure. I should have figured that."

But he was right. Sunday did seem a long way off. Saturday was a whole day closer, and with sudden inspiration she said, "I'm going over to the coast for the day. Maybe you'd like to come along?"

No hesitation or questions from Mitch. "What time?"

Mitch offered to take his SUV, and they settled on 8:15.

By that time, when Cate looked at the clock, she decided it was late enough to visit Willow's tree. She went to her bedroom to pick up a heavier jacket, but yet another phone call, this time on her cell, changed her plans. Rebecca. Her car had been running fine when she parked it in the hospital parking lot that morning, but now it wouldn't start. Could Cate come get her?

And by the time she and Rebecca got a mechanic who was willing to come after hours, and did, it was too late to go find Willow. Okay, tomorrow morning, then, and get there before the construction crew arrived. Cate set her alarm for 5:30.

10

Octavia opened one eye when Cate struggled out of bed the next morning, but she snuggled up to Rowdy rather than following. Cate took a quick shower and grabbed a bagel and coffee for breakfast. Rebecca was still asleep.

Remnants of storm clouds lingered in the before-dawn sky, but they were rapidly moving off to the east. Rainwater still gushed along street curbs, but that feeling of spring was back in the air. She expected all to be quiet at the construction scene at that hour of morning, but a police car angled into the sawhorse barrier, roof lights flashing. A spotlight from another police car targeted a tree down the street. Willow's tree! Even at this hour, curious people milled around on the sidewalk, and cars slowed on the street, drivers gawking. Cate couldn't park at the barrier, so she pulled around the corner to a side street and ran back.

From the lineup of sawhorses, she could see several police officers and workmen in hard hats clustered around Willow's tree. They were looking up at the spotlight beam in the tree.

"What's going on?" she asked a bystander frantically. "Is someone hurt?"

125

"They've been talking on a bullhorn to someone up in the tree," an older man in corduroy pants said. "One of those tree-hugger types. She don't seem to be comin' down."

"Good for her," a woman beyond him said. "If I were younger, I'd be right up there with her. It's a shame what they're doing here."

"Yeah, well, she's comin' down, you can bet on that. If they have to cut that tree out from under her." The man sounded gleeful, as if he'd happily supply the chain saw. "Dern-fool tree huggers."

Cate dodged around the end of the barrier, but she hadn't gone more than twenty feet when a hard-hatted worker stopped her with a raised hand. "Sorry. This area is off-limits to the public."

"But that's a friend of mine up in the tree!"

"Could you talk her into coming down?"

"I don't know. Maybe."

"Wait here."

Cate could hear the bullhorn herself now, an officer announcing that the occupant of the tree was in violation of a judge's orders and must come down immediately. He didn't say what would happen if she didn't comply. They surely wouldn't cut the tree down with Willow in it . . . would they?

The officers and several men in yellow hard hats huddled in a conference under the tree. The sky was growing lighter, and someone turned the spotlight off. Maybe they were going to start cutting! Cate dodged around piles of machinery already rumbling in readiness for the day's work, and almost fell over a chunk of asphalt. Members of the conference under the tree turned to look when she ran up.

"Please, I'd like to talk to her—"

"She's in violation of judge's orders," an officer repeated. "The construction crew needs to get to work here. And she's throwing shoes at us!" He grabbed a sneaker and held it up.

"Just give me a minute with her, okay? Maybe she's sick or hurt or something."

"There's nothing wrong with her throwing arm."

Without waiting for an okay, Cate ran to the tree trunk. Looking up, she couldn't see Willow. What she got was a falling faceful of raindrops collected on budding leaves and branches. She wiped her face with one hand. "Willow, are you up there? Don't throw any more shoes! Or anything else."

No answer.

"You have to come down. You can't save this tree, but there'll be others you can save."

No answer.

Cate turned to look at the officer. "Maybe it would help if I went up there. Not to stay," she added hastily. "I'm not a tree sitter."

Another conference. A man in a hard hat, apparently a supervisor, waved her upward. "Give it a try."

Cate spread her arms and embraced the tree trunk with a tentative grasp. She hadn't climbed a tree since she was in fourth grade, and she hadn't before noticed how big around this tree was. How had Willow managed to get up there? She tried for a foothold on the rough bark. Okay, that worked. Another foothold. She scooted her arms higher.

She was almost waist high now. So far so good!

Then both feet slipped. She dangled by little more than her fingertips, feet flailing. She struggled to wrap her legs around the tree, irrelevantly aware that she must look like a jeans-clad monkey clinging there. Probably an inordinately big-bottomed monkey. Then she lost a handhold.

And then she was on the ground. In the middle of a puddle she hadn't even noticed until she splatted into it.

"Better give her some help, Mike."

An officer strode up and helped her to her feet. She wiped muddy water off her face and tried to ignore the fact that she was wet from the waist down. He bent a leg, offering her a place to put her foot. She stood on his leg but still couldn't get enough of a hold on the lowest branch to hoist herself up.

"If I could get up on your shoulders?" Cate suggested.

"Whatever," he muttered.

She climbed awkwardly to his shoulders, balancing herself with a grip on his hair. He stood up, hands wrapped around her ankles. Would this all be written up in a police report? She finally grasped a bottom limb, and the officer shoved her upward with enough impetus to vault over it.

Barely stopping herself from a tumble right over the limb and another splat in the puddle, she looked upward and spotted a dark blob that she presumed was Willow. She took a deep breath and headed upward.

It was slow progress, finding foot- and handholds. More collected raindrops showered Cate's head and dribbled down her neck. But finally her head was just below Willow's feet. She could see now that Willow had tied herself to the tree with a piece of clothesline rope.

"You okay?" Cate asked.

"Do I look okay?" Willow snapped. Her hair hung like strands of unraveled rope, her nose was red, and her jacket soaked. She was also definitely shoe-less.

"How long have you been up here?"

"I climbed up about midnight last night."

"When it was still raining?"

"It seemed like a good idea at the time."

"I know it's disappointing, but you should come down now. One way or another, they're going to take this tree down. Since they got a judge to issue an order about getting you down from here, I'd say they mean business."

"You think I'm up here now because I want to be?"

"Aren't you?"

"Last night it was dark, and I just kept climbing. But this morning I looked around, and I'm . . . way up here." Willow scrunched closer to the tree trunk and looked back over her shoulder. "Way, way up here."

Cate, who had been concentrating solely on climbing, now looked around too. Willow was right. They were way, way up here. She could see out over the rooftops, out to flashing police lights and traffic on the street. Clouds still blanketed the mountains to the east, and the river cut a dark ribbon through the city. Up here, the tree trunk was slender and flexible, and it wobbled back and forth like a carnival ride with their every movement. Cate's insides sloshed with the sway. Had anyone ever become seasick in a tree?

"I tried to get down earlier, but it's even harder going down than coming up. My feet and fingers are numb . . . and I don't know what to do! I hate heights."

"Okay, don't panic. I'll come right up beside you."

Maybe not a good idea, Cate realized when she balanced on the branch just below the one Willow was sitting on, and it bent ominously under her weight. Here the branches were small and springy, suitable for birds, not budding PIs.

She had an unpleasant vision of two redheads tumbling to the earth below. *Lord, help me figure out what to do here!*

"Are you scared?" Willow asked.

"Of course I'm scared," Cate admitted.

"I suppose you pray when you're scared?"

"I pray when I'm scared. I pray when I'm happy. Or confused. Or thankful. God's always pleased to hear from us. You could pray too."

"God wouldn't want to hear from me. I've done . . . oh . . . things."

"God is in the forgiveness business. You don't have to get your life all straightened up before you talk to him."

"Hey, what's going on up there?" The big voice booming through a bullhorn made Cate grab another branch to keep her balance. "Judge's orders are that this tree be vacated immediately!"

There wasn't an "Or else" at the end, but Cate figured they had something in mind.

"Okay, we're coming down," she yelled back. She looked down, took a steadying breath, and instructed Willow to untie her rope.

"I can't. I'll fall! I wish Coop were here!"

"We don't need Coop. I'll be right below you. Face the tree. Keep your arms around it and back down, one foot at a time. I'll guide your foot so you don't miss the branch. By the way, you have a job waiting when you get down."

"A job?"

"Amelia's niece wants you to come back and house-sit for her. Amelia really did just fall down those steps. She was dopey from sleeping pills. And none of her jewelry is missing after all. They found it."

The news seemed to cheer Willow. She untied the rope, and Cate guided her shoe-less foot to the next branch down. She moved a branch lower herself, then guided Willow's other foot down another step.

"Doing great," Cate encouraged. "Don't look down."

Then a branch bent and cracked beneath Willow's foot.

She plunged downward, breaking Cate's grip on the trunk. Cate's arms windmilled, and she grabbed at branches as they scraped through her hands. Willow landed on Cate's head. Now she couldn't even see. They floundered among branches and a tangle of thrashing arms and legs.

A foot landed in the middle of Cate's midsection. A hand clutched her hair. She tried to yell "let go" but wound up with a mouthful of knee.

Note to self: avoid any future jobs involving trees and/or heights.

A larger branch finally stopped their fall. Looking down, Cate saw a cluster of upturned faces, like the petals on some bizarre people-plant.

"Everything okay up there?" an officer called, this time without the bullhorn.

Yeah. Lovely. Just out for a morning fall.

"We're coming down," Cate said. Of that she was reasonably certain; she just wasn't certain it was going to be a dignified descent.

But now that they were lower, Willow recovered her confidence. "I can make it okay now," she said, and with Tarzan-like agility she swung down through the remaining branches.

Cate was short on the Tarzan genes. Willow landed on her feet at the base of the tree. Cate, after a slower descent, made another ignominious splat.

She instantly scrambled to her feet. Whatever fear Willow had felt near the top of the tree did not translate into fear of police authority, and a fire of defiance now blazed in her eyes. She'd also reclaimed her shoes, and waved them like floppy weapons, yelling something about these people destroying what God had created.

Cate was gratified to hear Willow give God credit for the

trees, but she wasn't sure this was the time to proclaim it. She grabbed Willow's arm. "We're leaving now," she told the officers. "Thank you for your help."

"Hey," Willow objected. "I'm not—"

Cate propelled her look-alike forward. "We're leaving." Hopefully before Willow performed some brash action that would result in handcuffs for both of them.

Cate didn't let go of Willow's arm until they reached her car. "Sometimes you just have to accept temporary defeat and move on," she said.

Willow rotated her shoulders and looked down at her feet in muddy socks. "I'll have a better plan next time," she vowed.

❖ ❖ ❖

At the house on Lexter, Willow hooked up an electric heater and Cate backed up to it in her wet jeans. The house had a nice cinnamon-y smell, as if Willow had been baking again.

"I guess I haven't thanked you yet for climbing up to rescue me. I appreciate it." Willow spoke with her head under a towel, her voice muffled. "Not something every PI would do, I'm sure."

"It wasn't included in the job description, but I'm glad I could help."

Willow wanted to know more about the job offer, but what Cate said instead was, "I don't think you should take the job."

"You don't?" Willow peered out from under the towel. "Then why'd you tell me about it?"

"I didn't think it was something I could rightfully hide from you. And, up in the tree, I figured it might encourage you to come down."

Willow didn't berate Cate for that small ruse. "But now you don't think I should take the job?"

"Coop is still looking for you. Still *stalking* you. I think he's dangerous. I think you should leave Eugene as soon as possible." And, given that she couldn't quite let go of her suspicions about Cheryl, the job offer itself made her uneasy.

"I suppose I could go down to my grandma's in Florida." Willow threw the towel on the sofa and leaned her head over the heater, hair dangling like a red mop. Cate didn't like the reluctance she heard in Willow's voice.

"I was surprised, when we were up in the tree and you said you wished Coop were there. I didn't think you ever wanted anything to do with him again."

"I don't! It's just that I was so scared. I hate heights! Coop has a lot of faults, but . . . he's big and strong and competent at a lot of things." Willow's head disappeared under the towel again. "I mean, if you need protection from a rampaging bear or rescue from white-water rapids, or protection from some jerk trying to pick you up in a bar, Coop's your man."

"He came to see me."

Cate felt more than saw or heard the surprise in Willow's sharp intake of breath. "So he finally admitted he wasn't my great-uncle, Jeremiah somebody?" Willow asked.

"He said that, along with a few other things."

"Such as?"

Cate heard wariness in Willow's words. "He had a somewhat different version of your relationship and breakup than you did. He says he never hit you."

Willow gave an unladylike snort. Her head came out from under the towel again. "Of course he'd say that. What guy's going to come right out and admit he slaps and punches a girlfriend?"

"He also mentioned a belt buckle. His dad's, won in bull riding at a rodeo. He says you took it."

"Took it? That's a laugh. Coop loses everything. Watches. Wallets. Keys. He's also, if no one cleans up for him, perfectly happy to live in a pigsty of dirty clothes, dirty dishes, and greasy motorcycle parts. He could lose an entire motorcycle, to say nothing of one little belt buckle, in the mess. I'll bet he also had some story about my making off with his money."

"He mentioned that. Ten thousand out of a bank account and a bunch more on credit cards. He figured you bought lottery tickets. I didn't tell him you'd probably spent it on the Corolla because I didn't think he should know what you're driving now."

"There was money in the bank account, all right. But ten thousand? That's another laugh. And the money was mine anyway, a gift from my not-dead grandmother. I did put money into the lottery for a while, and it paid off too. Several times. My lucky numbers. But I needed all this money right away for a car." She paused. "Anyway, thanks for not telling him about the car. Anything else?"

"The credit cards?"

Another snort. "He has a grandiose idea about what I could get on those. Besides, Coop owed big on his credit cards when we first got together. I helped pay them off. When I left, I didn't take any more on cash advances than I had coming."

"He said you left because you were mad about his forgetting your birthday."

"Coop should be writing a fairy tale. He's good enough at making up stories."

"That's kind of what he said about you."

Willow gave a what-else-would-you-expect shrug.

"I didn't give him any hint where you were, and I told him Belmont Investigations was no longer working for him."

"Thanks. I appreciate that." Willow smoothly shifted gears

to another subject. "You told me up in the tree that Amelia's fall was definitely accidental?"

"That's apparently the official decision. I'm relieved. I'd been thinking . . . well, I had various ideas about people who might have pushed her."

Willow stood up and threw back her hair. Even wet, when Cate's hair tended toward a frizzed poodle effect, Willow's had a wild-woman attractiveness. She smiled. "Including me. Be honest now."

"It entered my mind," Cate admitted.

"I suppose I should tell you . . ."

"Tell me what?"

"That morning at Amelia's was a little different than I told you before." Willow pulled up a chair and wiggled her bare feet in the warmth of the electric heater. "I didn't actually . . . get fired. Though Amelia had threatened it enough times. The night before, she told me her book club was supposed to come for lunch the next day. I thought she'd called the deli, but she hadn't. They had to make everything, and I decided to wait rather than come back later. I was in my own car, and Amelia was really stingy about paying for gas. So it was at least a couple hours, maybe more, before I got back. I didn't see Amelia then, but I figured she was upstairs, sleeping late. I put everything in the refrigerator and got out the salad plates Amelia liked to use for serving lunch. She said people didn't eat as much if you gave them smaller plates."

Cate nodded. She remembered seeing that stack of plates in the kitchen. "So you didn't actually see Amelia at all that morning?"

"No. Then, after I'd been home awhile, I heard a fly buzzing at the window and pulled the drapes back to swat it. She always kept them closed, you know, because the backyard

135

looks so tacky. And there she was, lying at the foot of those old stairs." Willow rubbed her temples as if the memory hurt.

"You should have called 911 or an ambulance!"

"I know. But I could tell she was dead even before I ran out there. Then I just panicked. A while back I worked for that other older woman, the one I told you about who fell off her balcony. And back when Coop and I were together, we worked for an old guy on a dairy farm down in California, and he fell off his barn roof and got killed. I thought if the police came they'd find out I'd been around when these other deaths occurred, and they might think it was really odd. I mean, it *is* odd, three deaths, all by falling. And me right there."

Yeah. Odd.

Willow pushed a loose strand of hair out of her eyes. "I didn't have anything to do with any of them falling and dying, but people get convicted for crimes they didn't commit, you know? So I just picked up and ran."

The revised version of that day sounded like the truth. But then, Willow's first version about being fired had sounded like the truth too.

"This is why you looked for Octavia and wanted to take her with you? Because you knew Amelia was dead, and you were afraid no one would take care of her?"

"Yeah. But you got her, and that's even better. There's another thing. I guess it isn't important now that they know Amelia wasn't pushed, that she just fell." Although Willow had only moments before questioned that point, she'd apparently decided to go with it.

"What's that?" Cate asked, warily afraid of another corrected "truth."

"That guy Amelia was seeing—"

"The sleazy one?"

"Yeah. Radford. I saw his car a few blocks away when I was coming back from the deli that morning. I don't know that he'd been to the house. But I don't know why else he'd be in that area."

Which went along with Doris's suspicion of Amelia's boyfriend.

"Did he see you?"

"We didn't make eye contact, but I suppose he might have recognized my car."

"Doesn't that worry you? I mean, if he did push her, and he knows you saw him . . ."

"But Amelia wasn't pushed, she just fell, remember?" As if that settled the matter, Willow stood up. "I'm going to go put some conditioner on my hair, and then I'll call Cheryl."

"What about Coop?"

Willow waved a hand airily. "I'm not going to call Coop."

Which wasn't what Cate had asked, of course.

11

Driving home, Cate found herself both frustrated and annoyed with her look-alike. Willow hadn't yet been able to reach Cheryl by the time Cate left the house, but Cate had no doubt but what she'd accept the job offer. She wasn't taking Coop's stalking seriously enough! Unless Willow knew Coop wasn't actually stalking her . . .

Cate tended to believe Willow's version of her relationship with Coop more than she believed Coop's story, but she wasn't stake-my-life-on-it convinced.

This was not, she reminded herself, her problem. She'd accomplished what she set out to do. She'd found Willow. Although she was still undecided what to tell Uncle Joe about the various complications with the assignment. Maybe it would be best not to tell him anything.

After lunch, Cate drove over to the hospital. When she walked into the room, Rebecca was standing by the bed, holding hands with Uncle Joe.

"Cate Kinkaid, assistant PI, reporting in."

Uncle Joe held out his arms from the bed, and they shared an enthusiastic if somewhat awkward hug. "So, how do you like being a PI by now?"

138

"Interesting. Very interesting." She gave him a brief update on her success in finding Willow. "I'll write up a report for the files. Hey, I hear you'll be leaving here soon."

"A few weeks in a nursing home for physical therapy, and I'll be good as new. So they tell me. I keep thinking about those gutters and how they still need cleaning." Then, with no break to warn Cate of a change of subject, he said, "There's more to the Willow Bishop case than it originally appeared, isn't there?"

Cate tried not to reveal how much the question startled her. "What makes you say that?"

"I haven't been a private investigator all these years without being able to tell when someone is"—he broke off and studied her critically—"being evasive."

Evasive. Yes, he had her. Instantly. How did he do that? It was a talent she certainly didn't possess, since she still couldn't tell if it was Willow or Coop playing with the truth. She sighed and tucked that rebel spike of hair behind her ear. She started with the Whodunit ladies at Amelia's house. No Willow. Finding Amelia's body at the bottom of the stairs. Meeting niece Cheryl. The missing jewelry. Acquiring Octavia. Locating Willow's former employer. Missing ring. Finding Willow in the tree. Willow's different story about the identity of "Jeremiah Thompson." Cooper Langston's visit. Climbing Willow's tree. The jewelry not missing now. The niece offering Willow her job back. Cate advising Willow not to take it.

Uncle Joe blinked. "How long have I been in here anyway? I feel like old Rip Van Winkle, waking up after a twenty years' sleep."

"I hope you don't mind, but I told 'Jeremiah Thompson' the agency is no longer working for him, and we'll refund his money. And I didn't tell him where to find Willow, of course."

"Good. That closes the case, then." He brushed his hands together. Except that Cate could tell Uncle Joe was curious too. His tone was just a little too offhand when he said, "Did they ever find out how the woman happened to fall down the stairs?"

"Amelia's niece's husband Scott says the autopsy showed traces of sleeping medication in her blood. She was known to pop a lot of sleeping pills, which often made her really fuzzy-headed in the morning, and sometimes she even sleepwalked. So she must have just wandered out there to the stairs sometime in the night or early morning and fell down them. The police don't seem to be doing any further investigation."

Shrewd PI look. "But you don't think it was a fuzzy-headed accident?"

"I certainly don't know more than the experts! Although . . ."

"Although what?"

"Well, I was just thinking on the way over here. If someone knew about Amelia's habit of taking sleeping pills, and knew she was kind of dopey in the morning, it would be easy to take advantage of that. Someone could have led her out there and given her a push before she had any idea what was happening."

"So you think someone may be getting away with murder."

Cate jumped on that with an eagerness that surprised her. "Yes! There are a number of suspects—"

"Suspects are none of our concern," Uncle Joe interrupted. He also frowned. Not a normal expression on Uncle Joe's usually cheerful face. "Murder is not for amateurs. That isn't what Belmont Investigations does these days anyway. We only do low-key cases. Routine stuff. Nothing dangerous. No murder cases," he repeated.

"But I saw a gun in your desk—"

"You still have that thing?" Rebecca gasped.

"I don't keep it loaded," Uncle Joe said, as if that explanation made everything okay.

"But you used to take on more dangerous cases?" Cate asked.

"How do you think he got that limpy leg?" Rebecca snapped. "Not from falling off a ladder cleaning gutters."

"If I had a client, and there happened to be a murder involved, maybe an unjust accusation or something such as that, I might do some investigating. Sometimes there were unexpected complications. But now—"

"Another of those 'unexpected complications' was the time our Buick blew up." Rebecca sounded grumpy at the memory. "And there was the time that strange woman in the leopard catsuit took you hostage."

Cate gave Uncle Joe a quizzical lift of eyebrows, but he was not forthcoming with explanations.

All he said was a firm, "Even if it looks somewhat suspicious, this woman's death isn't our case. Leave it to the police."

"But if they're not even going to investigate, because they think it's an accident—"

"No. We don't have a client involved, and private investigators can't just rush out and stick their noses into something because it looks interesting or suspicious. That's very important, that whatever we do is for a client. Don't go sticking *your* nose into this. Besides, now that you've successfully taken care of your first case, I have a couple of other assignments for you. If you're interested in continuing with the job."

"Yes, of course." What else did she have to do?

Joe told her about the files to look at in his desk, and what she should do to investigate the cases. Both, he assured her, were routine—no murder, no mayhem, no tree climbing.

The fact that Uncle Joe now felt confident enough in her abilities to give her the new assignments made Cate feel good. But his "don't go sticking your nose into it" about Amelia's death put a definite damper on the trip to Murphy Bay on Saturday. She'd have to call Mitch and tell him it was off.

But Cate saw frustration in the flick Uncle Joe gave the hospital blanket covering him from the waist down, and she strongly suspected that if he'd found Amelia's body, and if he weren't stuck here in the hospital, he'd be sticking *his* nose into Amelia's death. She also figured that if he wanted to investigate a situation, he'd manage to find a client.

Cate had all those suspects walking around in her head. Unfortunately, none of them looked like potential clients.

But did a client necessarily have to be money-paying? Or human?

◆◆◆

Back home, Cate put the question directly to Octavia. "Are you interested in finding out if your former owner was murdered, thus depriving you of security, companionship, and a future supply of gourmet cat food? Because all you're going to get here is the ordinary stuff. No shrimp and caviar."

Octavia might not be able to hear, but she knew when she was being talked to. She looked up at Cate with her big blue eyes. *Mrrow.*

"And do you want me as an assistant with Belmont Investigations to investigate who may have done this dastardly deed? Payment to be made in snuggles, cuddles, and any other appropriate forms of feline affection?"

Mrrow.

Cate decided not to question whether those were affirmative responses—and not to test the authenticity of the answers by asking something such as, Do you believe scientists will figure a way around the limits of the speed of light in interplanetary travel? Because she had the feeling the answer would be that same complacent *mrrow*. Which might dilute the authority of the earlier answers.

"Okay," she said. "It's settled then. You're my client and I'm investigating."

The trip to the coast on Saturday was on again. That evening, before bed, she grabbed a book from the collection in Uncle Joe's office and read up on questioning reluctant witnesses.

◆◆◆

Mitch, in khaki shorts, white T-shirt, and a straw hat that looked as if it had spent most of its existence stuffed in the bottom of an old fishing box, arrived five minutes early. He loaded Cate's bags of food, bottled water, Thermos of coffee, maps, notebook, sun hat, raincoat, and sunscreen in his SUV without complaint. Cate noted all he'd brought was a windbreaker and a can of peanuts.

He didn't question their destination until they were headed across town to the highway to the coast. "Do we know where we're going, or is it just the coast in general?"

"Does it matter?"

He grinned at her. "Not really."

"It's a little place called Murphy Bay, population 514."

"Okay, I know where that is. I've never stopped, but I've been through there. I suppose this could be just a fun trip to

143

watch the surf and seagulls, et cetera, but I'm guessing that's just wishful thinking?"

"I need to find a woman named Texie. She has a friend, Lorilyn, who works at a real estate agency there. But I'm sure it will be a fun trip too," Cate added brightly.

"So, basically, it's PI business." After Cate murmured agreement, he added, "A new case?"

"Well, um, no."

"But you've solved the case of the missing Willow."

"There have been some additional developments."

Mitch questioned her with a curious glance, and she gave him a condensed rundown on Doris's phone call about Texie and Radford.

"So this trip to the coast isn't about Willow. This is about Amelia. And murder." Mitch tapped the steering wheel, apparently not thrilled with the implications of that. "What does your uncle think about your getting involved in this?"

"He said stay out of it," Cate admitted reluctantly.

"So isn't that what you should be doing?"

"This isn't really *involvement*," Cate protested. "It's just that I might be able to learn something that would be helpful to the police. I did find the body."

Although she'd found a textbook on microbiology back in college once, and she hadn't felt inclined to buy a magnifying glass and start prowling the campus looking for exotic organisms.

"Have you considered that poking around in murder could be just a tiny bit dangerous? That murderers tend to object, possibly unpleasantly, to finding a PI, even"—he shot her a sideways glance—"an attractive one, on their tail?"

Cate flashed him her most ingratiating smile. "Maybe that's why I wanted you along."

Flattery did not alter his lack of enthusiasm for her sleuthing efforts. "Are you thinking about becoming a full-fledged private investigator?"

"Uncle Joe will probably close Belmont Investigations and fully retire now, so I'm still looking for a real job."

He nodded as if he approved of that. "What do you usually do?"

Good question, Cate thought glumly. "I've been a Christmas elf, a costumed sign waver, and a stuffer of flyers under windshield wipers since I've been in Eugene."

"An admirable flexibility," Mitch said.

"Okay, I started out to be a teacher. My Aunt Delphie is a wonderful teacher. She still hears from students she had years ago. I saw teaching as a really worthwhile goal in life. Aunt Delphie encouraged me, even helped with my college expenses, and I got a degree in education."

"I hear a 'but' coming."

"But I discovered that, even if teaching may be the most noble profession in the world, and even if I liked the kids, I was not an effective teacher." She paused. "You might even say I was a lousy teacher."

"Maybe it was just the school. You could give it another try somewhere else."

"I was sick to my stomach on the way to school every morning. Some people like Aunt Delphie are Teachers. Capital T. I'm not."

"A borrowed dream that didn't work."

Cate had never thought of it exactly that way, but, bottom line, Mitch had nailed it. She'd latched on to Aunt Delphie's dream for her life, and it sank like her dad's old boat going down in the river one summer. They'd had life jackets to cope with the boat disaster, but no life jacket was available when her teaching career sank. She'd been disappointed with herself for failing as a teacher, saddened that she'd also disappointed Aunt Delphie.

"So what have you been doing since teaching"—he paused and then phrased it diplomatically as they passed a slow-moving log truck—"didn't work out?"

Cate told him about the companies where her jobs also hadn't "worked out," how she'd come to Eugene at Uncle Joe's and Rebecca's invitation, and found a job market tighter than the Gap jeans she'd once splurged on and now couldn't zip up. "So, at the moment, except for this temporary job Uncle Joe gave me, I seem to be basically unemployable."

"Beverly tells me God can do great things even with a crummy situation," Mitch said.

Not exactly a direct-from-the-Bible quotation, but "crummy situation"? Yeah, that fit. A job history that read like a self-help book on how to fail without really trying. A history of relationships scripted for a bad chick flick.

When Cate didn't comment, Mitch asked, "Was there a husband in there somewhere?"

"No. A fiancé for a while."

"Someone you met down in California?"

"We knew each other in grade school, but his dad transferred to serve as pastor at a church in another small town nearby. So we didn't go to the same high school or college. Then, down in San Diego, we ran into each other at a church event. My mom and his even became friends back home."

"A guy with a pastor for a father. Both of you with Christian beliefs. Parents who were friends. Sounds like a program for happily-ever-after."

Cate had certainly believed they were headed for happily-ever-after. "Kyle had slipped away from his Christian beliefs while he was in college. But he'd just lost a job and was feeling kind of lost, and he'd started going to this big church that I already attended. After we got together, we were involved in a lot of church activities together." They'd also prayed together and talked about how they could serve God with their lives.

"Very admirable."

"Then Kyle got a new, better job than the one he'd lost, a management position with a big satellite TV company. But he had to travel a lot, so he didn't have much time for church activities after that."

"So you had an ugly breakup? And it soured you on men forever?"

Cate turned to look at him, startled. "Why would you think that?"

He just shrugged, but she remembered his earlier comment about his impression of her "unavailability."

Her breakup with Kyle was dumb, really. An argument over a cappuccino machine started it. Kyle wanted one, the most expensive model on the market. Cate said they should be saving money to buy a house when they were married instead of buying overpriced gadgets. He grudgingly bought a cheaper cappuccino machine. He had some people from the satellite company over one evening. The machine turned out cappuccino that not only tasted as if it were made with a combination of sour milk and battery acid, it also shot a stream of foamy spray into the cleavage of a guest leaning over to look at the machine. Kyle blamed Cate. Cate said he hadn't followed the instructions. Kyle accused her of sabotaging his career. She accused him of being too interested in that cleavage. Later, words such as "unsupportive," "know-it-all," and "unsophisticated" were tossed around.

"The Cappuccino Conflict?" Mitch suggested after she'd given him a minus-cleavage version of the breakup.

The Cappuccino Conflict. Yes. "I thought we'd get back together. The whole thing just exploded all out of proportion. But before we got things straightened out, he got a surprise offer for a transfer to the company headquarters in Atlanta, and two weeks later he was gone."

"Apparently his career hadn't been sabotaged."

She nodded, but she'd suddenly had enough of putting her past failures with both Kyle and her career under a microscope. And she wasn't about to go into a study of the guys she'd dated after Kyle. "What about you?"

"No wife. Not even a fiancée."

"Working with computers was what you always wanted to do?" Cate asked.

"Pretty much. In high school I hacked into some sites I had no business being in, and got into big trouble. My folks were ready to ban computers forever, but one of my teachers was generous enough to think the hacking showed a certain potential and helped me get a college scholarship. Then Lance and I got together and have done pretty well with our own business."

"The Computer Solutions Dudes."

"We're in Eugene because that's where Lance was originally from."

"It must be nice to have your life's work all mapped out." Cate felt a little wistful. Here she was, almost thirty, still wondering what she was going to be when she grew up.

"Life's work?" Mitch sounded startled, as if he hadn't really thought of it as a lifetime commitment.

At the junction with Highway 101, without having to look at the map, Mitch turned north. A scent of ocean had teased them for some miles, but here it hit with an invigorating blast of salt-and-sea. Cate sniffed with the delight a visit to the coast always brought her. The scent hinted at exotic, far-off places across the ocean, adventures on the high seas, pirates and buried treasure. A stiff breeze swirled dissipating wisps of fog overhead, with glimpses of blue sky and sunshine. Sunlight lit patches of Scotch broom as if the golden blossoms were a special treasure deserving a spotlight, even though most coast locals considered them troublesome weeds.

A little after 10:00, Mitch turned the SUV into the parking lot of a café and gift shop. "Here it is." He pointed to a sign on the far side of the highway. "Murphy Bay."

Cate looked down the highway, which was also the main street of town. An assortment of stores and houses, gas station, church, and two motels. A bit shabby, perhaps, but all with a certain weather-beaten charm. A wind sock in the shape of a red dragon danced atop a pole outside an antique store. No bay that she could see. A good-sized hill to the west apparently blocked view of the ocean.

"Now what?" Mitch asked.

Deflation unexpectedly whooshed through Cate. Back home, finding Texie in a small town of 514 sounded as simple as picking white-furred Octavia out of a lineup of calico felines. She'd locate cowgirl-garbed Texie and ask her insightful questions that would produce a confession of her guilt or would lead Cate to a guilty Radford. The mystery of Amelia's death would be solved. Even though Uncle Joe had given her the temporary PI job out of charity, and didn't want her investigating this, he'd be impressed. But now that she was here, it felt more like the old needle-in-a-haystack quandary. She may have studied Uncle Joe's books, but what did she really know about investigating anything? The police apparently weren't suspicious of Amelia's death, so why should she be?

Mitch seemed to be waiting for instructions, and she couldn't think of any. "You think this is all some wild goose chase."

Mitch grinned. "I can't think of anyone I'd rather chase wild geese with than you."

Maybe this should simply be a fun trip to the coast. Find the bay, take a hike on the beach, get to know Mitch better. But once more that image of Amelia lying dead at the foot of the stairs jumped out and grabbed her. Surely it wasn't just an accident that Cate had been the one to find her. It meant something.

"How about we go have a cup of coffee?" Mitch motioned to the café, where a metal wind chime jingled cheerfully at the main door.

"I have coffee in the Thermos."

"You're missing the point. Don't hard-boiled detectives always go to some dark, smoky place and run into some sleazy character with exactly the information they need?"

"I think the sleazy guy is usually in a sleazy bar, but maybe this will work."

Inside, sunshine streamed through an east-facing window, and a fragrance of coffee and pastries wafted over maroon-padded plastic seats that lined a counter. A middle-aged woman in a pink uniform came over to take their order. The blond bun at the back of her head was watermelon size, but she didn't look sleazy.

Cate asked for iced tea and Mitch ordered coffee. Before the woman went away, Cate said, "I'm looking for a friend who's staying here in town, but I'm not sure where. She's an older woman, blonde, petite, and she usually wears cowgirl-type clothes?"

"Honey, we get all types here during tourist season. They come in wearing everything from shorts skimpy enough to make me want to throw a sheet over them, to T-shirts saying 'Membership Chairman, Alien Astronauts, Inc.' But a cowgirl? That doesn't ring any bells."

"How about a real estate agent named Lorilyn?"

"Oh her, yeah. Lantzer's Real Estate, down by the beauty shop." She waved a generously sized arm toward the south end of town.

Cate's confidence bounced back. Hey, maybe being a private investigator wasn't so difficult after all.

They finished their iced tea and coffee, and a minute later found the real estate office, stuck between the beauty shop and a hardware store, where the front window held fishing net and wire cages that Cate recognized as crab pots. A sign that simply said "Closed," without indication of an opening any time in the near future, hung inside the door.

The all-too-familiar "Now what?" snagged Cate again.

"Go next door," Mitch suggested. "Aren't beauty shops a universal gathering and distribution point of all female knowledge?"

Cate slid out of the SUV and pushed open the door of the beauty salon, half expecting she might be grabbed and herded into a chair for corrective hair surgery. The young, dark-haired woman did give that wayward spike of red hair a speculative glance, but she didn't offer emergency aid.

"Hi. I'm wondering about the real estate office next door?" Cate asked.

"Lori had to go down to Reedsport today. She'll probably be in the office if she gets back in time, or you can catch her at home later."

"Actually, it's a friend who's been staying with Lori that I'm looking for."

"Neva?"

Cate started to say no, but it occurred to her that if Texie was serious about hiding out here, she might be using a different name. "Yes, that's her."

"She might have gone to Reedsport with Lori. More likely, she's there at the house. She doesn't get out much. It's the big blue house on Denzler Street. Turn left at the next corner."

Doesn't get out much. Interesting. "Thank you."

Cate passed the instructions along to Mitch, and a few minutes later he braked in front of a three-story blue house, appealingly quaint, with maple trees, bushes with big balls of blue blooms, and a high hedge of shrubbery. Cate didn't ask Mitch to come along, but he opened the door of the SUV and followed her up the stepping-stone walkway. She felt unexpectedly apprehensive as she rang the bell, suddenly glad Mitch was beside her.

No answer to the bell. Was she disappointed or relieved? She wasn't certain.

"Let's go pick up something for lunch, find the bay, and come back later," Mitch suggested.

"I brought sandwiches. And some macaroni salad and chips. And some pickles and tomatoes and deviled eggs."

"A woman who's prepared. I like that."

They stopped at the gas station to ask for directions to the bay, and a few minutes later, down a rutted dirt road on the far side of the hill, they found it. "Bay" was something of an exaggeration for the inward bend in the rocky shoreline, but there was a narrow strip of sandy beach strewn with kelp and a couple of battered picnic tables on a grassy bluff. White spray shot over offshore rocks, surf attacked and retreated, gulls shrieked and dipped. They deposited their lunch on a table, and Cate took off her shoes, rolled up her jeans, and raced for the strip of beach.

She closed her eyes and dug her toes in the damp sand. Oh, much too long since she'd done that! Southern California beaches were wonderful, but the rugged Oregon coast had an appeal all its own.

They waded in the cold surf, inspected starfish clinging to rocks, studied odd creatures in a tide pool, squished the hollow bulbs on the strands of kelp, and tossed globs of sea foam at each other. They searched the pebbly areas for shells and agates. Mitch insisted only true agates were "keepers," which limited his take to two small stones. Cate gaily filled her pockets with pretty rocks, agates or not. Mitch told her about growing up in Tennessee, never seeing the sea until he was grown. They ate their lunch, tossing scraps to seagulls that expertly caught them in midair, walked to a jumble of rocks at the far end of the beach, and finally stretched out on a blanket in the grass by the picnic table. They decided they'd go back to the real estate office about 4:00.

Cate couldn't believe it when she woke to find she'd actually dozed off right there on the blanket, and Mitch was smiling and tickling her nose with a stalk of grass.

"It's 4:30," he said.

Cate jumped up and started looking for her shoes. She noted Mitch wasn't rushing to get into his. "Hey, we should hurry. The real estate woman might be back from Reedsport by now."

Mitch crossed his hands behind his head on the blanket. "How about we just forget Lorilyn and stay here a couple more hours before we head home? Maybe get some hot dogs and buns and stay even longer. Have a moonlight weenie roast on the beach."

Tempting as that idea was, Cate said, "But Lorilyn and Texie are the reason for this trip over here."

"Not my reason," Mitch said with a meaningful grin.

"Maybe we can come again sometime. Just for fun."

"Just tell me when."

They put their shoes on and gathered up leftover wrappers and cartons from their lunch. Just as Cate was opening the door on the passenger's side of the SUV, Mitch grabbed her arm and swung her around.

"This has been fun," he said. "I'm glad you asked me to come along."

"I'm glad too."

His arms slipped around her, and she looked up to meet his blue eyes. Wind had tossed his brown hair into ragged peaks, and sand glinted in his eyebrows. A surprisingly appealing combination.

"I'm thinking about kissing you," he said. But he didn't do it. He just kept looking at her, apparently undecided.

"You think too much."

She stretched up on tiptoes and gave him a quick kiss on the corner of his mouth. He grinned and did a much more thorough job of kissing her back. The wind whipped their hair together, and Cate's heart thumped faster than the incoming surf. And then an old pickup with a load of kids in back bounced down the rutted road and pulled up beside Mitch's SUV. Cate laughed and backed away from him, but he held on to her hand.

"Cate, I've been thinking."

"You know what I said about thinking."

"Maybe. But what I'm thinking is, we could really use another person in the Dudes office. How about coming to work for us?"

"Really? Doing what? I use a computer, of course. But I'm no expert."

"There's more work than our receptionist can handle. But if you're interested, you could work into the computer part of it. I could teach you. You could wear jeans or whatever you wanted to work. We're pretty casual."

Working for a company that was small but apparently stable. Learning something new. A steady paycheck. Working with Mitch! It all sounded great, until something lurking under the job offer poked out and jabbed her.

"Have you been looking for someone to fill this position?"

"Well, no, but—"

"Has there *been* a position, before about five minutes ago?"

"Lance and I have talked about it." Mitch's eyes dodged hers, and he sounded uncomfortable. "And I'll have to discuss salary and benefits and everything with him. But I'm sure we can come up with a good offer."

"A pity job. Because you think I'm too incompetent to find a decent job on my own!"

"No! I think you're sharp and intelligent and capable. It's just that it's a tough job market now and—"

"So you're going to pull a knight-in-shining-armor good deed! So I won't be standing on a street corner with a sign reading 'Will do private investigating for food.' "

"Don't be ridiculous."

"Offering me a job that doesn't exist is ridiculous!"

"And your chasing over here after a murderer isn't ridiculous?" he countered. "Cate, I can't understand why you're so involved in this. You're not really a PI—"

"Maybe I am. Maybe I've always had a dormant PI gene, and it's just now getting a chance to do something."

"People don't have dormant PI genes." He paused. "Okay, for all I know, maybe they do. And maybe yours is all awake and hot to trot. But this morning, there at the house, I saw someone moving at an upstairs window. I think this woman you're looking for was up there. She may be a murderer. And dangerous."

"So why didn't you tell me you saw her?"

"Because I don't think you should be involved in this! It . . . concerns me."

"That's very sweet, your being concerned and all, but this really isn't any of your business."

"It isn't any of yours either. Your uncle told you to stay out of it! Cate, you're no PI. You know that as well as I do. Just because you managed to find this woman you were looking for doesn't mean you're qualified to investigate *murder*."

"I have a client—" The statement burst out before Cate thought better of it.

"What client?"

"Client information is confidential."

She yanked the SUV door open to end the conversation, although the gesture lacked the effectiveness of a decisive slam. It didn't help that the window was open, and Mitch glared through it.

"Okay, forget it. I just wanted to help. I don't like the idea of your chasing around looking for murderers."

"It's none of your business," Cate repeated. "I'll thank you to just . . . butt out."

He stalked around the SUV to the driver's side door, slid inside, and slammed the door with enough muscle to rock the vehicle. It was also not a particularly effective gesture, since it merely put them together inside the SUV.

Mitch stared straight ahead. "The real estate office or the house?" he muttered.

"Real estate office."

They rumbled up the rutted road to the highway. At the real estate office, he pulled to the curb. The closed sign was turned to "open." Cate did a quick recalculation. If she went in to talk to Lorilyn, the woman would undoubtedly call Texie to warn her someone was looking for her.

"I've changed my mind. Let's go to the house."

Without further comment, although his hunched shoulders said volumes, Mitch drove back to the blue house.

"Wait here," Cate commanded. She slammed out, went to the door, and rang the bell. No response. Now what? If she hadn't been able to feel Mitch's eyes burning into her back, she might have quietly retreated. Even if Texie was hiding inside, Cate couldn't just storm the house like some one-woman SWAT team.

But since Mitch was watching her, she wasn't going to confirm her incompetence at being a PI. She marched around the house to the backyard, where the high hedge enclosed more green grass and a covered patio.

Texie sat in a lounge chair on the patio, a book in her hands. Cate was close enough to see the title. *The Bridges of Madison County*. A sad-ending romance? Not what she'd expect a Whodunit person to be reading, but Texie seemed engrossed in it. No cowgirl gear today. Texie's feet were bare, and slim white capri pants and a pink tank top emphasized her trim figure. A glass of iced tea sat on the table beside her. And beside the tea . . . Cate's eyes popped. A gun!

Cate stopped short, but she must have made some giveaway noise. Texie jumped up. Cate saw both fear and recognition on her face, but she couldn't tell whether Texie recognized Cate as herself or thought she was Willow. A split second later Cate saw her make a snap decision to fake non-recognition. She also stepped in front of the gun, hiding it.

"I'm sorry. Lori isn't here," Texie said. "She's at the real estate office."

"I'm not looking for Lorilyn. I came to talk to you."

Texie's eyes held Cate's, but her hands edged around behind her back. She was going for the gun!

12

Cate dodged behind the only available shelter, an oversized barbecue grill with a metal hood.

Before Cate could say anything, Texie yelled, "Get out of here! You have no right to—"

A crash and clatter—gunshot! The sound blasted through the quiet backyard like an explosion.

Am I hit?

Cate flexed body parts, almost frozen with shock, grabbed her thigh when something bit into it, then realized it was only the rocks still in her pockets. She warily peeked over the top of the grill. Texie just stood there, looking as stunned and shocked as Cate felt. They spotted something at the same time. The gun! It lay on the concrete patio, only a couple of feet from the grill. Cate lunged for it, and they met with a crash of heads. Cate saw spinning stars from the impact, but she managed to snatch the gun first.

She stood with the gun shakily pointed at Texie. Although she didn't really know what to do with it. Her dad had taught her to shoot a rifle, but she knew nothing about handguns. She wanted to look at it to try to figure it out, but she also didn't want to take her eyes off Texie.

159

"You shot at me," Cate accused, voice as shaky as her hands on the gun.

Texie snapped out of her daze. "I didn't shoot at you! I accidentally knocked that stupid table over, and the gun went off when it hit the ground. Now give it back to me." She held out her hand.

Cate realized now that the table was indeed sprawled on its side, but she warily backed away and just stood there, undecided what to do. She didn't have to contemplate the problem of her ignorance about guns for long. Mitch grabbed the weapon out of her hand and held it as if he definitely knew what to do with it. Cate didn't remind him she'd told him to wait in the car. She was too glad he was here beside her.

"Okay, what's going on?" he demanded.

Cate saw now where the bullet had blasted a ragged splinter off the side of one of the wooden posts supporting the patio cover. It had missed her by only a few inches. Shattered glass littered the patio, and iced tea spread an amoebic pattern dotted with ice chips over the concrete. Texie's book lay on the concrete too.

Texie didn't apologize about the gun. She held a hand over her eyebrow, apparently the impact point of their collision, and glared at Cate. "What are you doing here? Who told you I was here?" She didn't wait for an answer, and her voice gathered steam and volume. "It was Doris, wasn't it? Nosy old blabbermouth Doris! Did she tell Radford too? But I'll bet she didn't tell you she had just as much reason to kill Amelia as I did, and maybe *she* pushed her down the stairs!"

Cate tried to assimilate the barrage of questions and information. The first thing that hit her was that Texie was admitting she had reason to kill Amelia, but the next item was more startling. "Doris had some reason to kill Amelia?"

"Of course she did. All the Whodunit women did. Except Doris had the most reason of all. Now give my gun back, please." She held out a hand to Mitch, the gesture imperious rather than pleading.

"No."

Texie's mouth compressed in a frustrated line at the no-compromise tone of Mitch's one-word response. She looked back at Cate. "So why are you here?" she demanded. "What do you want?"

"What do you mean, all the Whodunit women had reason to kill Amelia? You're the one she stole Radford from, and from what I hear, you were mad enough to push her off the planet."

"Blabbermouth Doris told you all about Radford, of course."

Cate couldn't deny that. "Why did you call Doris, if you think she's such a blabbermouth? Especially if you think she may have killed Amelia?"

"Because I needed to find out if they'd arrested Radford yet." Texie hesitated. "And it wasn't until I was talking to her that I realized maybe she'd done it herself."

"So now you're packing a gun because you're afraid of Doris?"

"I have a gun because Radford threatened me. And if he'd kill Amelia, he'll kill me!"

"Why would he kill you?"

"To keep me from going to the police with what I know about him."

"So go to the police *now*." Cate took a step forward. "We'll go with you."

Texie looked as if she'd prefer to take off and run, but, in bare feet, with a minefield of broken glass around her, she stood rooted to the spot. Her toenails glittered with sparkly pink polish, somehow an incongruous touch for a gun-packer.

"Except maybe you don't want to go to the police because *you* killed Amelia, and you're afraid you might incriminate yourself some way if you talk to them," Mitch suggested, and both women turned to look at him.

Hey, I'm the PI here. But his accusation made sense.

"I didn't kill her," Texie muttered. "Even though I felt like it for a while."

In an effort to encourage her, Cate suggested, "But not so much after your niece investigated Radford and told you about his past, right? By then, you must have been grateful Amelia had him, not you."

"It was still a sneaky, underhanded thing to do," Texie said. Then, apparently realizing that comment didn't exactly reinforce her claim of innocence, she set the overturned table upright and became very busy picking up shards of shattered glass.

"I'd like to talk to your niece."

"No. I'm not dragging her into this. She could lose her job."

"Don't you want the police to find out who killed Amelia?"

"If it wasn't you?" Mitch put in.

"Yes, of course I do." Texie shot Mitch a baleful glance as she stood up, hands full of shattered glass. She set the shards on the table and reluctantly added, "I suppose maybe I should go to the police. Would they give me protection, so Radford couldn't get to me?"

"I don't know," Cate had to admit.

Texie planted her hands on her hips, the lift of her chin defiant even though the gun was in Mitch's hands. "And if Radford found out I'd gone to the police, and then it turned out they wouldn't protect me, and he came after me, and I'm lying there dead, it would be a little late to realize I *shouldn't* have gone to the police, wouldn't it?"

True.

"Besides, even if I don't go to the police," Texie added, "they're surely investigating Radford already, aren't they? I mean, isn't the boyfriend an obvious suspect? They'll find out about his past too."

"I don't think they're investigating anyone. Amelia had traces of sleeping pills in her system, and they've decided it was an accidental fall. No one saw anything."

"So he's going to get away with it," Texie said. She wasn't mentioning her suspicions of Doris now.

"You could go to the police and keep that from happening."

"And then Radford finds out I did that, and I'm dead meat."

They were back to that unpleasant point. "Where is Radford now?" Cate asked.

"Who knows? Maybe he picked up and left the country. Isn't that what killers do?"

It was also more or less what Texie had done, though she hadn't managed to cross any borders yet.

"Where does he live?" Cate asked.

"He had an apartment in Shadow Rock Terraces, out on the west side of town. But it wasn't exactly high-class, and after he got Amelia in his clutches . . ." Texie tilted her head and squinted off into space. "Or maybe it was the other way around, after she got him in her clutches. Whatever. Anyway, he moved. I don't know where."

"But why do you say Doris, and all the other Whodunit women too, had reasons to kill Amelia?"

"Money." Texie nodded meaningfully. "Follow the money. See who lost the most. I lost some too, but not like the rest of them. Especially Doris. Ask about how she and Amelia got into a shouting match at Krystal's, with Doris yelling that Amelia wasn't going to get away with it. Doris was mad enough then to push Amelia out of a ten-story building."

"Get away with what?" Cate asked, but before Texie could answer, if she intended to answer, the sliding glass door from patio to house shot open. A woman, smartly dressed in white slacks and high-heeled sandals, charged outside. Cate assumed she was Lorilyn. Her body stiffened when she saw Mitch with the gun in his hand, but she didn't panic.

"What's going on here?" she demanded, less intimidated than Cate would have been in her situation, even though the gun in Mitch's hand drooped off-target now. Cate remembered Doris saying Lorilyn was into self-defense lessons. Right now, she looked capable of going on a high-heeled offensive. "Texie, are you hurt?"

"No, but—"

Lorilyn stepped forward, broken glass crunching under her sandals. She jabbed a finger at Cate and Mitch. "Get off my property. You're trespassing and harassing my guest."

Texie nodded vigorously. "Yes. Asking nosy questions. Harassing! And that's my gun."

"Set it on the ground," Lorilyn commanded Mitch crisply. "And then get off my property."

Mitch looked momentarily undecided, but he didn't follow orders about the gun. Lorilyn whipped out a cell phone as if it were also a weapon.

"I'm calling the police."

"No! Um, wait." Texie grabbed the other woman's arm. "I'd rather not—"

"You don't have to talk to these people. They have no authority to question you." Lorilyn raked Cate and Mitch with an acid glare. "In fact, who are they?"

"She's some kind of private investigator," Texie said. "I don't know who he is."

"Well, whoever they are, they're not welcome here. I told you you'd be safe at my place, and I intend to see that you are safe."

"We'll leave the gun around front," Mitch said.

Cate wanted to ask more questions about the Whodunit women and the money, but Mitch grabbed her arm and marched her around the house. About halfway down the front walkway, he emptied the bullets out of the gun and set the weapon on the grass. He looked at the bullets for a moment, then stuck them in his pocket. Cate glanced back when they reached the end of the walkway. The gun was already gone. Neither Cate nor Mitch said anything until they were back on the highway. Cate fingered the lump that was sprouting like some alien appendage on her head.

"Are you okay?" Mitch asked.

"Texie and I bumped heads when we were trying to get the gun before you got there."

"We can stop and find a doctor."

"I'll be okay. I'm just feeling a little . . . disoriented." Maybe as much from the startling encounter as from the head collision. "That was . . . odd."

"Just another day in the life of the private investigator," Mitch muttered.

Cate didn't hear actual sarcasm in his tone, but there was a definite suggestion of disapproval. "I suppose you're going to say I told you so. That it isn't safe to be tracking down a killer."

"You don't think I'd miss a chance like this, do you?"

He didn't actually say the "I told you so" in words, but Cate felt them hanging like a storm cloud between them. She purposely ignored both cloud and Mitch. She squirmed in the seat until she could reach the beach rocks in her pockets. Out of the water, they weren't nearly as bright and pretty as they had been. But they were still worth keeping, she decided stubbornly.

"What if I hadn't come along with you today?" Mitch said.

Cate wasn't sure what a hackle was, but she felt hers rise. "You're implying I'd be helpless if I were alone?"

"I didn't mean that. But you had hold of that gun as if it were a live snake. And you weren't sure which end was the head."

Cate gritted her teeth. "Okay, I appreciate your male presence. Very impressive. Thank you. But I don't think Texie would really have shot me. The gun going off was an accident when it fell."

"Having a gun within grabbing reach, when all she's doing is sitting in a backyard, reading? Looks like someone willing to pull the trigger to me. And you might have been hit when the gun fell even if she didn't deliberately aim at you."

"And maybe I'd have found out more from her if you hadn't dragged me away!"

He apparently decided to ignore that. "So what do you think now?" he asked. "Is Texie hiding out solely because she's afraid of Radford, or because she's guilty herself?"

"I think she's mostly afraid of Radford. But it might be in a different way than she told us," Cate added slowly as a new thought surfaced.

"Like what?"

"Maybe Radford really was in love with Amelia. Maybe Texie knows that he knows Texie killed her. So now Texie figures he's out to get her. And maybe he is."

"Sounds possible." Mitch sounded, if not approving of

the new perspective, grudgingly impressed that she'd come up with it. "What about the other woman she mentioned, Doris?"

"Doris McClelland. I have no idea what Texie was talking about, the money thing. Maybe I'll ask Doris."

"Brilliant," Mitch muttered. It was not a compliment.

Cate again ignored him. Texie's suspicions about Doris now put a different spin on both Doris's words and actions. Doris's willingness to go upstairs when the other women were not. Maybe that was because she already knew Amelia was dead and couldn't object to the intrusion. Doris's quickness to tell the police she and Cate had found the door open, and her suggestion about a heart attack. The way Doris had mentioned that the other Whodunit women might tell Cate that Doris and Amelia had exchanged harsh words. A preemptive strike, so if Cate heard about the arguments, she wouldn't think Doris was hiding something because Doris had already mentioned the confrontations herself.

But Doris was hiding something. She hadn't said anything about a hostile money connection with Amelia.

"Cate, stay out of this." Mitch's tone suddenly grew urgent. "You have no idea what's going on with these people, who did what or who's after who. But if Amelia's fall really was murder, not an accident, sooner or later you *are*, if you haven't already, going to meet up with a killer. And I might not be there."

Cate touched a hand to her chest. "Oh my, poor, helpless little ol' me." She gave a melodramatic sigh. "Whatever will I do if I don't have a big, strong man around to rescue me?"

The facetious comment drew an exasperated grunt from Mitch. He reached over and turned on the radio as if he wanted to drown her out. She burrowed in the litter bag hanging from a knob until she found a discarded plastic sack, dug the last of the rocks out of her pockets, and dumped them in the sack.

Mitch snapped the radio off. "You aren't going to try to find this Radford guy, are you?"

"If I am—"

"I know," he growled. "None of my business."

They exchanged only a few excessively polite words on the remainder of the drive back to Eugene. At the house, he gathered up her oversupply of gear and carried it to the door.

"Thank you. I can manage from here," she said politely.

"Okay." He glanced at what now felt like an avocado-sized lump at the edge of her hairline. She resisted probing it with her fingertips again. "How's your head?"

Cate's head pounded like the stereo system Coop had offered to install in her car, and the emotional aftereffects of encountering a woman with a gun were beginning to catch up with her. That stray bullet *could* easily have hit her. But all she said was a stiff, "I'm fine. Thank you for driving your car and all your help today."

He didn't squeal tires when the SUV pulled away from the curb, but his foot was definitely heavy on the gas pedal.

◆◆◆

Cate and Rebecca went to the first service at church the following morning, and afterward Rebecca headed for the hospital. Cate's head was still tender from the impact with Texie, and the lump was now eggplant purple, noticeable enough to draw curious glances at church, but it was painful only when she touched it. Cate had given Octavia an investigator-to-client report on her day at the coast, but the cat had been more interested in batting at the beach rocks Cate had given her.

Cate was thinking about spending the afternoon in a lounge chair in the backyard, but soon after Rebecca left the house, Willow called. She said she was back at Amelia's house now. She'd found another big sack of cat food in a cupboard, and Cate might as well have it for Octavia.

"C'mon over and get it any time."

Cate briefly thought about Mitch's earlier plan to clean the gutters on the garage this afternoon, but after their icy parting the day before, that wasn't going to happen. The knight had downsized his shining armor and put his white horse out to pasture. So, now that she had new questions for Willow about the Whodunit ladies, she said, "How about this afternoon?"

"Great! I need to run over to Nicole's house and pick up the rest of my stuff, and you can come along."

"Am I being drafted as an assistant mover?"

"Well, yeah," Willow admitted. "But I'll make peanut butter cookies afterward."

"Okay. See you in a few minutes."

Cate changed from her church clothes to denim shorts and a tank top. Cheryl's silver BMW stood in the driveway when she arrived at the house, Willow's Corolla beside it. Cate parked down on the street so she wouldn't block the steep driveway, and Willow, waiting for Cate in the car, zoomed down the short hill. Cate hopped into the car.

Willow did a double take when she spotted Cate's face. "Hey, what happened to you?"

Cate echoed Mitch's statement from yesterday. "Just another day in the life of a private investigator." Which reminded her: someday she was going to ask Uncle Joe exactly how he got that limpy leg. And what made the Buick blow up. Now she decided she didn't want to go into the subject of yesterday's ill-fated excursion and how she'd acquired the eggplanty lump. "Confidential stuff." She made a quick change of subject as she fastened her seat belt. "Everything going okay at the house?"

"Cheryl's treating me like a long-lost best friend. She and Scott are there going through stuff today. She said if I wanted any of Amelia's clothes, I was welcome to them. They're probably miles too big for me, of course, but I thought that was nice of her. I told her you were coming over, and she said she wanted to talk to you before you left."

"Talk to me? About what?"

"She didn't say. Maybe she wants to thank you for, you know, finding Amelia's body or something. Or contacting me for them."

At the house on Lexter Street, they loaded household things Willow had stored in the garage. Apparently Coop had been right about her taking anything not nailed down. She must have made several trips when she moved out of the cabin she'd shared with him. They wrestled the TV into the backseat of the Corolla and piled silverware and dishes, plus a toaster, blender, and waffle iron around it.

"What're you going to do with all this stuff?" Cate lifted the straps of her tank top off her sweaty back. "You don't need it there at Amelia's house."

"It's mine," Willow replied, as if that were explanation enough. "Coop didn't have any right to it. I can sell it or give it away or something. I'll store it in the garage at Amelia's house for now."

Apparently the important thing was that she'd gotten the stuff away from Coop. Perhaps not the most admirable attitude, but Cate was relieved to hear it. Willow had several times sounded dangerously nostalgic about Coop, as if she might be remembering the good times and forgetting the bad, but Cate didn't hear any lingering affection for him in this sharp statement.

Cate paused to bend over and stretch her back after they managed to stuff a coffee table partway into the trunk. "How long do you think this house-sitting job will last?"

"Cheryl will get rid of the house as soon as she can. That's what she said when I first talked to her about the job. But I get the impression now that there may be some complication."

"What kind of complication?"

"Who knows?" Willow giggled. "Maybe Amelia's will says they have to preserve it as a monument to her. Bring that big portrait of her in the bedroom down to the living room and curtsy every time they pass it."

"Maybe she left the house to Radford instead of them, and they just found out."

"You suppose? Wouldn't that rain on their parade, as my grandma says. A real downpour, actually. I think the place is probably worth a bundle, even in these hard times. It's a huge piece of land, for right here in town."

Cate would guess Cheryl knew to the penny what the property was worth long before Amelia's demise. Which kept her firmly on Cate's suspect list. Radford was at the top, but Texie and Cheryl, and now Doris too, were jostling him for position. Willow wasn't up there with them, but she definitely hadn't disappeared from the list. After they packed sheets and towels around the coffee table, they took a break to go into the house for cold drinks and Cate found an opening to ask about the reading club.

"Do you know anything about the women in the Whodunit Club losing money in some way that involved Amelia?"

"I remember one time after lunch they played cards instead of talking about books." Willow laughed. "I thought it was bridge or pinochle, but when I went in, there they were, all these old ladies, huddled over their cards like gamblers in some old Western saloon. Playing poker!"

"Gambling?"

"Oh yes. Using buttons instead of chips, but dead serious about it. I think Amelia was pretty good at it. I saw her rake in a whole mountain of buttons. But I don't think the stakes were very high."

So maybe that was all Texie was talking about. A game of poker where Amelia had taken all her friends' buttons. But surely not enough of a loss to motivate murder. Although gamblers had been shot at poker tables . . . Had one of the Whodunit women used a shove instead of a gun in some outburst of poker vengeance?

"But there may have been something else," Willow added. She pressed a glass of ice water against her cheek. "I think they were all in some investment thing together. But they weren't losing money. When I first started working for Amelia, they had a Whodunit meeting at the house and someone, Krystal, I think, brought a bottle of champagne to celebrate some big dividend or payoff or something they'd all gotten."

"An investment Amelia was involved with?"

"That's what it sounded like. I had to uncork the champagne for them, and they all made this big fuss toasting her. They were talking about using their profits to take a cruise together. I was wishing I could have gotten in on it." Willow hesitated and then gave a little laugh. "Actually, I looked around in Amelia's files to see if I could find out what it was, but I never found anything. Not that it mattered, I suppose, since I couldn't have scrounged up more than $1.98 to invest."

A great investment that went sour? And the Whodunit women, especially Doris, who'd lost the most, blamed Amelia and were unhappy, maybe murderously unhappy, with her?

Now Cate realized her head was pounding again. Probably lugging stuff from garage to car in the unseasonably hot sun wasn't the smartest move for someone with a head bump that now felt the size of a cantaloupe. But, thankfully, Willow decided they had a big enough load for today, and they tied the trunk lid in a half-open position to hold the coffee table safely inside, and headed back to the house.

Not one but two BMWs stood side by side in the driveway now, silvery clones, and behind them was a red Mustang. With the driveway already full, Willow parked her car behind Cate's on the street, and they both slid out.

"We can unload the stuff later," Willow said. "I wonder what ol' shyster Radford is doing here? That's his car."

Cate wondered too. Shouldn't Radford be running for the border now? The front door of the house flew open, and a big, dark-haired guy stormed out to the Mustang. Cate was glad she wasn't standing in his way. He looked capable of mowing down a team of Superbowl winners. The Mustang shot down the driveway and past them, and Cate caught a glimpse of a jaw that looked chiseled in concrete. Then, to her surprise, the vehicle shot back just as fast, and the guy jumped out. He walked up to Willow.

"You're Amelia's—" He paused as if undecided what to call her. "Helper, aren't you?"

"I was. She let me go shortly before her death. Her niece has hired me to caretake the house now."

He had the anger under better control now, the set of his jaw no longer hard enough to smash atoms. He was more than good-looking, Cate realized. A twenty-first-century

173

Rhett Butler. Tall and rugged, tanned, dark hair, and amazingly green eyes. Blue Dockers and a lighter blue polo shirt emphasized an impressive acreage of muscles. A real lady-killer type. Maybe in more ways than one, unfortunately for Amelia.

"I'm glad to hear that," Radford said. "Not good for the place to be sitting here empty. Amelia wouldn't want her house to be neglected." Radford gave Cate a passing glance, then a sharp second look, as if startled by the similarities in appearance between the two women. Or maybe it was the bump, like a purple headlight on her forehead.

"This is Cate Kinkaid," Willow said. "She's a pri—"

Oh no! Willow was blithely going to tell him Cate was a private investigator. Or that Cate had found Amelia's body. Cate hadn't time to consider why, but both facts were information she'd prefer Radford not know. She whacked her foot against Willow's ankle.

Willow gave her a blank look, then apparently got the meaning of the whack and took off on a wild tangent. "A real prima donna tree climber," she said, effectively turning the "pri" beginning into something different. Although odd. "Right to the top." She swooshed a hand over her head to emphasize the height of Cate's climbing abilities.

Radford's dark eyebrows scrunched in confusion at these out-of-the-box comments, but he held his hand out to Cate. "Radford Longstreet," he said.

Cate, figuring she'd rather have Radford confused than knowing she was suspicious of him, said, "Maples and oaks are friendly, but poplars are terribly unsociable."

"That's, uh, interesting," he murmured, and Cate could see him mentally slapping a "kook" label across her purple lump. Good. He turned his attention back to Willow. "I won't keep you. I just wanted to say hello. It's been a difficult time, coping with the tragedy of Amelia's death. I was out of town at the time, so it was a terrible shock to get back and find out what had happened."

Hey, that wasn't true! "But Willow saw—"

This time it was Cate who got the swift kick in the ankle, and she hastily changed direction. "Willow saw all these lovely old trees that were being cut down, and you could almost hear them crying. A terrible tragedy."

Still looking baffled but turning a shoulder to ignore kook Cate, Radford said to Willow, "Perhaps we could get together sometime, so we can share our memories of Amelia." He looked up at the house. "Sometime when her niece isn't around." His acid tone suggested *niece* wasn't the word he would have liked to use, that he was thinking something considerably more descriptive.

It sounded like a strange suggestion to Cate. Willow made a noncommittal mumble. Radford headed back to his Mustang, and Cate suddenly realized that as a PI she was again failing here. Radford topped her suspect list, and she was letting him get away without extracting so much as a smidgen of information out of him.

"Maybe you should give Willow your address, in case she needs to get in touch with you," Cate called after him.

He turned. "Why?"

"In case she, um, hears something about Amelia's death. Or needs to talk to you."

"What's there to hear?"

"Have the police talked to you?"

"They had a few questions. Nothing important." Radford strode up to Cate and stared at her. "I don't know who you are or what this is about, but I find this dialogue . . . upsetting.

Amelia and I were deeply in love, and I'm extremely distressed by her death."

"You came here today to offer your condolences to Cheryl?" Cate suggested.

"Condolences? To that greedy . . . woman?" Again he sounded as if the word he used were a poor substitute for what he wanted to call Amelia's niece. Obviously no lost love between Radford and Cheryl. "Cheryl completely cut me out of the funeral. I didn't even get to say good-bye to Amelia properly."

His distress sounded sincere—or he was experienced at faking sincerity.

"It was a private service," Willow said. "I don't think it amounted to much anyway."

"I'm not surprised," Radford muttered.

Still no clue why he was here today. Cate fished. "So you came here today to ask where Amelia is buried?"

"Why I'm here is none of your business."

Radford stalked back to the Mustang, jumped in, slammed the door, and squealed the tires as he roared down the street.

"I think you ticked him off," Willow observed. "Though he was already ticked off at Cheryl, wasn't he?"

"He was *lying*. He wasn't out of town. You saw him that very morning Amelia fell down the stairs, on your way home from the deli."

"I suppose I could have been mistaken." Willow was still gazing down the street, where the Mustang had disappeared around the corner. "But I don't think so. And I just thought of something. I don't remember Amelia ever actually using that old back stairway. But Radford smokes, and she wouldn't let him smoke in the house, so sometimes they went out and sat together on that rickety old landing at the top of the stairs so he could smoke there."

Willow seeing him in the area the morning of Amelia's fall put Radford Longstreet in the vicinity at the time of her death. This new information put him at the top of the stairs with Amelia, if not specifically that morning, at least occasionally. And, if he was also included in the will . . .

Was that why he was here today? Checking on what Amelia had left him? But Cheryl must have won today's round, whatever it was, or he wouldn't have been so angry when he left.

Inside the house, Cheryl moved across the room toward them. The drapery at a front window fluttered behind her, as if she'd been standing there watching their encounter with Radford. Angry lines cut deep parentheses around her mouth. A streak of dust decorated her pink T-shirt, and several straggly strands hung out of her sleek hairdo. A large cardboard box stood near the bottom of the stairs, the head of a stuffed owl sticking out the top of it. Apparently Cheryl and Scott were in the process of discarding mementos of old husbands.

Cheryl rolled her eyes. "I cannot see what Aunt Amelia saw in that man." She shuddered delicately.

"Love is blind?" Willow suggested.

"As an infatuated bat." Cheryl made a dismissive swish of manicured hand, as if she were clearing an unwanted picture from an Etch-a-Sketch screen. She smiled and reached out to clasp Cate's hands warmly. "I'm so glad you're here. I was going to call you later if I missed seeing you today."

"Willow said you wanted to talk to me?"

"First, I must apologize for my actions the day we first met. I was so very upset that day. I still am, of course, but I was really in a daze that day, so soon after Aunt Amelia's death." Cheryl put a hand to her throat as if reliving the traumatic experience. "It was just a terrible day."

"No need to apologize. I understand."

"Anyway, I don't know what in the world I was thinking, letting you take our sweet kitty. I've just kicked myself ever since. Olivia meant a great deal to Aunt Amelia, and of course I want to give her a good home."

Cate, even though she'd first felt nimbly maneuvered into accepting Octavia, now had the unexpected feeling she was being maneuvered in the opposite direction. Warily she said, "*Octavia* has a good home with us. There's no need to be concerned about her."

"I'd really like to have her back," Cheryl said. "She belongs with me, you know. And she needs the special diet Aunt Amelia provided for her. I'm so fond of her, and it's important to me that she's happy and well cared for."

Cate hadn't seen any signs of fondness or concern about Octavia's welfare when Cheryl shooed the cat out of Amelia's office and complained about her excess of white hair. Nor had Cheryl struck her as being particularly "dazed" that day.

"I think she's happy with us," Cate said. "I'm taking good care of her." Octavia might like her high-priced cat food, but they'd discovered she'd also happily chow down on almost anything edible.

"I want her back." Cheryl smiled, but her voice took on an edge. "In fact, I really must insist on it."

"You gave her to me," Cate pointed out. With an edge of her own, she added, "I intend to keep her." She wasn't about to give Octavia back to someone who couldn't even remember her right name, someone who'd planned to dump her at an animal shelter. What was this all about anyway?

A man appeared at the top of the stairs. Cate assumed he was Scott Calhoun. Not quite as good-looking as Radford, but definitely in the tall, dark, and handsome category. Was

there some family trait—like aunt, like niece—that gravitated to this genre of men? The touches of silver in Scott's
neat beard and dark hair gave him a distinguished maturity,
but Cate placed him as several years younger than Cheryl.
A preference for younger men another family trait? He wore
jeans and a sweatshirt, scruffy enough to be mildly disrepu-
table looking, but taking nothing away from a man-in-charge
confidence. He came down the stairs and crossed the room to
stand by his wife. She immediately snuggled under his arm
and put a hand on his chest.

"Is there a problem here?" he asked, his tone genial. He
gave Cate's purple-headlight bump a glance but didn't make
any reference to it.

"This woman is refusing to give the cat back," Cheryl said.

"You must be Cate Kinkaid, the woman I talked to on the
phone. Cheryl said you and Willow looked so much alike, and
there is a remarkable resemblance, isn't there?" His glance
flicked between them before he stepped forward and held out
a hand. "I'm Scott Calhoun."

Cate shook the hand, still wary in spite of what appeared
to be his effort to defuse an uncomfortable situation with
Cheryl.

"We do want to thank you for putting us in touch with
Willow. Having her here to look after the house is a great
relief for us," Scott said.

Cate didn't mention that she'd tried hard to talk Willow
out of the job. "You're welcome."

"About the cat—"

"I'm very fond of her, and she has a good home with me."

"I'm sure she does, and this is really just an awkward mis-
understanding. Cheryl was so upset that day. She just wasn't
thinking straight when she let you take the cat."

"She didn't 'let' me take Octavia," Cate pointed out. "She gave her to me."

"I'm sure you can understand how distraught Cheryl was that day," Scott said, smoothly sliding over the differences in their versions of Cate's acquisition of the cat. "We really want to make Amelia's beloved pet a part of our lives. We can come to wherever you live to pick her up. We don't want to inconvenience you in any way."

"That won't be necessary. I'm glad to have her."

"This is quite important to us. The cat is family, you know, as beloved pets are."

Family? When Cheryl didn't even know her right name, and all he could call her was "the cat"? "I'm sorry, but I'm really quite attached to Octavia now."

A faint line cut between Scott's dark brows. "We don't want to be unpleasant about this, but we really must insist that the cat be returned." His tone, like Cheryl's, had hardened, but in a more conciliatory tone he added, "We'll be glad to pay you for your time taking care of her, or any expenses you've incurred."

"No," Cate said, her own resolve hardening. "She's a part of my family now." *And I'm not giving her back.*

Cate had first tried to give Octavia away to any neighbor who'd take her. But now she was accustomed to the furry body snuggling up to her back or feet at night. She liked having Octavia there to greet her whenever she got home, even if the greeting might be a yowl of complaint. And no matter what either Cheryl or Scott said about fondness or wanting her to be a part of their lives, Cate couldn't see Octavia comfortably sprawled on one of those burgundy velvet chairs in the Springfield home. Something else was going on here, and whatever it was, Cate didn't like it.

"The cat is, of course, part of Amelia's estate," Scott said. "So it really wasn't Cheryl's prerogative to let you take her. We apologize for that. But it is, at this point, a legal matter. She must be returned."

"No."

"If you refuse to return the cat, we'll have to take up the matter with the legal firm handling Amelia's estate," Scott warned. "In fact, if you refuse to return the cat, now that we've given you ample opportunity, this might even have to be pursued as a criminal matter."

"Criminal?"

"Theft."

Cate suddenly had visions of a major assault: lawyers brandishing legal papers, cops storming in with a cat net. No matter. No way was she letting these people have Octavia.

Cheryl stepped forward, her stance threatening. "If you let anything happen to Olivia—"

"Octavia."

Cheryl ignored the correction. "There will be serious consequences. I'm warning you—"

"I'll consider myself warned," Cate shot back. "But I'm not giving Octavia back."

Willow had remained silent during this exchange, and she didn't now mention the sack of cat food. Cate gave her a stiff nod and headed for the door, but she was only a few blocks from the house when her cell phone rang. She pulled over to the curb to answer it.

"Cate, it's me, Willow," Willow said, her voice a conspiratorial whisper. "I don't know what's with Cheryl and Scott. Cheryl hates cats, and Octavia in particular. She never could stand all that shedding hair. I'm glad you didn't let them scare you into giving her back."

181

"It sounds as if they may have me arrested for catnapping."

"It's weird, isn't it? But Cheryl doesn't know anything about that sack of cat food, so you can have it anyway. That's what Amelia would want, I'm sure. It's that special, high-priced kind Octavia likes. You can come get it some other time, when they're gone."

"Well, we'll see."

"And I'll see what I can find out about why Radford was here, and why Cheryl was so upset about it."

"How?"

"Don't you know? Eavesdropping is a fine art among the hired help. Maybe I'll turn into a PI myself!"

"Willow, I don't think you should get involved—"

"Gotta go. Cheryl's coming. I'll let you know what I find out."

◆ 13 ◆

Cate drove to the hospital, but Uncle Joe was asleep when she reached his room. Rebecca was sitting patiently by his side, a magazine open on her lap. She whispered that he'd had a bad day, and Cate tiptoed out without waking him.

Back home, she was startled to see a familiar SUV parked at the curb. She dashed through the aisle between the house and garage. A neatly tied black lawn bag stood by the back of the garage. The ladder leaned against the house now. Cate stopped short. Mitch stood at the top of the ladder, another black bag in hand.

"What are you doing here?" Cate yelled up at him. Dumb question. It was obvious what he was doing. Cleaning gutters. Just what he'd said he was going to do.

He tossed the partly filled bag to the ground and came down the ladder. He was in his old paint-blobbed coveralls, now with a couple of soggy leaves stuck in his hair instead of paint on his face. "After I finished with the garage, I noticed the house gutters needed cleaning too." He took off his gloves and slapped them against the ladder.

"But I thought . . . I mean . . ."

"You didn't think I was coming?" he challenged.

"Well, after yesterday—"

"I said I'd be here. Yesterday didn't change that."

Cate wavered between appreciation that he'd come in spite of their confrontation, and exasperation that he'd shown up when she assumed he wouldn't. A man who lived up to his word, no doubt even if he had to climb mountains, swim rivers, or crawl through walls of fire, and she'd skipped out. A one-upmanship banner waving right at the top of the flagpole.

"I'm sorry I wasn't here to help," Cate said. Although he obviously hadn't needed help. He'd also brought his own lawn bags in which to stash the gutter gunk. She knew he wouldn't accept payment, so she made another offer. "Maybe we could donate something to your church's Helping Hands project?"

"The project can always use donations."

"Okay, then. Well, uh . . ."

Mitch grabbed the partly filled bag and put a foot on the bottom rung of the ladder. "I hope you don't mind that I'm doing the house gutters too. They looked as if they needed cleaning just as much as the garage gutters."

"That's very thoughtful of you."

He snapped his head around to give her a sharp look, as if he suspected the statement was something other than complimentary, and Cate had to admit she wasn't sure what it was. He dropped his foot back to the ground. "Look, I may have come on a little strong with my concerns about your work. As you pointed out, none of my business."

As an apology, it wasn't all that great. But he was admitting he'd overstepped boundaries. He probably deserved an apology too. She'd been a little over the top with her sarcastic "big, strong man" retort.

"I may have . . . overreacted," she said.

"Even though it was none of my business, I did a little surfing on the internet last night and before church this morning. I found out a few things that might interest you."

"About what?"

"People."

"Knight in shining armor galloping in on his white horse to rescue helpless damsel in distress again?"

Something momentarily flashed in his blue eyes, but he stayed above her level of snideness when he said, "I'm fairly adept at galloping around on the internet."

No doubt much better than Cate. She could find some good shopping sites, and she had to admit that she'd checked up on her ex-fiancé and his current fiancée a few times, but she was no expert at going beyond shallow surface information. "I don't want to be involved in anything like illegal hacking."

"What I found might be information the people involved would rather you didn't know, but I didn't do anything illegal."

They eyed each other as if neither could decide where to go from that point. Finally Cate said warily, "There are steaks in the freezer."

"Steaks?"

"I think I mentioned something about a barbecue." She motioned to the gas grill sitting near the back door. "We should be safe from gunshots here."

He didn't quite grin, but almost. "I barbecue a mean steak. If that wouldn't be too much big, strong man help."

Cate's not-quite-a-smile acknowledged her sarcastic words from yesterday. "I'll go thaw the steaks in the microwave."

He touched her arm lightly as she started to walk away. "How's the bump on your head?"

"It draws attention. I don't think it'll ever catch on as a fashion statement, though."

She thawed T-bones, tossed a salad, buttered slices of French bread, and made iced tea. By the time she went back outside, a second bag bulging with gutter trash stood by the garage, and Mitch had the gas grill going. Octavia dashed out with her.

Mitch, as he'd said, did indeed barbecue a mean steak. The T-bones came out just right, neither overdone leathery nor underdone bloody, and he grilled the toast to perfection. They ate at the picnic table in the backyard, spring sunshine filtering through the trees, with a pleasant accompaniment of kids splashing in a kiddie pool in a nearby yard, a lawn mower running farther down the street, and the scent of lilacs drifting from the bushes along the back fence. Octavia industriously tongue-washed her hind leg under the table, occasionally pausing for a luxurious roll in the grass.

Their conversation, about Uncle Joe's condition, the weather, and the state of the economy, was a little stilted but not hostile, and the tightly reserved atmosphere between them loosened by small degrees. She asked for an address to send a donation to Helping Hands at his church and he said he'd check on it for her. He didn't mention her working at Computer Solutions Dudes again, but he did offer to mow the yard, where yellow dandelion blooms already loomed over the grass. After they'd eaten, he presented the leftover bone from his steak to Octavia, who pounced on it as if she'd just captured dangerous prey. Cate showed him the mower in the garage, admitting she didn't know anything about starting it, but a few minutes later he had it revved up.

A handy kind of guy, Beverly had said. Cate watched him cut a smooth swath around the perimeter of the yard, carefully avoiding the daffodils Rebecca had planted at the edge of the grass. Beverly was right. Very handy. When he took a break from the mowing, they sat at the picnic table, drinking more iced tea, and he had her laughing about a handyman job he'd had as a kid, when he was supposed to build a doghouse for a neighbor's dog named Maurice, but he got carried away and built what came to be known as Maurice's Mansion.

After he finished the mowing, he got his notes from the SUV on what he'd found on the internet.

"My search was rather restricted, because I didn't have that many names to work with, but on those I had, no one comes up with a rose-scented 'I am innocent' badge attached." He spread the papers on the picnic table. He had, of course, been able to find information Cate hadn't.

The information he had on Radford Longstreet was similar to what Texie's niece had found, except he'd turned up an additional marriage. The Radford name was a morph from Romar Lomax. There was an even greater difference than Cate had guessed between Radford's and Amelia's ages. There was some suspicion about him in the deaths of former wives, and he'd definitely come out a winner after each marriage, but no actual charges had ever been filed. The Mustang wasn't paid for, but he had an impeccable credit record under the Longstreet name and no black marks on his Oregon driving record. He had a local address at an upscale condo complex, and Mitch had also found a cell phone number for him. No job record of any kind.

"What do you think?" Cate asked.

"He may have just had really bad luck with wives and wanted to start a new life with a new name here." Mitch said. "He may have a comfortable income from investments that I couldn't locate. And I guess a guy really can fall for a woman twenty years older than he is."

Mitch didn't sound convinced Radford had changed from

serial husband to solid citizen. Neither was Cate. A little gruffly, he added, "I don't want to pull some big, strong man interfering act, but if you want to talk to him, I could come along."

"If I do decide to contact him, I'll let you know. I appreciate the offer."

"Peace?" he said.

She smiled. "Peace."

His findings showed that Doris McClelland lived frugally off Social Security. She'd formerly owned a hybrid Toyota Prius, but it hadn't been paid for, and she'd recently traded her equity for a much older Ford Escort. She had some past-due bills, and she was behind on her property taxes. Which suggested she had, as Texie said, lost some sizable amount of money she'd had available when she bought the Prius. Cate remembered Doris saying that day at Amelia's house that she could buy a new car with what Amelia had spent carpeting the place. The observation took on a more ominous meaning now.

Cate pictured a scenario: Doris confronts Amelia at the top of the stairs. They argue. There's an angry shove. All followed by a good acting job from Doris when she and Cate "discover" the body together later that day.

But no, it couldn't have been that way. Doris had said she'd never been upstairs before.

Yeah, right. As if killers were bound by some vow of truth.

Mitch had found that Willow's legal name was Winona Bishop. She had traffic violations in Oregon, a shoplifting arrest in California, a bad credit rating, and an award of appreciation from Save Our Tree Friends. Mitch didn't have a full name for Texie or Coop, or the names of the other Whodunit women, so he hadn't been able to come up with anything there.

But altogether, it was a rather impressive showing for a limited search time. A handy man indeed. Cate asked about two more names.

"What about Cheryl and Scott Calhoun?"

"Who are they?"

Cate explained their part in her list of suspects, and he said he'd see what he could find out. The cell phone in Cate's pocket jingled as she was gathering up his notes. He'd said she could keep them.

"Cate?" The woman's voice sounded vaguely familiar, but Cate couldn't place it until she'd said, "Yes, this is Cate," and the woman said, "I got your phone number from your mother. Am I calling at a bad time?"

"Mrs. Collier?"

Cate realized Mitch was looking at her, as if he heard something strange in her voice. As he definitely had. Kyle's mother . . . calling *her*? She dropped back to the bench by the picnic table.

"Yes, this is Emily. It's been a long time, hasn't it? Your mother told me you were in Eugene now. They sound happy with their retirement in Arizona. How are you doing?"

"I'm fine." A generic answer to a generic question. At one time she and Kyle's mother had talked fairly often, but she surely hadn't called after all this time to check on whether Cate was gainfully employed and getting her teeth cleaned regularly.

"You're probably wondering why I'm calling," Mrs. Collier said, and Cate managed an ambiguous murmur. "Kyle asked me to."

"Kyle?"

"He's just moved to Portland to take a new position with a gourmet foods company. He'd like to drive down to Eugene to see you this coming weekend. Under the circumstances, he thought it would be best if I called first. To pave the way, I guess you might say."

"What about his fiancée?" *Is she coming too?*

"Kyle and Melanie are no longer together. I think you know how sorry Doug and I were when you and he broke up. We're hoping . . . Well, I'll give you his number, and you can make arrangements with him about this weekend."

Cate picked up the ballpoint pen Mitch had been using when they'd looked at his notes. She hesitated when Mrs. Collier gave her the number. Kyle wasn't calling her himself. He had his *mother* do it? She wasn't sure what that said about him, but it made her uncomfortable. But when Mrs. Collier said, "Did you get that?" and repeated the number, Cate scribbled it on a corner of the notes.

"He's anxious to hear from you," Mrs. Collier said. "I hope you'll call him right away."

Cate stared uneasily at the number. So why wasn't Kyle calling her, instead of asking that she call him? "I'm not sure this is a good idea. Things are different now . . ."

"Your mother didn't say anything about your being involved with anyone." She sounded alarmed.

"I'm not, but . . ." Cate glanced at Mitch. She'd been so startled by the call that she hadn't even thought to move away to talk in private, but he'd taken care of that. He was on the other side of the yard now, laying the ladder down alongside the garage. They weren't "involved." They weren't much more than acquaintances. He was heavy-handed with his "concern" over her. And yet . . .

"I can call back later," Mrs. Collier said quickly, as if she didn't want to give Cate an opening to say no. "I know this comes as a complete surprise to you."

"Look, I just don't know about this. It's a . . ." More than a surprise. A shock. "I'll call you back, okay?"

"Thanks, Cate."

Cate dropped the phone back in her pocket. Kyle. After all this time. Was God sending him back to her as she'd once been so certain he would?

Mitch came back to the picnic table. "There's an expression: 'She looked as if she'd seen a ghost.' Now I know what it means."

"That was Kyle's mother."

"Kyle, major player in the Cappuccino Conflict?"

Cate nodded. "He's just moved to Portland. He isn't engaged now. He wants to come down and see me."

"But he had to have Mommy make the call for him?"

Cate jumped to her feet. Octavia, startled, skedaddled away from under the table. "It was thoughtful of him! He didn't want to—to put me in an awkward position by calling me himself."

Mitch gave a "whatever" shrug. "When's he coming?"

"I told her I'd have to think about it and call her back."

"Is this what you've been waiting for?"

"I'm not sure."

At the beginning, she'd been so certain God had brought the two of them together. She usually went to the 9:00 service at that big church down in San Diego, but she happened to go at 11:00 that day. There was a big crowd coming and going between services, no reason for them to meet, and yet they'd bumped right into each other, almost falling into each other's arms. After a moment of don't-I-know-you-from-somewhere awkwardness, they'd shared startled recognition. Wasn't that meeting a God thing? Eventually she'd been certain God intended them to spend their lives together. And now was he giving them another chance, because he had a plan to get them back together after they'd messed up before?

Mitch waited a minute while she just stood there with thoughts racing and colliding like an emotional demolition derby inside her head. Then he came to some conclusion and nodded briskly.

"Okay, I'll be on my way then, so you can get on with your thinking." He paused. "I apologize for the snarky remark about Kyle's mother making the call. And any other uncalled-for snarkiness."

He grabbed the two big lawn bags as he went by the garage, one in each hand. She'd have had trouble dragging one bag off. She managed a moment of scorn. Showing off with the big, strong man stuff.

But she had to resist an urge to run after him.

◆◆◆

By the next afternoon, after she'd thought her way through much of a sleepless night, Cate was still undecided. Thinking about Kyle. Thinking about Mitch. Wishing a big voice from God would boom out of the sky and tell her what to do.

And now the bump on her head, which she'd almost forgotten for a while yesterday, throbbed again.

She decided she should get away from thinking for a while. She had an address for Radford now. She could go see him. If he wasn't guilty, maybe she could enlist him as an ally in finding Amelia's murderer. If he was guilty, going to see him was about as smart as walking unarmed into a grizzly's den. Where the bear was perhaps not sleeping but sharpening its claws.

Okay, how about Doris? Ask her about the money connection. Cate couldn't see her as being as dangerous as Radford, but the conclusion about charging in to question her was the same. Not smart. She might find herself smothered by something purple.

But how could a PI get information, if she didn't step into danger once in a while?

Okay, she wasn't ruling out danger indefinitely. But not today, while her head felt as if Octavia was batting beach rocks around inside it.

She dug out the list of numbers she'd taken from Amelia's little red book. She passed over Texie and Doris. Hannah. Who was she? Maybe the short one, with the squeaky voice? Or how about the next one, Emily? Cate frowned. She couldn't even remember an Emily. Krystal. Yes, Krystal! The woman who did volunteer work at the hospital, the most sophisticated looking of the Whodunit gang. Cate grabbed her cell phone and had half the number punched in before she stopped, remembering something she'd read in one of Uncle Joe's books. Often an investigator was better off surprising people and catching them off guard than setting up a formal appointment.

She didn't have either an address or a last name for Krystal, but a few minutes on the internet in a reverse phone directory provided both. After briefly wondering what was appropriate clothing for a prowling PI, she changed to conservative blue slacks, white blouse, and sandals, and headed out.

2978 Vista View Drive turned out to be in an area of nicer older homes, a substantial brick with ivy climbing the walls, mature maples in the front yard, and two white columns flanking the entryway. A formal rose garden bordered a side fence, and a newer Cadillac stood in the driveway. Cate hesitated after she pulled up to the curb.

She'd come close to getting hit by a bullet on Saturday.

What would happen today? Maybe Krystal had a hidden arsenal of major assault weapons.

Cate resolutely discarded that possibility. She slid out of her car, walked up to the double doors with leaded glass inserts, and pushed the doorbell. She halfway expected to encounter a barrier of household help, but Krystal Lorister opened the door herself. She was dressed in pink capri pants and a scoop-necked tee today, but she looked ready to step onto the runway of a fashion show of casual outfits for older women. Her white hair was as perfectly coifed as before, elegantly immovable.

"I don't know if you'll remember me . . . ?"

"Of course," Krystal said. She eyed the bump on Cate's head, her gaze curious, but she didn't follow up with nosy questions. "The private investigator. The woman who was at Amelia's that day looking for Willow and found a body instead."

Not necessarily the way Cate wanted to be remembered for posterity, but at least no assault weapons were in sight. "I'm wondering if you'd have time to talk with me for a few minutes?"

"Concerning?"

Cate started to toss out the names that interested her. Amelia. Doris. Texie. Willow. Cheryl. Radford. Instead, afraid of alarming Krystal, she said, "I won't take much of your time."

"Are you here in a professional capacity?"

"Well, I, um, have a client whose . . . future is involved in the situation."

"I see." Krystal tilted her elegant head, but her reserved expression finally softened to a smile, and her tone even took on a touch of playfulness when she asked, "Anyone I know?"

Cate tried to make her return smile both friendly and professionally mysterious. Somehow she doubted offering the information that her client was a deaf cat would enhance her PI status.

Krystal seemed to be granting her professional status when she said, "I know. A client isn't something you can discuss with me. I've encountered a good many private investigators in books and on TV, but I've never known one in person before. It must be a fascinating occupation."

"It's just a job," Cate said modestly. She refrained from using the "ma'am" that seemed to go with the line.

"We can go back to my reading room to talk."

Cate followed her through an immaculate living room decorated in white and delicate coral and blue pastels. Coordinating fresh flowers stood on the coffee table and fireplace mantel. They passed several closed doors down a white-carpeted hallway. Krystal opened a door and stood aside to let Cate enter. The room held floor-to-ceiling bookcases, with books precisely aligned. A lamp on a white end table flanked a recliner, and two wing chairs were set at precise angles to it. Landscapes of serene meadows and flower gardens hung on the walls.

"I spend a lot of time here," Krystal said.

Cate had never known anyone who had a room just for reading. It was a lovely room, serene and soothing. Although overly neat, by Cate's standards. She'd have had books strewn all over, but here a lone book lay on the arm of a recliner. The paperback with a corpse on the cover made a lurid island in the tranquil room. Cate started to take a seat in a wing chair, but she stopped short when she saw a very pretty, dark-haired girl of seven or eight sitting in a child-sized rocking chair beside a floor lamp, a book open on her lap. Cate hadn't expected anyone else to be here.

"Oh, is this one of your—" Cate broke off before she got to the word *grandchildren* and did a double take. Not a little girl. A doll. A life-sized doll. In a demure blue dress with a white collar and cuffs, rather old-fashioned, and black shoes in a Mary Jane style.

Krystal smiled, apparently pleased with Cate's reaction. "Isn't she realistic? Does she look familiar?"

Familiar? Why would a doll in the reading room of a woman she barely knew look familiar?

Krystal stroked the doll's dark hair. "A woman who lives out south of town makes them. Face, arms, legs, everything. She's very talented. She did Camille using this old photo for guidance."

Krystal picked up a silver-framed photo and handed it to Cate. The photo was black and white, but the resemblance to the doll was truly remarkable. The doll maker had caught the shape of face and ears, the round cheeks, the firm jaw, and wide-eyed gaze. The photo might have been taken of the doll, not the other way around.

"She's really beautiful."

Krystal knelt and put her face next to the doll's. "Do you see it now?"

Cate didn't see anything except an extremely real-looking doll.

"Camille is me, of course." Krystal smiled again as she made a fractional adjustment of the old-fashioned locket hanging around the doll's neck. "At eight years old."

Cate's glance darted between doll and woman once more. No remarkable resemblance jumped out at her, but there could be a trace of Krystal's seventies elegance in the face of the girl-sized doll.

"That's, uh, very nice," she said.

In a macabre kind of way. Sitting here reading with the company of a younger version of yourself in the chair beside you. Cate suddenly wondered if Krystal was perhaps a little odder than she appeared on the surface.

Of course, there was nothing really *odd* about owning a single life-sized doll. Some women had collections of dozens, even hundreds of dolls. Beverly made teddy bears.

Krystal motioned her to a wing chair, and Cate perched on the edge of it. Now she had the uneasy feeling the doll might lift its head and stare at her straight on, a maniacal gleam in its eyes. Or suddenly produce some Twilight Zone cackle of laughter.

Krystal sat in the other wing chair and held her hands neatly in her lap. "You wanted to ask me something about Amelia, perhaps? Or her niece?" She sounded pleasantly encouraging.

Cate decided to go straight to the focal point of this visit. "Actually, I really wanted to ask about the Whodunit ladies. I understand that in addition to the book discussions you shared, there was something like an investment club you were in together?"

"Where did you get this information?" The question didn't sound hostile, but it held a hint of frost.

Cate decided not to give a name. "It came up in my investigation for my client."

Krystal seemed undecided for a moment, but then she gave an almost imperceptible shrug. "It wasn't really a club. Just an opportunity we all had to make what appeared to be an excellent investment. Unfortunately, that didn't turn out to be the case. But I was fortunate in that I'd invested only a small amount and didn't lose much."

"You had misgivings about the investment?"

"Before his death my husband put much of our money into

good mutual funds. He left me quite comfortable. Although Amelia's pressure to get us all to invest was very intense." A small line cutting between her perfectly arched brows suggested she hadn't appreciated that pressure.

"What kind of investment was it?"

"A company developing a totally different type of car engine using some easily available alternate energy source. Hydrogen? Nitrogen? I'm afraid the technicalities escaped me. The investment wasn't yet open to the public, so investors who got in early could expect a tremendous profit. Amelia said it was the opportunity of a lifetime."

"Apparently you made a wise decision not to invest a large amount."

"I saw no reason to place much trust in Amelia's judgment about an investment. I'm sure you saw that painting in her living room." She wrinkled her nose delicately.

"The one with three eyes?" Gazing out of what appeared to be a cauldron of bad chili.

"That was also one of her investments. Some upcoming artist whose work is supposed to make a spectacular jump in value as soon as he becomes better known. I wouldn't put the thing in my laundry room." Krystal's reserved elegance took a hit with the catty-sounding comment, and another not un-catty comment followed. "I've always wondered if he was a friend of Radford's."

Which suggested she also questioned Amelia's judgment about the current man in her life. Everyone but Amelia seemed to have had reservations, to put it kindly, about good-looking Radford. "Did Radford get in on this investment?"

"I don't know." Krystal's already perfect posture straightened in the chair. "That's an interesting question, isn't it? I hadn't thought about it before."

Cate saw something out of the corner of her eye. Did that doll move? No, of course not. Cate jerked her attention back to Krystal. "Did Scott also pressure everyone to invest?"

"No, not really. It was something he was handling outside normal office channels. A rather large minimum amount was required to get in on it, but Amelia said she'd persuaded him to make an exception for her friends, and we should take advantage of that."

"That's why everyone blamed her, not Scott, when the investment tanked? Because she was the one who pushed it?"

"Scott said that knowledgeable investors were jumping on it, but he warned us that any investment involved risk. He didn't seem eager to let us in on it."

"Maybe that was a clever sales technique."

Krystal's delicate eyebrows lifted. "You're suggesting he knew all along that it was a bad investment?"

"I don't know much about investments," Cate admitted. The closest thing she had to an investment portfolio was an envelope of coupons for toilet tissue and buy-one-get-one-free at Burger King.

"Scott called each of us to tell us personally how sorry he was when the company went under. He seemed quite distressed about it."

"How about Amelia?" Cate asked. "Did she feel bad that the investment she'd promoted lost money for everyone?"

"She went on and on about how sorry she was, that the company was just ahead of its time. Et cetera, et cetera." A small gesture of Krystal's manicured hand suggested a certain lack of faith in Amelia's distress.

"Did she lose money too?"

"That's the big question."

"What do you mean?"

"I'm not sure this is any of your client's business."

Krystal moved slightly in the chair. Not really a squirm in one so elegant, but almost. Cate, afraid the woman might be about to end the interview, jumped away from the subject of investments. "I was quite fascinated by Doris's unique . . . look. Does she always wear purple?"

"Not always. It is her favorite color, and she always wears at least one accessory in purple. But we managed to talk her out of painting her house purple." Krystal's lips twitched in a suppressed smile. "I could just see it. Like a square eggplant on that little lot."

The comment suggested there was a certain amount of caring among the Whodunit ladies, in spite of the hostility Cate had felt that day at the house. And Cheryl's comment about seeing them as piranhas ready to pounce on each other over a good quiche.

Krystal shook her head. "Poor Doris."

Cate used the connection to edge back into the subject of investments. "She was the one who lost the most money?"

"Her loss might not have been an exorbitant amount to some of us, but it certainly was to her. I didn't care to discuss details of my finances with the other women, so I didn't ask for specifics about theirs. I do know she had her money in CDs, and she took it out to make this investment."

"Doris didn't seem like a person who'd invest in anything questionable."

"The interest rates are so pathetic now, as you undoubtedly know, and Doris needed more income than what she was getting off the bank CDs. She loved her hybrid Prius. She's really into the going-green thing. She recycles everything. So she jumped on the idea of a vehicle with an even more advanced engine and an alternate energy source. She said the first thing she was going to do with her profits was buy one of those cars as soon as they were available."

"Instead she had to give up her Prius."

"And now she's driving that ghastly old clunker and having to watch every penny." Krystal reached over and adjusted the doll's skirt by a fraction of an inch. "You think Doris pushed Amelia down those stairs, don't you? That she was so angry about losing all that money that she just lost control."

"I'm not convinced Amelia's fall was an accident," Cate admitted. "Even though the police apparently think it was. There was something in the autopsy report that showed her mental faculties, and probably her balance, I suppose, were impaired by sleeping pills."

"So she wasn't pushed."

"Do you think she was?"

"It had entered my mind, of course." Krystal unexpectedly laughed. "Which only proves I read way too many murder and thriller novels." She motioned toward the paperback with the lurid cover. "Knowing she wasn't pushed is a relief, of course. We wouldn't want to think our dear friend Amelia had fallen victim to foul play."

"Dear friend Amelia" might express affection in words, but it came out with all the warmth of an ice cube down the back. The piranhas were coming out to play now?

"You said something about it being a 'big question' whether Amelia had lost money like the rest of you did on the investment."

"We're pretty sure she was getting a . . . I suppose it might politely be called a commission on anything the rest of us invested."

"But it might be called something else?"

"A kickback. For every dollar she talked us into investing,

she got a kickback." Krystal didn't sound so casual now about the money she'd lost.

Losing money was no doubt enough to make all the Who-dunit ladies unhappy. But then to find out Amelia had *made* money on their losses. Maybe that took the unhappiness to the anger of murder. However, there was a point of logic against that.

"But why would Scott give Amelia a kickback when he didn't even want to let the Whodunit ladies in on this investment anyway? Could they have been in on something together?"

"You're saying Amelia and Scott may have had a deliberate plan to defraud us?" Krystal touched a hand to her chest. "That's a very serious accusation!"

"I'm not accusing," Cate said hastily. "Just, uh, thinking out loud. Of course, another thought is that maybe Amelia's financial situation wasn't as plush as everyone believed, and Cheryl talked her husband into helping her aunt out with a schedule of commissions."

"I never saw much evidence that Cheryl was all that concerned about Amelia's welfare. She's so busy trying to hold on to that husband of hers that she didn't have much time for Amelia."

"They have marriage problems?" Cate hadn't seen any signs of discord. Scott had, in fact, seemed quite solicitous, determined to get the cat back if that was what Cheryl wanted.

"He's younger, of course," Krystal said, as if that made for obvious suspicion. "There are also rumors Scott has a roving eye. Of course, that may simply be malicious gossip."

"Malicious gossip among the Whodunit ladies?"

Krystal waved a hand, dismissing the question. "Of course, we may simply have been wrong about the kickback thing.

I'm trying to remember how it first came up . . ." Krystal stood and paced to the window. "It was Texie who said it, I think. Yes, definitely Texie."

"Where would she get that kind of information?"

"She said at the time that she had a 'confidential source.' But she may have just made it up because she wanted to cause trouble for Amelia."

"Because of Radford."

Krystal's genteel laugh came out more of a bark this time. "Maybe someone should have pushed Radford down a flight of stairs. We were a much happier group before he came along and caused trouble."

"At this point, do *you* think there were kickbacks involved?"

"At this point, what does it matter? Amelia's dead."

"Scott isn't. Maybe you should go to the police. Aren't kickbacks illegal?"

"Look, Miss Kinkaid, I'm planning a trip to Connecticut to visit my sister in a few weeks. I am *not* going to get stuck here in some long, drawn-out court case concerning Scott Calhoun's business dealings. Which were probably perfectly legitimate anyway. At this point I'm thinking Texie did just make up the whole thing about kickbacks."

Krystal suddenly yanked the book out of the doll's hands. "I have a lovely spring outfit for Camille. I don't know why I haven't changed her into it before now. I always keep her up to date with the seasons. So if you'll excuse me, I'm going to unpack her spring things right now. You can show yourself out?"

"Of course. I did want to ask—"

"I've already given you more time than I have available." Krystal lifted her arm and made a point of looking at the gold watch on her left wrist, as if dressing Camille was more important than bad investments. Or murder.

"Well, thanks for your time." Cate found herself giving the doll a little good-bye wave as she left the room.

As she drove home, Cate felt more confused than ever. She didn't have Uncle Joe's talent for detecting evasiveness, and separating the good guys from the bad ones seemed to be getting even more difficult. It occurred to her that Krystal herself wasn't above suspicion. She could be considerably angrier with Amelia over the investment loss than she was letting on. *Kickback* had enough venom in it to stock a viper's den.

◆◆◆

The next couple of days were taken up with getting started on the new cases for Uncle Joe. One involved a client in Seattle who, in doing genealogical research on her family, had discovered she had several relatives in Eugene. She wanted photos of their homes before she contacted them. Apparently she didn't want to claim relatives who turned out to live in old trailers with wheel-less cars on concrete blocks in the yard. Cate took three photos, all of satisfactorily upscale houses, printed them out with the computer, and mailed them to her.

She applied for a job with a local plant nursery, but they were not favorably impressed with her past experience, which consisted solely of weeding her dad's garden years ago. And she didn't even confide in them that she'd pulled up all the young radishes because she couldn't tell them from weeds. But she did find a new site on the internet on which to leave her résumé.

Mostly she tried to decide what to do about Kyle and the coming weekend. She discussed it with Rebecca. She prayed about it. *Hey, Lord, straighten me out here. What am I supposed to do?* She even asked Octavia's opinion. But she received no helpful instructions anywhere. Octavia even stalked off, dragged Rowdy to her cat bed, and slept there that night. Apparently she specialized in PI problems, not advice to the lovelorn.

The following morning, Willow called. She wanted to bring Cate some things she'd gleaned from Amelia's closet. Cate was not particularly interested. She murmured something about a report she had to write for the files on the genealogy woman and added, "I don't think I could wear anything of Amelia's anyway. She was rather larger than I am."

"Amelia was always intending to lose weight, and she had this whole section of skinny clothes in her closet. I think she had this fantasy of getting back the figure she had when she was twenty or something. I also found out what Radford was doing here that day and why he and Cheryl were so furious with each other."

Which did interest Cate.

◆ 14 ◆

Cate gave Willow directions to the house, and she arrived in less than twenty minutes. She came to the door lugging a cardboard box. The first thing she said was, "You know what? I forgot that sack of cat food. But I did bring chocolate chip cookies."

She tilted the box, and Cate caught the plastic bag of cookies before it hit the floor.

"Octavia can wait for the cat food," Cate said. "She isn't going hungry."

The well-fed feline sniffed at the clothing when Willow spread it on Cate's bed. Cate wondered if she recognized Amelia's scent. Did cats have sentimental thoughts about the past? Maybe. Octavia picked out a fuzzy sweater and curled up on it.

Even if the clothes were from Amelia's "skinny" wardrobe, they were still too large for Cate. But there were a few items she could actually use. A cashmere scarf with metallic strands. A chain belt with a length that adjusted to Cate's waist size. A loose muumuu thing in a tropical pattern, one size fits all, that Rebecca might be able to use. Cate set them aside to keep.

"And then there's this!" Willow pulled a last item from the box, a blonde wig, the hair long and tousled.

"I'm not going to wear that!"

"I know. I just brought it along to show you because I was so astonished when I found it." Willow giggled. She tossed it on the pile of discards.

Cate boxed up everything except the sweater Octavia had chosen, and set the box aside to donate somewhere. Then at the last minute she rescued the wig. Who knew when a PI might need a blonde disguise?

"Have Cheryl and Scott given everything else away?" Cate asked.

"Not yet. The closet is still jammed with stuff. Actually, they haven't been around much the last few days. I was beginning to think I wasn't going to get a chance to eavesdrop on them."

"But then you did."

"Oh yeah. I got an earful. I tippy-toed up to Amelia's office when they were in there. Carrying my can of window-cleaner spray and a roll of paper towels, of course, so I could look all innocent if they caught me." Willow made a mischievous little gesture of spraying and wiping in the air. "But they were much too engrossed in arguing and worrying about Radford to notice me. Ply me with a Pepsi, and I'll tell you all about it."

Cate felt uneasy about listening to Willow's eavesdrop information. Although it probably beat walking into personal encounters with hostile gun toters. She got Pepsis from the refrigerator, and, taking the cookies along, they went out to sit on the webbed lounge chairs in the backyard.

"Okay, Radford was there about an engagement ring he said he'd given to Amelia. Two carat, emerald-cut diamond in the center, two diamonds on each side, white gold setting."

"Expensive!"

"He told them he and Amelia were supposed to get married in a couple months, but, under the circumstances, he wanted the ring back. Cheryl told him she'd never seen any such ring. He accused them of having the ring and cheating him out of it. They accused him of making up a story about a ring and trying to con them."

"Con them how?"

"By trying to make the estate reimburse him for a ring that never existed."

"Is that possible?"

"Who knows? Radford is sleazy enough to try something like that. But I wouldn't put it past Cheryl to claim the ring doesn't exist even if she found it somewhere. But I can't imagine that if Amelia had such a ring, she wasn't flaunting it."

"You never saw it?"

"No. Amelia had mentioned we'd be throwing a big party soon, though, so maybe she was managing to keep the ring under cover until she could have a big unveiling at an engagement party."

"So maybe it's a question of who's trying to con whom."

But another thought unexpectedly jabbed Cate. She didn't want to distrust Willow. She liked her look-alike. But Willow had been known to dance around the truth, and now there was another missing ring. Could Willow be letting Cheryl and Radford feud over the ring . . . and she had it?

"And you didn't want me to take this job and miss all these soap-opera doings." Willow socked Cate with a playful punch on the shoulder.

"They aren't saying anything yet about how long the job will last? Maybe you should start looking for something else before this one ends. Cheryl will probably give you a good recommendation letter to add to those you already have."

"About those letters, I've been wanting to tell you . . ."

"I have copies, if you need them."

"Actually, I kind of . . . wrote those letters myself. I didn't want to bother Beverly when I had to leave there in such a hurry because of Coop. Then it just seemed more efficient to do the others myself."

Phony reference letters. *Efficient.* Sometimes the truth seemed to get ever more flexible with Willow. Although flexibility with the truth seemed to be everywhere, not only with Willow.

"I may not stay until they sell the house anyway," Willow said. "I'm thinking I'll go down to Florida and stay with Grandma for a while. A long time ago we talked about opening a little café or coffee shop together."

"That's a wonderful idea! The way you can cook, you'll make a fortune." And a continent between Willow and Coop would be a smart move. "How soon?"

"I can't leave for a while. I have to collect some money I have coming first."

"You mean a paycheck from Cheryl?"

"Not that. Big money!" For a moment, with the sparkle in Willow's eyes, Cate thought she was going to share some exciting information about the money, but then she turned cagey. "I just have to wait a few days."

"This doesn't have something to do with Coop, does it?" Cate had never been convinced Willow's feelings for Coop were quite as dead as she claimed.

"Coop? What makes you think I'd ever want anything to do with Coop again?"

Okay, maybe what she'd been thinking was unfair. "Maybe

because I'm, um, thinking about getting in touch with the guy I was engaged to once. Actually, he got in touch with me."

She paused. Was she being foolish for even hesitating about seeing Kyle again? Kyle was no Coop. He had his flaws, sure. The Cappuccino Conflict had been about as mature as five-year-olds squabbling over a rubber duckie. Even more immature was the way the original argument had escalated into arguments popping out about everything from where they should live after getting married to who their friends should be, Kyle's new car and Cate's old one, even which TV shows they should watch.

"What did he have to say?"

"It was his mother who called me. He wants to see me this weekend."

"He had his *mommy* call?"

Mitch had sounded derisive, as if this were something no real man would do. Willow just sounded incredulous. Cate had doubts about this herself. But now she found herself responding with the same defensiveness.

"I see it as a thoughtful gesture," she said.

"Yeah, I guess it could be. So are you going to get back together with him?"

"I've met this other guy. Although we're kind of . . . on the outs."

Willow swung her legs to the side of the lounge chair so she could face Cate. She clapped her hands. "Cate, I had no idea you had such an interesting love life!"

"It's not a love life. It's just a couple of guys I know."

"This guy who wants to see you, he's the one you thought God intended you to spend the rest of your life with?"

"Yeah. Kyle Collier."

"And the other guy?" Willow asked.

"Mitch Berenski. I met him at Beverly's. He was painting the inside of her house. Beverly thinks he's God's gift to women. Me in particular."

"How come she never produced a guy like that for *me*?"

The thought occurred to Cate that if Willow hadn't left the job working for Beverly, maybe she would have met Mitch. "Well, he acts like I'm some kind of incompetent, helpless female. Always thinking he has to jump in and rescue me."

"Hey, Superman was a rescue-type guy. Sounds good to me. Coop rescued me once, when I got mad at him and jumped off the edge of a dock into the river." When Cate frowned at that comment, Willow shrugged. "Maybe neither one of them is right for you. Maybe God has in mind someone else entirely. The world is full of men."

"But why would he send Kyle back into my life if he didn't mean for us to get back together?"

"Maybe he sent the guy back so you could let go of something you should have let go of a long time ago. Like I dyed my hair jet black for a while. I thought it was so dramatic looking, kind of Cleopatra-ish. I kept it that way until Coop told me I looked more like Davy Crockett in a bearskin cap."

Cate got a little tangled in a story that combined Cleopatra and Davy Crockett, and she was uneasy with these frequent mentions of Coop, but the hair fiasco did point out that you could hang on too long to something that was wrong to begin with. Mitch had sensed an "unavailability" about her. She'd wondered herself if she'd dated those guys from Creeps-R-Us because her subconscious was stubbornly holding out for Kyle. Now Kyle was back . . .

Did God want her to grab onto him again?

Or let him go for good?

Did God have some plan for her with Mitch?

Or was Mitch just a speed bump in her life?

"Would you rush to get Kyle back if this Mitch guy wasn't in the picture?" Willow asked.

Cate mentally eased Mitch out of the picture. But maybe he was already out. Actually, he'd never been that much *in*. So, did she want to see Kyle this weekend? Well . . .

"I'm not sure I should be taking advice from you," Cate muttered.

"Well, thanks a lot!" Willow scooted around and leaned back in the chair. "Here I'm trying to use my vast experience to help you, and you don't even appreciate it."

"Sorry."

"But you could be right. What do I know? It's not as if anything in my love life is going down in history as the Romance of the Century." Willow sighed and grabbed another cookie. "Or even Romance of the Week."

"Maybe you'll meet someone wonderful down in Florida."

"Hey, you think?" Willow's blue eyes brightened. "I'm not sure I can tell a creep from a wonderful guy, though. I've been wrong more often than right. But I still don't think you should rush back into anything with Kyle."

"And you base this on . . . ?" Cate challenged.

"Maybe it's a message from God to you through me." Willow tilted her head and stared at the overhead leaves. "Or maybe it's more like Grandma and one of her sayings: 'Even a stopped clock is right twice a day,' and this is one of the times I'm right."

Maybe she'd call Mrs. Collier this evening. Or she could play Kyle's game and have Rebecca call him.

And say what?

Before she left, Willow stopped by the bedroom to give Octavia the kind of roughhouse petting she liked. Willow said she'd call when the coast was clear and Cate could come pick up the cat food.

Later that afternoon, Octavia perched on the desktop in Uncle Joe's office while Cate was looking through the file on the next assignment he'd given her. The cat moved over to the phone, looked at it expectantly, and a second later it rang.

"No way," Cate said, not realizing she'd already picked up the phone when she said, "Coincidence."

"Coincidence?" an unfamiliar voice on the other end repeated.

Cate decided not to explain that she was talking to her deaf cat, who had this uncanny ability to—

Then she broke off that thought. No uncanny ability involved. Just coincidence. So now, in her most professional manner, she said, "Belmont Investigations, Cate Kinkaid speaking."

"This is Roger Ledbetter, from Winkler, Ledbetter, and Agrossi, Attorneys-at-Law—"

"I'm sorry, but Mr. Belmont isn't currently accepting new clients, but if you'd like him to contact you later—"

"No, it's you to whom I need to speak," he said.

Cate hadn't dealt much with lawyers, but she recognized a voice of authority when she heard one. A voice ominously pinpointing *her*. Cheryl had done what she'd threatened. She'd called in the big legal guns about Cate's refusal to return Octavia.

"You're Amelia Robinson's lawyer?"

"I am executor of her estate, yes. I understand that you have in your possession a certain white cat by the name of . . ." Pause while Mr. Ledbetter rustled papers. "Octavia."

Cate resisted an urge to say, "Yes, would you like to speak with her?" Instead, in her most noncommittal tone, she said,

"Yes, I do." She reached out and gave Octavia's white fur a reassuring ruffling.

"Mrs. Calhoun says that you removed the cat from her aunt's home—"

Cate's determination to be cool, calm, and professional evaporated, and her words came out in an indignant yelp. "I didn't 'remove' her, Cheryl gave her to me! She wanted to get rid of her. She was going to take her to the pound."

"I see." Pause, as he no doubt collected powerful legal phrases to hurl at her. Pro bono. Corpus delicti. Habeas corpus.

Unequipped with legal phrases of her own, Cate settled for simple stubbornness instead. "And I intend to keep her."

"Mrs. Calhoun does not, at this point, have authority to make disposition of any portion of Amelia's estate. The cat is part of that estate. The will must go through the proper process of probate."

A lot of words to say . . . what? You've got the cat and you're in big trouble? "But Cheryl inherits everything, doesn't she? Including Octavia?"

"I am not at liberty to disclose details of the will, but as executor I must abide by its terms. It is my duty to conserve assets of the estate and distribute them properly."

Conserve assets. Like not letting one stray white cat escape his clutches?

"I'm sorry, but I'm not giving her up. I'm just not. And if you don't like it, you can . . . sue me."

Great going, Cate. You just suggested a hotshot lawyer sue you. What came next on this legal eagle's schedule? A bombardment of court papers? Stolen cat complaint to the police?

"Are you looking for money, Ms. Kinkaid?" Mr. Ledbetter inquired suddenly. "You want payment for return of the cat?"

The question astonished her. Her indignation ballooned. "Money? No, I do not want money. I am not a cat kidnapper." Inspiration! "Look, since you're handling the estate and are concerned about money, how about if I pay you for Octavia? Estates sell things, don't they?"

"You want to buy the cat?" The dignified attorney sounded taken aback. And, unexpectedly, momentarily human. Then, as if wary but curious, he added, "What's she worth?"

Cate eyed the blue-eyed cat now regarding her from atop the nearby filing cabinet. "Well, I, um, don't know. She's a wonderful friend and companion, so that's worth a lot. She was a stray, but she might be some fancy breed for all I know. She has beautiful blue eyes. She's deaf, but she seems able to tell when a phone is going to ring."

Dumb, dumb, dumb, Cate chastised herself. She should be bringing Octavia's value down: she's overweight, lazy, and loud, and you could knit a pair of leg warmers out of all the hair she sheds. Instead she was making her into Super Cat. And making herself sound like an irrational nutcase with the phone thing. At least she hadn't mentioned the door opening.

"She must be a most extraordinary animal," the lawyer said. Cate couldn't tell if he was being facetious or patronizing. "Perhaps quite valuable."

"I guess I probably can't pay what she's really worth," she muttered.

"I see. But you absolutely refuse to return her?"

"I absolutely refuse," Cate stated with more confidence than she felt. "But if you'll set a price on her, I'll try to come up with the money. Maybe I could make monthly payments?"

He ended the conversation smoothly and noncommittally. "Thank you, Ms. Kinkaid. As executor of the estate, I'll give your offer careful consideration."

And no doubt check her credit rating.

"We could run away," Cate suggested to Octavia after the end of the conversation with the lawyer. "Disappear where they'd never find us."

Mrrow. Was that asking when? Or how big a supply of cat food Cate intended to take on the trip?

❖❖❖

By evening Cate knew she had to call Kyle or he might just show up on her doorstep. And she definitely didn't want that. Okay, she'd call Mrs. Collier and tell her that this weekend was out, but maybe sometime. That way she wouldn't have to explain anything to Kyle. Maybe because she wasn't sure what her explanation was? She got as far as looking up Mrs. Collier's number on her phone. Then she changed her mind. She wasn't going to hide behind Mommy. Before she could change her mind again, she punched the number Mrs. Collier had given her for Kyle into her cell phone.

"Kyle Collier here."

After all these years, there he was. She felt a little light-headed. She didn't know if she'd have recognized his voice if he hadn't identified himself. Familiar, but different. More mature? "Hi, Kyle. It's Cate."

"Cate, it's so good to hear from you!"

"Your mother said you've moved to a new job in Portland."

"Yes. I'm really excited about it." He talked about the new job with the gourmet food company and his apartment with a view of the Willamette River. He didn't mention his broken relationship with Melanie in Atlanta or ask what Cate was doing now. "We have an awesome line of specialty teas. I remember how much you like to try different kinds. I can bring some along this weekend—"

"About this weekend," Cate interrupted. She'd intended to say not this weekend, but maybe later, but it came out differently. "I don't think that's a good idea."

A moment's silence until he said, "Are you saying not a good idea for this weekend, or not a good idea for *any* weekend?"

"Any weekend, I think."

"I see." He sounded mildly stunned by that reaction. "Any particular reason?"

"Um, no. Just . . . um, no." Brilliant dialogue, Cate. Any more um's and you'll have a catchy new song: um, um, um. Clap, clap. Um, um, um. She tried to be more articulate. "It didn't work before, and I don't think it would work now."

"I wasn't asking for a lifetime commitment, Cate. I just thought we might enjoy seeing each other again."

Reproach. Oh yeah, Kyle had always been good at reproach. And now she felt like a total idiot. As if she had some overblown idea of her own hotness, and all he had in mind was a cup of tea.

She stuck to her decision anyway. If her relationship with Kyle had been God-solid, would their Cappuccino Conflict have exploded the way it had back then? "I don't think so. But it was nice of you to think of me."

"We had such plans, Cate." A long silence from Kyle, as if he was thinking over their past together. "I think the breakup was a big mistake."

"Maybe it's the breakup with Melanie that's a mistake."

Huff of breath, as if he hadn't realized this topic would come up. "Melanie is what this is really all about, then?"

Cate felt a splash of dismay. Was it? Was she letting some petty jealousy thing sabotage a wonderful possibility?

"You figure Melanie dumped me, and that's why I'm

running back to you? And now you're going to give me the brush-off? Well, that isn't what happened. I finally realized Melanie and I were no more right for each other than you and I were, and I had to get out. How did you know about Melanie anyway?"

"Your mom. My mom."

"Oh yeah, the good ol' Mom hotline."

"You used it to get in touch with me!"

A couple of minutes on the phone, and they were squabbling again. And they didn't even have a cappuccino machine to get it going. Kyle apparently decided to back off and start again with a new, less confrontational tactic.

"What are you doing now, there in Eugene? Have you gone back to teaching?"

"I'm a private investigator. I'm involved with a murder. I have a blonde wig. I'm buying a deaf cat."

It took him a bit of time to absorb all that. Finally he said warily, "Are you all right, Cate? You sound . . . different."

Was she all right? A high-powered lawyer was after her for catnapping. A good-looking knight on a white horse had walked out on her. She was tangled in a hotbed of could-be killers. Which added up to . . . what?

"I'm fine, Kyle." She said the words out of reflex, but with some astonishment she realized they were true. In spite of the temporary weirdness of her life, she *was* fine. But Kyle was obviously feeling down, and she didn't want to sound as if she were clicking her heels with exuberance, so she toned down her enthusiasm. "I'm looking for a different job. My health is great. My car's running good. So everything's fine, it really is."

"I'm glad to hear that," Kyle said, even though he didn't sound convinced.

"Kyle, look, I know that back then, down in San Diego, we both thought our relationship was ordained by God. That he choreographed our meeting, and he meant for us to be together. But people make mistakes about God's will. I think we did. You said it just now. That you and Melanie weren't any more right for each other than you and I were."

"I said that?" He sounded surprised.

"You said that."

"This really was a mistake, wasn't it?" Kyle said. He actually sighed. "I'm sorry I bothered you. I guess I've just been feeling kind of lost and looked for something familiar to grab on to. But don't tell me to grab on to God," he added roughly. "I've already been through that with my dad."

Okay, she wouldn't tell him that, although it was what she was thinking. Neither would she tell him she'd pray for him, because she'd do that, whether he wanted her to or not.

"Actually, I appreciate your contacting me. It's helping me straighten out my head about some things too."

◆ 15 ◆

Yes, her head was straightened out about Kyle. No more letting her subconscious sabotage her present by dragging around something from the past. So, should she call Mitch? Although it wasn't as if she'd chosen Mitch over Kyle. She'd just un-chosen Kyle.

Two days later, when she was still waffling about calling Mitch, he called her with a brisk rundown on what he'd dug up on the internet about Cheryl and her husband.

Cheryl Calhoun was fifty-six. She'd had two years at the University of Washington and an eighteen-year marriage that ended when the husband divorced her and quickly married another woman. She had a son and daughter, both living back East. Cheryl's interior decorating business wasn't going under yet, but neither was it flourishing. Their Springfield home was valued by the county assessor's office at $625,000, less than what they'd paid for it. Scott Calhoun was fifty-one and had been with the local branch of a national stockbroker firm since coming to Eugene five years ago. He was active in a couple of civic organizations. He had grown children, but Mitch hadn't been able to pinpoint where they lived. Neither Cheryl nor Scott had anything except minor traffic citations on their police records. They'd been separated briefly a year or so ago, but the court action was dropped. They'd taken a Caribbean cruise together shortly afterward.

"I can probably locate his children," Mitch added. "If you think it's important."

"No, that's fine. I don't think it matters."

On the surface, the Calhouns looked like any ordinary divorced-and-remarried couple. Middle-class, law-abiding, conservative lifestyle. With their twin BMWs, they obviously liked status symbols. So did a lot of people. The house value looked high to Cate, but it was in an area of similarly valued homes. The fact that it had dropped in value was probably more an indication of lower property values all over the country, not bad judgment on their part.

Nothing there to suggest Cheryl was desperate enough to concoct a push-auntie-down-the-stairs scheme.

However, there could be some under-the-radar problems. Troubles with Cheryl's business. Scott's earnings might also be dropping in an uncertain stock market. They could be in over their heads on the house even if not on a cliff brink of losing it. There was also Krystal's close-to-vicious comment about Cheryl being so busy trying to hold on to her husband, and the possibility of his "roving eye." Could Cheryl have figured a hefty inheritance would add some twinkle to her marriage?

Mitch didn't bring up the subject of Kyle and the previous weekend, and before Cate could decide how to do so, he said he'd be out of town for a couple of days on business. End of conversation.

Cate stared at the silent phone in frustration. He'd done it again. He'd said he'd look up information about Cheryl and Scott, and he'd done it. The man who lived up to his word, even if he had to plow through ex-fiancés to do it. Commendable.

Cate touched her finger to her tongue and drew a five-pointed figure in the air. *Give the man a gold star. Sure, give him two.* She drew another star with her finger, then punched both with her fist.

◆◆◆

Cate and Rebecca moved Uncle Joe from the hospital to a rehabilitation center. In his condition, he couldn't literally drag his feet about going, but he certainly did so verbally. He wanted to come straight home. Cate spent the next day working on the case from the files, an old situation concerning a daughter adopted out at birth.

She went for a run that evening. Usually a run both invigorated and relaxed her, and this was a beautiful time of day. She slowed to a walk as she neared home. The setting sun turned clouds into streaks of pink and gold, and birds twittered in the trees. But she felt neither invigorated nor relaxed. Maybe she should take up bird watching. She apparently wasn't going to need any time for male relationships. Then she was annoyed at herself for the grumpy attitude and took off at a hard run.

As she rounded the corner a block from the house, she almost ran over the older couple who lived two doors down from Uncle Joe and Rebecca. The Martins? Madsens? They walked hand-in-hand almost every evening. Cate skidded to a halt and apologized.

Mrs. Martin/Madsen waved off the apology. "I just wish we had the energy and ability to do what you do."

"It's a great evening to be out."

"I'm glad we ran into you," the woman added. "In fact, I

222

was thinking perhaps I should call you. A man came to the house yesterday asking about you."

Cate tried to squelch a mild flicker of alarm. "Asking where I live?"

"No, he knew where you live. He wanted to know about you. Something about a background check. How long you'd lived there and if we knew where you worked and what hours, and if you'd been in any trouble, what kind of people came to the house. What other people lived there, were there pets, or noisy parties, all kinds of nosy things. He even peeked in the trash barrel Rebecca had set out for the garbage truck."

"Some man wanted to know all that about *me*?" And he checked the *trash*?

"We thought it probably had to do with a job you'd applied for," her husband added.

Cate couldn't remember applying for any job involving national security, corporate secrets, or government contracts. It seemed unlikely the people at Wily Coyote Pizza would care if she indulged in noisy parties at home. Or what was in her trash.

Yet simply because the man said a background check was what he was doing didn't mean that was actually what he was doing. But, if he wasn't running a background check for a job, what *was* he doing? And what did he intend to do with the information?

"We told him we didn't really know much about you, but from what we'd seen you were a very well-behaved young woman of exemplary character. And that Joe and Rebecca are lovely people too."

A nice report, even if it did make her sound like an elderly spinster. "Thank you."

"He went to a couple of other houses." The husband pointed across the street. "The Carmichaels over there, and the new people next door to them."

"You didn't ask for identification?"

The couple exchanged glances.

"We should have, shouldn't we?" the woman said, her tone apologetic. "But he seemed so nice. Very polite. We wanted to help, you know? Rebecca said you've been looking for a job for quite a while."

"What did he look like?"

"Six-foot-one or two," the husband said, his tone going important. Witness stuff. He looked off into space, concentrating. "Lean build. Narrow face. Heavy eyebrows. Dark hair, good length, not straggling around his shoulders. Blue slacks, short-sleeved white shirt, gray tie with red stripes. He was quite tan, as if he'd been somewhere other than here for the winter."

The wife looked at him with an expression somewhere between amazement and skepticism. "I didn't see all that."

He didn't quite polish his fingernails on his shirt front with satisfaction, but he definitely looked pleased with himself.

"Anyone can have a tan these days," his wife scoffed. "At any time of year. You go to one of those tanning booth things. Or buy that stuff in a bottle or spray can. It doesn't mean you've been somewhere."

"The tan looked real," the husband insisted.

"Did you see a car?" Cate interrupted before this escalated into a full-scale Battle of the Tans. Even as the couple squabbled, she noted they were still holding hands.

"I didn't see one," the woman said.

"I did. It was parked down in the next block. A dark sedan." The husband obviously prided himself on his powers of observation. But "dark sedan" was about as helpful as "green grass."

"He had a little notebook and wrote everything we told him down in it. A black notebook," the woman said. Her glance at her husband said she may not have noticed the car, but she'd noticed that notebook. Had he?

The notebook thing made Cate remember that the police officer asking questions after Amelia's death had used such a notebook. Could a plainclothes detective be investigating *her* in connection with Amelia's death? A more ominous possibility loomed, someone with darker and more dangerous motives than the police. Radford Longstreet? He was tall and dark-haired. Coop? No, he was blond. Unless he had someone asking questions for him. Actually, anyone, male or female, could hire a snoop. Did someone think that because she'd found the body, she knew more about Amelia's death than she actually did? Or that she'd acquired incriminating information since then? *Did* she know something that she didn't even realize she knew?

"Did he ask about my daily schedule, when I come and go?" Was he trying to pinpoint her movements so he could ambush her?

Exchanged glances again.

"No, I don't recall that," the husband said.

Okay, don't complicate this with wild speculation. It probably did have to do with a job she'd applied for at some time, maybe even weeks ago. Maybe that cashier job at the big warehouse store. Or the application with the vacuum cleaner manufacturer. Maybe they wanted to be sure their employees weren't out to steal parts and construct dangerous new vacuum weapons.

She thanked the couple and headed on home. Her cell

phone rang just before she reached the front door. She dropped to the steps to answer it. Willow. With a surprising announcement. Radford had called her late the previous evening, the call apparently timed so it would come when he was sure Cheryl wasn't at the house.

"He wants to talk to me," Willow said. "He wanted to come over right then, but I wasn't about to go for that, of course. But I did say I could meet him somewhere."

"I can't believe he wants to get together and reminisce about Amelia."

"No. It's something else."

"Willow, why would you meet with him at all, anywhere, any time, for any reason? He may be a killer!"

Radford's call to Willow struck her as worrisome for another reason. Someone was canvassing the neighborhood asking questions about *her*. Was there some connection?

"He says he has a business proposition for me."

"What kind of legitimate business proposition could he have? I don't like this. Just give him the brush-off."

"He says he'll pay me $250. And it's nothing illegal or dangerous. So I said I wasn't agreeing to anything, but I would talk to him. We're supposed to meet in the food court at the mall tomorrow afternoon."

"You said you had all that 'big money' coming from somewhere. Why bother with this?"

"A woman can always use an easy $250."

Cate gave a snort of exasperation. "So why are you telling me? You've already made up your mind, haven't you?"

"I was hoping you'd come with me."

"No way."

"Please, Cate? I'm uneasy about meeting him alone, even if it is a public place."

"Then don't."

"Maybe it's something about Amelia's fall. Maybe he knows something. Doesn't that interest you?"

Yes, Cate reluctantly admitted, that did interest her. "But why would he be willing to pay you money if *he* knows something? Maybe he's more than sleazy. Maybe he's a weirdo psychopath."

"I know it sounds strange," Willow said. "Maybe the strangeness of it is a reason you *should* come along."

"Maybe he won't talk if I'm there."

"Then we'll know he's really up to something no good."

Cate wavered between curiosity and thinking that meeting Radford was the worst idea ever, right up there with bungee jumping on a cord of dental floss. Also a certain concern that if she weren't there to stop it, maybe Willow would get involved in something foolish and probably dangerous. "Okay, I'll do it," she finally said reluctantly.

"Food court at the mall, 11:30 tomorrow. Order something expensive. We'll get him to pay for it."

◆◆◆

Cate parked at the mall at 11:25. She hadn't had lunch. Inside, the food court was not busy at this hour on a weekday afternoon. Willow waved at her from a corner table. Before they had a chance to say more than hello, Radford bore down on them. His dark brows melded toward an ominous-looking unibrow when he saw Cate.

"I intended this to be a private meeting."

Cate was undecided whether to leave politely or stubbornly glue her anatomy to the chair.

Willow gave him a winning smile. "You remember Cate, don't you?"

"The woman who climbs trees."

"Yes! It's okay if she's here. We share everything. She's my twin sister. We didn't know it until just recently, but isn't it wonderful?"

Cate gaped in astonishment at this incredible story. Truth with Willow was indeed flexible. "Willow, I don't think—"

"I know. We don't usually tell people." Willow patted Cate's hand. "But I'm sure it's okay if Radford knows. Radford can keep a confidence, can't he?" She didn't quite bat her eyes at Radford, but not far from it.

Radford didn't look happy about the situation, but he didn't stomp off. He glanced between them and apparently accepted the twins story. He scooted a chair back and sat down. "Yes, certainly, I can keep a confidence. And what we're discussing here today is also completely confidential. Is that understood?" There came the unibrow again.

"Of course." Willow leaned her elbows on the table, steepled her hands together, and gave him a primly expectant look.

Radford looked at Cate for confirmation of the confidentiality agreement, and she managed to echo Willow's words. "Of course."

"What I have in mind is this. Amelia and I were engaged. I gave her a ring. She wasn't wearing it yet because she wanted to throw a big engagement party and show it off then."

"She'd mentioned a party," Willow offered encouragingly.

"But now that niece is refusing to give the ring back. And it's *mine*. An engagement ring is a promise to marry, and there wasn't any marriage. But she's claiming there isn't any ring, that I'm just making it all up. Maybe she's told you all this?"

"Not really, no," Willow murmured.

So true. The Calhouns hadn't *told* Willow anything.

"Anyway, what I need is the receipt on the ring to prove it does exist. It must be somewhere in Amelia's belongings."

"Why would Amelia have a receipt for the ring?" Cate asked.

Radford threw her an annoyed glance, but he answered the question. "She wanted to add the ring to her insurance policy, and she needed the receipt to prove its value."

How romantic! Demanding a receipt to prove the value of your engagement ring. If Amelia needed to know its value, why hadn't she discreetly had it appraised?

As if he'd heard Cate's mental question, Radford said, "I don't know why she didn't just have the ring appraised. She wanted the receipt, and I gave it to her. So what I want you to do"—he planted his arms on the table and leaned toward Willow—"is find the receipt for me. There's $250 in it for you."

"Cheryl and Scott have been all through Amelia's office," Willow said. She sounded disappointed in this as a business proposition. "If it were there, they'd surely have found it already."

"Can't you get a copy of the receipt from the store where you bought the ring?" Cate suggested.

His glance at Cate said, What business is this of yours? But he gritted his teeth and answered. "It was a private sale. The woman simply wrote out a receipt for me, and that's what I gave Amelia." He turned back to Willow. "Maybe you could get hold of the insurance company and see if she'd added it to the policy. Tell them you're, oh, working on the estate or something. I'd do it, but I have no idea who her insurance was with."

Willow shook her head. "I'm sure Cheryl took any insurance papers that were in Amelia's files, so I don't think there's any chance—" She broke off, a thought just occurring. "But she kept cancelled checks in a box there in her office. At least until the bank stopped doing the cancelled check thing. Cheryl might not have bothered with cancelled checks. I might be able to look through them and find an insurance company name. And she'd probably have written the policy number on the check."

"I'll give you $100 right now to do that. And another $250 if you can get proof about the ring."

Willow looked at Cate. Cate started to shrug, then asked a question instead. "Is the ring paid for?"

"Of course it's paid for!" Radford snapped. He hesitated, his gaze studying Cate as if he were reevaluating her. "But I paid in cash, so I don't have a check to prove that."

Which might or might not be true, since flexibility with the truth seemed rampant as an infectious virus here. Radford pulled out his wallet, opened it, and fingered a hundred dollar bill as he looked at Willow.

She reached over and plucked the bill out of his fingers. "I'll see what I can do." She inspected the bill as if it might be phony, then stuffed it in her purse.

Radford stood up. "Call me when you find out anything."

Willow's gaze followed his tall figure as he walked out of the food court. "I thought he'd at least buy us lunch," she grumbled.

"Why in the world did you tell him that crazy story about our being twins?"

Willow's grin was mischievous. "I don't know. Sometimes I just get this crazy impulse to make things up. Maybe I'll write books or movies someday. Besides, I always thought it would be fun to have a twin. Now I have one!"

"Don't tell anyone else, okay?" Cate muttered.

At the outside doors, just as they parted to go to their cars,

Willow said, "You want to come over and help me look for the receipt?"

No, she did not want to look for a receipt that might or might not exist. "I have to . . ." She juggled excuses. Wash my hair. Clean the lint out of my belly button. Weigh Octavia. "Go see Uncle Joe."

"I didn't mean now. Cheryl was there when I left. Come over late tonight."

"I really don't approve of this whole venture."

"Okay, whatever. But will you come?" Willow asked, as if approval were irrelevant. "I'll fix something to eat afterwards. We'll make it a midnight party! How about tacos?"

Bribed by a taco. No. Although cheesecake might have done it. But Cate suddenly realized she had a very good reason of her own for peeking into Amelia's files.

"Okay. I'll be there about 10:00."

◆◆◆

Cate paused on the front steps and looked around cautiously when she left the house at 9:30 that night. She'd gone with Rebecca to see a grumpy Uncle Joe, and weary Rebecca was already in bed. Cate didn't spot anyone waiting in ambush. But ambushers probably didn't wear DayGlo vests with name tags. She ran for her car parked in the driveway and locked the doors the instant she was inside. She was equally cautious when she slipped out of the car at Amelia's house. An ambusher could have followed her.

But she made it safely to the door. Willow opened it a crack. The door didn't have a peephole. "What's the password?" she whispered.

"Tacos." Willow opened the door and Cate stepped inside. "You're the only one here?"

"Cheryl went home hours ago. The good housewife is always there when her husband comes home from work, you know. But she was a busy little heiress while I was gone this afternoon."

"Busy doing what?"

"Carting stuff out. Amelia had a bunch of antiques in there." Willow motioned toward the curtain of wooden beads at the door to the turret room. "It's almost as if Cheryl didn't want me to see her taking the stuff."

"That's strange. But doesn't everything have to be inventoried for some kind of report for estate taxes? Maybe she's trying to fudge on that."

"Could be." Willow shrugged. "Doesn't matter to me. They can pull out those fancy faucets in Amelia's bedroom and sell them for scrap metal for all I care. You want a cup of coffee or tea or something before we go upstairs?"

"No, I'm fine. You haven't looked for the receipt already?"

"I thought it would be more fun to do it together."

Cate noted as they crossed the living room that, except for a couple of missing lamps, the room looked the same as before. Cheryl hadn't yet feng-shuied it into acceptability.

The box of canceled checks was no longer behind the copy machine, where Willow remembered seeing it. It also didn't take them long to determine that Cheryl had also been a busy little heiress here. No folders concerning insurance, the will, bank accounts, investments, or anything else concerning assets or finances remained in the file cabinet.

"I wonder why they didn't just haul the entire file cabinet home?" Cate said. "It would have been easier than trying to go through everything here."

"I think maybe they tried. It's a few inches over from where it used to be. But it weighs a ton, that's why. Just try to move the thing."

Cate put her shoulder to the file cabinet. Willow was right. She could barely budge it, and it was missing a lot of folders that had originally been there, which would have made it even heavier. What remained was an odd collection of folders that attested to Amelia's peculiarities. Each old husband had a separate folder. Inside were mementos. A menu from a restaurant in New Mexico. Some crumbles that had once been a flower and still retained a sweetish scent of old love. A cruise ship itinerary. And some less romantic details: a daily record of cash spent on the cruise, with check marks to show what she'd spent and what the husband had paid for. A list of gifts at one of her weddings, with a name and value attached to each. Her letter of complaint to a funeral home concerning charges on a husband's casket.

No folder on Radford, however. Did that mean a man didn't rate a file of his own until he reached husband status? Or had Cheryl taken Radford's file? Or had Radford himself snatched it after he killed Amelia, afraid it might contain incriminating information?

The Whodunit Club had its own file, with lists of books they'd read, and a list of members, with many names crossed out, apparently signifying they'd left the group. There were dozens of files with clippings on houses, furniture, recipes, menu plans, landscaping, indoor plants, fashions, cats. Amelia had an eclectic range of interests, with more files on movies she'd seen, complete with caustic reviews. Astrology. Solar power. Climate change. Reincarnation. Skin-care advertisements.

"There's nothing here about the ring." Willow slammed a file drawer shut in disgust. "There goes my $250. Let's go make tacos."

"You go ahead. I'll keep looking a little longer."

Then, as she flipped through the contents of some files,

Cate discovered another of Amelia's peculiarities. Mixed in with the old clippings were scraps of paper with disconnected bits of information. She guessed Cheryl hadn't bothered to look through these. She found a receipt for a $798 dress. Had Amelia hidden that from some old husband? A sketch of a guy . . . Radford! Was Amelia a budding artist, not yet confident of her skill to show it to anyone? Perhaps with good reason. Radford was identifiable, but the oversized smile made him look as if he were auditioning for a toothpaste ad.

Another receipt, this time for a thousand-dollar handbag. Maybe there was a receipt for Radford's ring in here somewhere!

She found several more unlikely items, as if Amelia had dropped items into folders at random more than in an effort to hide them: a lock of brown hair, the strands held together with scotch tape. The page of a calendar from July, 1997, the 17th circled in red. And then, in the back of a file on koi in the bottom drawer, torn pages of a notebook covered with scribbled letters and dates and numbers. Amelia keeping track of . . . what? She started to drop the sheet back in the file, then took a second look.

The letters could be initials of names. O. M. didn't mean anything to Cate, but K. L. jumped out at her. Krystal Lorister? T. R. She didn't know the last name, but T. could be Texie. F. M.—Fiona Maxwell! Cate dug back in a labeled file of Whodunit ladies and checked names. Several crossed-out names corresponded to initials on this much more cryptic list. And if you put a dollar sign in front of the figures after the names . . .

And the initials with the largest dollar amount? D. M. Doris McClelland.

Cate sat back on her heels. Krystal was right. Amelia had

been getting kickbacks on what her friends invested, and this was a record of them. Undoubtedly not a record she offered to her tax accountant. Something she kept hidden, and perhaps not dropped into this unlikely file at random. Krystal had played down the amount she'd lost, but what Amelia had received from Krystal's investment was not insignificant. Although Doris's amount, and a couple of the others, was much higher.

Perhaps, if the investment had turned out well, none of them would have cared about Amelia making money for herself with a kickback. They might even have thought she deserved it for getting them into such a good deal. But to realize Amelia had raked in payoffs while they were losing every dime . . . Any one of them could have been angry enough to shove her down the stairs.

Whodunit ladies en masse now scuffled for top place on Cate's suspect list. But what should she do with this information? Take it to the police? She studied the cryptic scribbles again. She saw proof of the kickback scheme here, definite motive for murder, but there was nothing to prove to anyone else what this was about. She heard Willow coming up the stairs, nothing tippy-toey about her steps now, and she hastily stuck the notebook pages in a pocket of her jeans. She wasn't sure why, but she didn't think sharing this with Willow was a good idea.

Willow's chicken tacos were excellent, the salsa homemade with fresh tomatoes, and Cate took a couple home to eat for breakfast. Rebecca would be appalled, of course, but Cate considered cold tacos right up there with cold pizza as an excellent breakfast item.

◆ 16 ◆

Cate worked on her assignment for the next two days, visited Uncle Joe, took Octavia in for a vet checkup, and thought a lot about that list of initials and dollars, and what she should do with it, if anything. She even considered calling Mitch to see what he thought. He might be annoying, but he was sharp and knowledgeable, and he could do things with a computer that would never occur to her. But she was stopped by two thoughts: if she called on him for help, it would look as if she needed rescue again. The other was that he might think she was feeling desperate because the reunion with Kyle hadn't worked out, and she was trying to jump-start some romantic relationship with him.

About mid-morning, Willow called again. Cate was beginning to think, without Amelia there at the house to keep her busy, Willow had way too much time on her hands.

"Why don't you come over and have lunch with me?" Willow asked. "Cheryl isn't around. She said she has a house to stage today. She's been doing that, working with some real estate outfit, since her decorating business is on the skids. Though she'd never admit her business is on the skids, of course."

"I need to go visit Uncle Joe—"

"Oh, c'mon," Willow wheedled. "All these cupboards are full of stuff that's been here since before Amelia hired me. It ought to be used up. Sometimes I think she was poor as a kid and vowed when she was rich she'd never run out of food again. And some of it's really fancy. We can have smoked oysters! Pickled asparagus! Those fancy truffle mushrooms. There are even jars of caviar."

"Cheryl will probably want them. Does she know the stuff is there?"

"She went through the cupboards, but all she said was, 'Toss the cat food.'"

Which said what about Cheryl's scheme to get Octavia back? Apparently she didn't think it was going to happen. Maybe the lawyer had told her he could squeeze some ridiculous price out of Cate for the animal, which would add to the value of the estate.

"She can donate everything to a homeless shelter or rescue mission, then," Cate said.

Willow giggled delightedly. "Wouldn't they be surprised? Caviar for the homeless! But okay, I can fix something else."

"I'm kind of busy—"

"You can pick up this sack of cat food for Octavia too. You know how much she likes it."

True. The Furry Gourmet. "The cat food actually belongs to Cheryl now. You can't just give it to me."

"Sure I can. I told you, she told me to toss it. And I'm just tossing it to you. You don't want it to go to waste, do you?"

"Well . . . okay." Cate was about to add that she'd drop by for a few minutes after lunch, but Willow was already dancing ahead.

"We'll eat outside. I was poking around in the garage looking for a little step stool that used to be here in the kitchen, and I found this cute patio set. Table and chairs and umbrella. I can't imagine Amelia ever using it, but I've already got it all set up out back."

So, at 11:30, Cate was on her way over to the house. She hoped Willow wouldn't come up with some strange pickled asparagus and smoked oyster casserole for lunch. Even though Willow could probably make even that taste good.

Cate sniffed a wonderful scent when Willow opened the door to let her in. Spicy. Tomatoey and garlicky. "What *is* that?"

"You didn't sound enthusiastic about the gourmet goodies, so I made spaghetti. One of Beverly's favorites. Grandma told me this secret about putting in just a sprinkle of cinnamon."

"You need to rush right down to Grandma's and open that café."

"Soon," Willow said.

"Still waiting for that money?" Okay, she was curious.

Willow didn't fall for her subtle fish for information. "It won't be much longer. Hey, I'll set out that cat food so you'll be sure to get it this time."

Cate followed Willow to the kitchen, where Willow pulled what looked like at least a twenty-pound sack of cat food out of a lower cabinet and set it in the doorway between kitchen and dining room. Octavia would be in kitty paradise. She'd eat anything, but that particular cat food generated the loudest purrs.

Today Willow had both the dining room drapes and windows open, and the table gleamed with fresh polish. The light from outside brightened the gloom of the dark room considerably. Although with the drapes open, that rickety stairway was much too visible.

"The spaghetti sauce needs to simmer a little longer. Let's go out in the backyard. I made lemonade." Willow was in a pink halter top and hip-hugger denim shorts ragged at the bottom.

She filled two glasses, and they went outside. The unkempt grass needed Mitch and a lawnmower, although Willow had trampled a space for the patio set. She'd also tilted the umbrella and arranged the table and chairs so they wouldn't be looking at the scene of Amelia's demise.

Willow moved a chair into the sun and stretched out her legs. "I think I'll ask Cheryl if we can get someone in to clean up the backyard. They'll need to do it so they can sell the place anyway."

"Maybe they could tear down that old stairway too."

"Good idea." Willow closed her eyes.

Cate sat in the other chair, but even with her back to the stairs, no way could she be unaware of their existence. Visions skulked in her head. Amelia at the top of the stairs . . . talking with someone she trusted . . . the surprise of a ruthless shove. She couldn't identify the shadowy shape behind Amelia in her vision. It could be Cheryl, Radford, or one of the Whodunit ladies. And, even though she'd almost discarded the possibility, maybe Willow herself. Or perhaps someone totally unknown to Cate.

Cate tried to distract herself with a different thought. "Don't you get a zillion more freckles if you sit in the sun like that? I do."

"Yeah, but I don't mind." Willow laughed. "Coop used to like to count them on my back. He said each one was a little gold star of approval from the sun."

Again that hint of nostalgic affection for Coop. Another subject that disturbed Cate.

"Hey, what about your old boyfriend. Or fiancé, wasn't he? Did you see him over the weekend?" Willow asked.

239

"No, I called and talked to him. We're off, for good."

"Are you brokenhearted?"

"No."

"What about that other guy, the one Beverly thought was so great?"

"He's just an acquaintance." Actually, Cate realized, she'd rather talk about Amelia and murder than this. "The police have never talked to you about Amelia's fall?"

"Actually, they did. Didn't I tell you? They were here the day after I moved back in. It wasn't any big deal. They just wanted to know more about how often Amelia took sleeping pills and did she ever sleepwalk, and I told them, oh yeah, she took a lot of pills. And the last time she sleepwalked I found her in the turret room with a window open. It looks out on that steep drop-off to the road down below. She could have leaned out and fallen head over heels right then."

"Did they ask why you moved out that morning?"

"I told them Amelia fired me. I didn't want to, you know, confuse the issue by saying I had seen her body before I left."

The fact that Willow hadn't told the police the truth disturbed Cate. She looked at her watch and stood up. "Hey, you know what? Maybe I shouldn't stay for lunch. It's getting late."

"Oh, c'mon. The spaghetti sauce should be ready by now. You mad at me or something?"

"No. I just sometimes think you know more about Amelia's fall than you're letting on. That maybe you know something that might look bad for Cheryl. And she hired you back as kind of a bribe so you wouldn't tell."

Willow jumped up. "Cate, you're overdoing the PI stuff. Looking for bad guys and killers where there aren't any. You've got suspects and motives and opportunities all running around in your head like so many scrambled eggs."

Could be, Cate admitted reluctantly. Although what she said was, "Scrambled eggs don't run."

"C'mon, let's go eat."

They went back to the kitchen. Willow was just dishing up the spaghetti when the doorbell rang. "Get that, would you?" Willow asked.

Cate went to the door. She would have instantly slammed it shut, except a booted foot jammed inside stopped her. With a big smile and a strong hand on the door, he pushed it open.

"Ah, we meet again," he said. "The lovely but uncooperative PI from Belmont Investigations."

"Who is it?" Willow called.

"Nobody," Cate said.

"Me," Coop corrected.

Willow apparently recognized the voice. She came through the dining room, spoon dripping spaghetti sauce in hand, a strange look on her face.

"Coop," she said.

"Willow," he said.

Cate did not like the sound of that. Too much like star-crossed lovers calling to each other across some gap of time and space.

"How did you find me?" Willow asked.

Coop walked up to her and held out his arm, fist closed around something in his hand. She held out her hand, and he dropped something into her palm. Cate moved closer for a look. The object was black, flattish, smaller than Willow's palm. Innocuous looking, but it skittered a shiver up Cate's spine.

"What's this?" Willow held up the object to inspect it.

"I just took it off the underside of your friend Cate's car."

Willow gave Cate a questioning glance. Cate blinked, blank.

241

She'd never seen that thing before. Had he done something to disable her car, removing some essential part she didn't even know existed? But why . . .

Then she knew. She'd read about it in one of Uncle Joe's books. "It's a tracking device. You used it to track me here!"

Coop grinned. "Give the PI a gold star." He tapped a finger on Cate's forehead, as if he were planting the gold star there. Then he reached over and retrieved the object from Willow's hand.

"You did this?" Willow gasped. "You put this thing on Cate's car so you could follow her here to me?"

Cate also didn't like the sound of the accusation. Because it came out more admiring than angry or frightened.

"It's illegal to track someone without their knowing it," Cate accused. She wasn't sure of that, but if it wasn't illegal, she figured it should be.

"Anyone can buy one of these gadgets over the internet," Coop scoffed, unperturbed about legality. "Fifty-nine ninety-nine. Plus shipping, of course. Runs twenty hours on a built-in battery. You put it on a vehicle, then take it off and plug it into your computer. It shows you everywhere the car's been, complete with map. Not as handy as the kind where you can follow a vehicle's movements in progress, but that system costs big bucks, and you have to sit there and monitor it."

"It looks as if you made this one work pretty well." Again Willow sounded admiring.

"I had to put it on and take it off several times to check it on the computer." Coop smiled at Cate. If a snake could smile, she figured that's what it would look like. "And you were always considerate enough to leave your car out where I could get to it. Though it took me a while to connect with this place. I lost time looking up addresses where you'd been before I figured out this was the place. And I didn't realize you'd be here when I arrived."

Willow suddenly seemed to have second thoughts about admiring his stalking technique. She backed up a step. "You wanted to find me to get your money back?"

"You did take money that belonged to him?" Cate asked in dismay. Willow had denied this.

No one paid any attention to her.

"I don't want any money back. I just wanted to find you. I miss you. I never did know why you left."

"You don't remember what a cheapskate you were about getting a new car? Or how many times I asked you not to leave your dirty clothes scattered all over the floor? Or our big argument about that woman who kept calling you?" Willow demanded.

A woman? Willow had never mentioned a woman. Had their big breakup been not about abuse and fear, but jealousy? And dirty clothes?

"She was nothing," Coop said. "Nobody. I tried to tell you that."

"I thought you'd try to find me."

"I did try to find you. I hired this detective agency, didn't I?" He waved a hand at Cate. "And I'm here now."

"It took you long enough!"

To Cate's dismay, they smiled at each other.

"Don't I smell some of that awesome spaghetti you used to make?"

Willow smiled again. "I was just dishing it up. I'll get another plate."

"Willow, don't do this," Cate begged. "Pick up and leave. Now! Go down to live with your grandmother in—" She broke off before she let "Florida" slip out.

243

Willow's eyes flicked back to Cate. "Well, going down to Grandma's was just an . . . option."

"I wouldn't object to going down South somewhere," Coop said. "Magnolias, mint juleps, Southern sunshine . . . sounds great! But I have another idea that might interest you."

"Remember what this guy did to you!" Cate said. "He hit you. He threatened you."

Coop shook his head. "Willow, babe, you told her all that? How melodramatic can you get?"

"You did punch me once," Willow said to Coop.

"It was self-defense. You were pounding on me at the time."

"A gentleman wouldn't hit back!"

Coop grinned at her, and, after a moment, Cate was dismayed to see Willow grin too. Coop gave Cate a smug smile. "She exaggerated."

"But most of it was true," Willow insisted. "You did want to know where I was every minute. And that sob story you told Cate about my taking your dad's belt buckle. You hocked it yourself when we were up in Seattle."

Coop shrugged. "I guess I forgot about that. But I think I used the money to buy you some earrings. I always suspected good ol' Dad stole it instead of winning it anyway," Coop added, as if that justified forgetting whatever he'd done with the buckle. Or maybe it was just another lie.

"And then you told Cate I ran up thousands of dollars on your credit card," Willow accused. "You didn't even have a credit card, remember? Both of them were canceled."

Cate blinked. She felt caught in a whirlpool of lies and counter-lies. But Coop and Willow were looking at each other, and again they started to smile at the same time. Then they were laughing.

Cate had kept wanting to believe in her look-alike. Because they looked enough alike to be twins? A bad reason, a truly lousy reason.

And yet she didn't want to see Willow make another big mistake in her life.

"Willow, don't let him talk you into going back to him!"

"Ah, c'mon, Cate," Coop said. "Are you trying to stand in the way of true love?" He looked at Willow. "We ought to do it up right and get married this time."

Cate groaned. Playing the high card. Marriage. "Willow, this is a worse idea than . . . than sitting in a two-hundred-foot tree while they cut it down."

"You should probably leave now," Coop said to Cate. He draped a proprietary arm across Willow's shoulders. "Willow and I have things to talk about."

"There's lemonade in the fridge to go with the spaghetti," Willow said.

"This is a bad idea, Willow." Cate wanted to throw a pitcher of lemonade or a plate of spaghetti . . . something! . . . over Willow's head. Anything to wake her up or shield her from Coop's manipulation. But she knew it would take more than a cold splash of ice cubes to shield Willow from herself. "A really bad idea," she repeated even as she knew how useless the warning was.

"I'll walk you to the door," Coop said to Cate. It sounded more like a get-out threat than a polite offer.

"Don't bother."

Outside the door, Cate heard the lock click behind her. Willow was going to go back to Coop. She knew it as surely as if Willow was holding up a diagram with her initials carved with Coop's inside a heart. And there wasn't a thing Cate could do about it.

Except pray. Which she did fiercely on her way out to the car. *Hammer some sense into her head, Lord. Please!*

Cate was in her car and at the end of the block before a thought occurred to her. Not a persuasive thought to make Willow change her mind. Something considerably more petty. Willow had given her that sack of cat food, and she'd stomped out without taking it.

Suddenly that seemed the last straw piled on top a whole lot of other straws of disillusionment today. That cat food belonged to Octavia, and she was going to claim it.

She U-turned at the end of the street and zoomed up the sloped driveway, right up beside Coop's big bike. His flashy, flame-painted helmet still hung on a handlebar. On the porch she decided to ignore the doorbell. Willow and Coop were probably already in the backyard sharing lemonade and spaghetti and cozy plans to reunite. She'd just run in and grab the cat food.

That wasn't going to happen, she realized a moment later. She'd forgotten Coop had locked the door behind her. Coming back for the cat food was a dumb idea anyway. Cate turned away from the door. Then she remembered something.

She ran back to the car and rummaged through her purse. Yes, there it was.

She stuck the key in the lock, opened the door, and tiptoed across the living room. Yes, the sack of cat food was still leaning in the doorway between the dining room and kitchen. She hefted it into her arms and braced it on her hip. A murmur of voices came from the backyard through the open windows. A sudden burst of Coop's husky laughter fueled Cate's already simmering anger.

"I can't believe it. You really told her that mom-and-pop-raised-me-in-a-carnival story?" Coop asked. "And she bought it?"

"I was going to tell her the truth one of these days. She's sweet, Coop, she really is. But sometimes, I don't know, I just can't help making up things."

"Yeah, I know. You told me that whopper the first time we met. Along with some others." He sounded affectionate, not critical, and Cate had no trouble picturing a hug around her shoulders.

Cate clutched the sack. Gullible, that's what she'd been, she groaned at herself. She shifted the weight of the sack in her arms and turned to head back to the door. They wanted to tell lies, let them tell lies to each other. But Coop's next words stopped her.

"I have an interesting project in the works. Something you'll like, I think."

"You'd cheat your own brother," Willow scoffed. "In fact, I think you did cheat your own brother. So why should I be interested in any 'project' with you?"

"You know I'd never do anything to cheat *you*," Coop said. "And this deal is worth big bucks."

Cate tried to get her feet moving. She was not interested in Coop's deal. But curiosity trapped her. A punch of that familiar protective feeling for her look-alike also kicked in. Would it do any good to storm out there and again try to persuade Willow to tell him to get lost?

"Except that your 'big bucks' never seem to materialize," Willow said.

"We've had some bad luck, but we're good together, babe. Remember how we lived in that high-class Houston apartment and worked the rare coin thing? That was fun, wasn't it?"

Rare coin thing? Somehow that did not sound like an endeavor endorsed by the Better Business Bureau.

A suspicion affirmed when Willow said, "What I remember is that we left town with the cops practically snapping at our heels. So what kind of deal is it this time?"

Cate rested the heavy sack of cat food on the edge of the oblong dining table as she listened.

"I've been looking at apartments because Jeff says he wants to live in the cabin himself, and I met this old guy with a sixty-unit apartment complex over in Springfield. He and his dead wife have had it for years, so he owns it outright, no mortgage. He'd like to sell it, because he's got arthritis, lumbago, whatever. He can't keep up on repairs or manage the renters. He says they're driving him crazy."

"He'll need a super salesman and lots of luck, the way real estate is selling now."

"Right. So he's kind of stuck. He was thinking about hiring a management company to handle the rentals, but he's suspicious of companies like that, and I think we could talk him into something else."

"You want to buy an apartment building?" Willow sounded astonished.

Cate was surprised too. Buying an apartment building was an admirable enough project. Was she mistaken about Coop? Then Willow raised an obvious objection.

"We couldn't come up with the money to buy an apartment building. With our credit rating, we couldn't finance a doghouse."

"Not exactly buy it. Though we'd need some money to get the deal started. Show the old guy our good intentions and all."

Again Cate was surprised as Coop outlined what he had in

mind. She didn't know much about business deals, and this sounded as if it might be classified as "creative financing." But not necessarily dishonest.

They would approach the old guy with a combination sales and partnership deal. They'd put up some money as down payment and also evidence of their credibility and good will, then live in and manage the apartments, with a percentage of the rents going toward their buying the place.

"So, basically we'd be apartment managers," Willow said when he was done. "I'd go for that."

"The problem is, we'd need some money to get the deal started."

A long moment of silence until Willow said slowly, "I might be able to come up with some money."

Although Cate had been intrigued by what sounded like a viable possibility, now she silently wailed, *No, no, no! Whatever money you have coming, don't let Coop get his sticky fingers into it until you're positive this isn't something shady!*

"Whatever you're making on a job like this isn't going to do it, babe," Coop said, not unkindly.

"Bigger money than that."

"You pushed the old lady down the stairs, didn't you?" Coop laughed. "I wondered if you'd done it. You got cash she had stashed?"

"No! I did not push her! How'd you know anything about Amelia's fall?"

"Various addresses showed up when I was tracking Cate. I researched them on the internet and asked some questions here and there until I figured out this was the right place. It's no big deal to me if you did push her, you know."

"But I didn't," Willow said, and her insistence reassured Cate. Given Coop's charitable attitude toward murder, she'd have no reason to lie now. "I'd been away from the house, and I came back and found her lying right over there at the bottom of the stairs, dead. I got scared, you know? Another elderly woman I worked for fell off a balcony—"

"Like that old dairy farmer who fell off the roof?"

No comment from Willow on whatever that was about. "So I decided I'd better get out, before they accused me of having something to do with her falling. But before I left I thought about all the jewelry Amelia had. I figured a few pieces wouldn't be missed, so I ran upstairs to grab some. But the valuable stuff was all gone."

"You mean somebody else killed her and stole the stuff?"

"Somebody killed her, all right. Her fall was no accident."

"Like who?"

Cate leaned toward the window, balancing the sack of cat food on the table with an outstretched hand. Yes, who? Willow hesitated, and Cate wondered as if she was considering possibilities or perhaps not yet certain enough of Coop to share something this important with him. Then Willow said something, but her voice had lowered. Cate moved closer trying to hear, but all she caught was Coop's surprised word.

"Black—"

Willow apparently cut him off before he could finish the word. Cate puzzled over it. Black? Black what? Blackberry? Black widow? Black sheep?

Blackmail! Willow's "big money" was coming from *blackmail*?

More unintelligible murmurs from Willow. But Cate knew what Willow must be telling him. She either had always known, or knew now, that Cheryl had pushed her aunt down the stairs. And Cheryl either knew or suspected that Willow knew. Was the job offer so they could keep an eye on

Willow? Or had Cheryl hoped the job offer would buy Willow's silence? But it obviously hadn't been enough. Willow wanted more.

No gold stars for Willow. Not a murderer, but definitely a blackmailer.

But what about Amelia's jewelry? The hide-and-seek jewelry that sometimes seemed to be missing, sometimes wasn't. What kind of game was Cheryl playing there?

"Good work," Coop said with satisfaction at whatever figure Willow had told him. "That ought to be enough to do it."

"*If* I decide I want in on your deal," Willow said. "We used to talk about going down to Mexico to live. Cabo, maybe."

"We can still go to Mexico, and after the apartment house deal, we'll have enough money to live there as long as we want. In style. The old guy is in no position to check out repairs we charge for. Or how many units we tell him are empty and not bringing in rent. There'd be all kinds of opportunities to skim off a larger share for us."

A scam. This was more like the Coop Cate knew and suspected.

"Doesn't the old guy have kids or family or a lawyer who'd jump in and nail us?" Willow asked.

"Wife's dead, no kids. He thinks his nephews and nieces are lazy bums and he won't even talk to them, and he calls lawyers 'vultures in expensive suits.' It's an awesome setup. Chance of a lifetime."

"What makes you think he'd go for a deal with us when he doesn't trust anyone else?"

"Because I've been buttering him up. Helping out with the rental repairs. He's thinking of me as the son he never had." Coop sounded smug.

"So what do you need me for?"

"I love you, babe. Don't you know that yet? I could find a partner for a deal, but I need *you*."

Love and marriage. Coop was pulling out all the big guns.

"And think about the payoff in the end," Coop went on. "As part of the partnership, we set up one of those big insurance policies that pays off the other partners if one partner dies. Plus, if we handle it right, something that gives us ownership of the apartments if anything happens to him. And I'd bet anything he has a bundle of cash stashed under his bed or in his cookie jar. He's a stasher kind of guy."

Cate saw what was coming. It sent a shiver to her toes.

But Willow seemed oblivious. "Even if his health is bad, it might be years before anything happened to him."

"Years? Oh no, babe. Just long enough to keep it from looking suspicious."

"Keep what from looking suspicious?"

"Poor old Mr. Linkbetter's untimely death. Or timely, depending on your point of view."

"You're talking about—" Willow almost hissed a gasp. "About *making* him die?"

"Don't sound so shocked. It wouldn't be the first time."

"What do you mean? We maybe . . . did some stuff we shouldn't have. We pulled some scams. But we never killed anyone."

"Oh, c'mon, babe. Remember the old dairy farmer we were working for? You really think he slipped and fell off that barn roof all by himself?"

"You're telling me . . . you pushed him?" Willow sounded as if she choked over the words. "Coop, I don't want to be involved in anything like that. Not ever. I won't do it."

"You didn't seem to mind grabbing the cash he had hidden in the attic."

The words zapped Cate like a fist to the belly. Coop had just admitted murder. Murder not just contemplated, murder accomplished. And murder gotten away with. She touched her lips to cut off the gasp or yelp building there.

And in doing so, she let go of the sack of cat food . . .

It leaned. Tottered. Cate lunged for it. Too late—

Crash!

And that's why she forgot the sack of cat food. Yeah, that's it. Cate forgot the sack of cat food.

◆ 17 ◆

Cat food blasted out of the sack as it hit and broke. Cat food on the floor, cat food hitting Cate's face, cat food bouncing off the wall! A veritable explosion of cat food.

Frantically Cate looked around for some way to scoop it back into the sack. Then she realized that was the least of her worries.

"What was that?" Coop's voice, knife-hard and dangerous.

She couldn't let them catch her here! Run! No, she could never make it out the front door in time. Hide! Behind the drapes? Under the table?

Cate lunged for the drapes. Too late, because there was Coop staring at her from the doorway, Willow right behind him.

"I, uh, forgot the sack of cat food Willow gave me. I came back to get it, but I guess I . . . dropped it."

"You were listening to our conversation?" Willow's forehead creased in dismay.

"No, I couldn't hear anything—"

"She was listening." Coop stepped up beside her, looming over her. Cat food crunched under his boots. It sounded like old bones breaking. "She heard."

"I'm sorry about the mess." Cate eyed the doorway. She stood up. "I'll just get a broom and—"

Coop barred her way with the single thrust of a muscular arm.

"It's okay." Willow stepped over and touched Coop's arm. "I did give her the cat food. I'll help her put it in a plastic bag and—"

"Forget the cat food," Coop commanded, his gaze never leaving Cate. "She heard."

"I couldn't hear anything," Cate insisted, but even to her own ears the words sounded shrill and phony.

"So she heard us talking about the ridiculous deal on the apartments." Willow threw up her hands and kicked the tattered cat food sack across the room. "It's just another of your lamebrain, get-rich schemes that would never work."

"She heard the part about the farmer's fall off the barn."

"No, I didn't," Cate said, but these words sounded even worse. She put her hands behind her back, trying to keep them from shaking, and clenched her lips to keep them from trembling. But she knew what showed on her face. Her mouth might deny it, but her face made a banner headline of it.

"She'll turn us in." Coop's big hands clenched into fists. "Then the cops will know it wasn't an accident and nail us."

Willow rubbed his arm in a soothing gesture. "No one's going to pay any attention to some wild story about a dead farmer way back when."

"Two years isn't that long." Coop's fists flexed. Open. Shut. Cate's throat thickened, no breath passing through, as if those hands were closing around her neck. "With new information, they reopen cases that are two decades old."

"But Cate isn't going to say anything, are you, Cate?" Willow's face had paled under her sprinkling of freckles, but she gave Cate a nod of encouragement that plainly said "Tell him!"

Cate shook her head and stuttered agreement at the same time. "I-I don't know anything t-to say to anyone. I just came for the c-cat food."

"One thing you better remember, babe. If they nail me for pushing that old farmer off the roof, you go down too, as an accomplice. You want to spend the rest of your life behind bars? Or waiting to sizzle in the electric chair?"

"But Cate's my friend," Willow protested. "She rescued me from a tree once. I can't—"

Cate's heart hammered. Can't what? What did Willow think Coop had in mind?

"Look at it this way, babe. It's her survival or ours. I vote for ours. How do you vote?"

Plain enough. Cate's life or theirs.

"We can't take any chances. We need to make sure she can't talk. Babe, you better be with me on this," Coop warned. "But I'll do it alone if I have to."

At the moment Cate surely couldn't talk to anyone about anything. Her mouth felt as if the exploding cat food had filled it. Her tongue was trapped, immovable.

Willow folded her arms across her chest. "So what do you have in mind?"

Coop's gaze flicked to the window. Cate knew what he saw. The stairs.

"Falls seem to work."

Willow flung her hands in the air again. "That's crazy. *Two* people getting killed on those stairs, and the cops will investigate like there's a maniac serial killer on the loose. And who'll they investigate? *Me.*"

"So you tell 'em the old lady was murdered and who did it. And then you don't know anything about clumsy-footed Ms. PI here stumbling down the stairs."

"And you just waltz on out, free as a bird, while I'm stuck here taking all the risk!"

"You have a better idea?" Coop challenged.

Tell him, Willow. Tell him a better idea is to take his crazy schemes and get out of your life!

But what Willow said, her eyes avoiding Cate's, was, "A fall is . . . good. But not here."

"Where, then?"

"Over on the coast. There are lots of places to push someone off a cliff into the ocean."

Cate managed a dry-mouthed gasp. "Willow!"

"It's a long ways to drive, but, yeah, that might work." Coop's eyes narrowed as he studied Cate as if she were merely a problem in logistics. "We put her in the trunk of your car. I drive. You follow in her car. If anyone sees, they'll think it's her driving."

Willow picked up the plan. "We get to the coast and find a good spot. We leave her car parked there. It'll look like she just got out to look at the view and stumbled off a cliff. People fall off those coast cliffs all the time."

Not all the time, Cate objected. But often enough that it probably could look like an accident.

Coop had a sudden second thought. "Yeah, but if someone knows she came here, they'll wonder why she suddenly decided to rush over to the coast."

Willow eyed Cate as if expecting her to volunteer a useful explanation. Then she remembered. "She thought she was going to get back together with some old boyfriend, but then he broke up with her again."

"Smart guy," Coop muttered. "So if anyone questions you later, you tell them she was here, but she was upset about the guy and said she was going over to the coast to get away and think about it. Where's your car?"

"In the garage."

"How much gas is in it?"

"I filled the tank yesterday."

"Good. Let's get going."

Cate planted her feet on the cat food. She couldn't think what to do, but no way was she helping with a cooperative trot out to the car.

However, it was not as if she had a choice. Coop simply threw her over his shoulder as if she were an oversized sack of cat food and headed for the garage. She pounded his back with her fists and battered her knees against his chest, she yelled and screamed, but she may as well have attacked a bulldozer, and there was no one to hear her in the garage. Willow, following, also ignored Cate's flailing and yelling. Coop carried her past Amelia's Mercedes and dumped her upright beside the trunk of Willow's Toyota. He instantly wrenched her arms around behind her body. A jolt of pain shot through her shoulders.

"We need something to tape her hands and feet. And her mouth. We don't want her yelling and somebody hearing. Duct tape'll do it. You got some duct tape?"

"Duct tape!" Willow indignantly planted her fists on her hips. "Why would I have duct tape? And what's the point in tying her up if she's going to be in the trunk? What's she going to do? Tap Morse code messages on the lid and some satellite will pick them up?"

"I heard about somebody in a trunk managing to rip out the lights and stick out a hand, and somebody saw it."

Willow rolled her eyes. "I'll be right behind you. If I see her making obscene gestures at passing cars I'll let you know."

Willow's objection to tying her up gave Cate momentary hope. If she could just get Willow alone for a moment . . .

Willow might have moral deficiencies in the pulling-a-scam and blackmail departments, but she was no killer. Cate had heard the horror in her voice when she realized what Coop had done to the farmer.

"I'm not taking any chances," Coop insisted. "Just our luck she'd let out a banshee yell and some busybody would hear her. Now get something to shut her up. And there's a gun in the left saddlebag on my bike. Get it."

Willow disappeared back into the house. Coop yanked Cate with him when he went around to the driver's side door to click the trunk latch, yanked her along again when he went back to the trunk.

Willow returned with a mean-looking black gun and a roll of narrow white tape.

Coop grabbed the gun but he muttered an oath when she handed him the tape. "That isn't duct tape. It's masking tape! Nothing but sticky paper. Nowhere near strong enough."

"So I'm not a tape expert. It's all I could find in the storage room."

Coop grumbled as he wrapped the tape around Cate's wrists. He might consider it of inferior strength, but it felt all too sturdy to Cate. The tape was too narrow to cover her mouth shut with a single length of tape, so he used short pieces crisscrossed from cheeks to chin.

Willow watched him, and Cate's blood chilled when Willow unexpectedly giggled. "That looks like a four-year-old did it."

"Sorry. The Boy Scouts didn't offer a badge in mouth taping." Coop sounded grumpy, but Cate also heard the tease in his voice. They were making a fun outing of this. What next . . . pack a picnic lunch to take along?

"Are you going to do her feet too?" Willow asked.

"You think I should?"

"Nah. She won't be doing any hiking in there."

Coop picked Cate up and stuffed her in the trunk. Her feet dangled over the edge, and helpful Willow stuffed them in too.

"What about your bike?" Willow asked. "Should we bring it inside the garage?"

"It'll be okay. Let's get this show on the road. Just go out there and get her car started."

"Her purse is in the car. I looked when I went to get the gun out of your bike. But there's no car key."

"So it must be on her. Look for it."

Cate, stuffed in the car trunk with tape over her mouth, was in no position to object when Willow extracted the keys from Cate's pocket.

"I need to change clothes and get a jacket," Willow said. "The coast can be chilly."

"Okay. But hurry up."

They were hauling Cate to a cliff to shove her into the ocean, and Willow was worrying about her wardrobe.

The trunk lid slammed shut. The blackness of a cave engulfed her. Instant claustrophobia pounded the blood in her ears. Her throat closed. Bands of fear cinched her chest. She couldn't breathe. They wouldn't have to push her off a cliff. She was going to die right here, right now.

Lord, help me! I don't know what to do. I can't do anything!

A moment later the car door slammed. The garage door rumbled open. The car vibrated with the start of the engine.

A journey of a thousand miles starts with the first step.

A death drive to the coast starts with the first roll of the wheels.

The car started rolling.

❖ 18 ❖

The car rolled down the sloped driveway. Hands bound, Cate skidded across the hard floor of the trunk and banged into the wall. The rough carpet burned her cheek.

Helpless. Like a nightmare from which she couldn't awaken. A big swoop when the car reached the bottom of the driveway and turned to head down the street. A turn to the left at the corner. A few blocks and a swerve to the right. Then more turns, and she was totally disoriented, all sense of direction lost.

She started praying, sometimes a conscious prayer, sometimes like a program on a computer running continuously in the background. She lost track of time there in the cave of blackness. The ride was rough, the rumble of tires on the road close to her ears, the floor of the trunk unyielding bedrock against her bones. A sour scent of something once spilled on the carpet rose around her. A seasick nausea fluttered in her stomach.

Coop turned on the radio. Sound vibrated from the backseat speakers when he hit a hard rock station. Boom, boom, boom! Thankfully he moved on, finally stopping on the last music choice Cate would have expected. Coop liked golden oldies? Somehow she'd never imagined that she'd spend her last hours on earth listening to Tony Bennett singing "Fly Me to the Moon."

She managed to roll onto her side, and then her neck crinked as her unpillowed head flopped sideways to the floor. The arm under her went numb. She rolled to her other side. Would her body show carpet burn and incriminating fibers to alert the police?

Now there was a cheerful thought.

The ride went on and on. The sway of curves, the bump of a stretch of potholes, a smell of oil or grease rising from the underside of the car. The roar of a truck passing, a honk. Neil Diamond warbling "Song Sung Blue." Fuzz from the carpet tickling her nose. She sneezed, one, two, three times, cramping the muscles across her stomach. The tape across her mouth shrink-wrapped her lips. Bruised muscles, crick in her neck, sore bones.

She'd be sore for days from this—

No, she realized. She wouldn't.

In spite of that bleak thought, a peculiar sense of indignation unexpectedly welled up in her. This wasn't fair. Perhaps she shouldn't have muddled around in Amelia's murder. Both Uncle Joe and Mitch had warned her not to. But here she was . . . helpless in the trunk of a car, mouth and hands taped, headed for an appointment with a cliff . . . and it had nothing to do with Amelia's death. It was all because of a murder she hadn't even known existed until today. That and her dropping a sack of cat food.

She thought about the passing traffic. Who would guess Willow's innocent-looking Toyota held a trussed-up captive inside? She'd never look at passing cars the same. She'd always wonder, is someone in there, bound and helpless?

No, she wouldn't wonder that, she realized as the raw reality slapped her again. She kept missing the important point here. This was her final ride.

She thought of many other things there in the darkness. The deep and profound: *Lord, I believe in you. I believe there's an eternity beyond whatever happens to me here. Will I be seeing you soon? I'm so glad I know you. I trust you. But I'm so scared.*

The mundane: Her parents. Uncle Joe and Rebecca. Octavia. This would hit them all hard. Maybe even Mitch and Kyle would have a few regretful thoughts about her.

And there were regrets about things undone in her life. Blonde. She'd always intended to try being a blonde for a while. Not now. So, big deal. There were more important things undone. Marriage. Kids.

Sometimes her muscles went rigid with panic as the reality of what was happening . . . what was going to happen . . . rolled through her. Once a shiver grabbed hold of her like a live thing with tentacles and claws that wouldn't let go. She pictured herself taking that plunge into space . . . heard the air whistle in her ears as she somersaulted downward . . . saw the horizon revolve like some strange new rotation of earth and sun.

Her face itched under the tape. Her dry mouth and throat screamed for something to drink. A memory of the iced tea she and Mitch had shared in Uncle Joe's backyard surfaced. The icy tang, the sweetness. Oh, how she longed for a sip of that tea!

And Mitch. *I'm sorry I never got to know you better. I hope you'll find your way, all the way, to the Lord.*

Yet sometimes, incredible as it seemed, her brain slumped into boredom. Her muscles numbed. The hum of the road lulled her. Nat King Cole soothed her with "Unforgettable."

Eventually, even in the enclosed trunk, she sensed a change in the air. A scent of sea mingled with the sourness of the soiled carpet and the reek of her own scared sweat. A difference in temperature too, a cool freshness. Willow was right about needing a jacket over here. She could use one herself. Though she had to admit that was the least of her troubles. Once she thought she heard the boom of surf on a beach.

And she could really use a restroom about now.

Then a pull to the side of the road. Was this it, the place they'd chosen to fling her off a cliff? Her stomach clenched and started to lurch into reverse. She battled it down. Voices murmured right outside the trunk as her captors apparently got out of the cars and met there.

"What's going on?" Coop's voice, muffled by the lid of the trunk. "Why were you blinking your lights at me?"

"I needed to tell you I'm going to have to stop and put gas in this car. I'll go on ahead, and you can follow when I pull into a station."

"I can just keep on going down the road, and you can catch up with me."

"No, I don't want to go in there alone!"

"Okay, okay, don't panic. I'll be there. Should we check on her? There's no one around to see."

"It's not as if her comfort is any big deal," Willow pointed out. She laughed. "Considering what we have planned."

A hint of chuckle from Coop too. "Yeah, right. Is there a credit card in her purse?"

"I don't know. I can check."

"Use it if there is. That'll back up your story of her saying she was driving over here."

Slam of car doors, the car moving again. Swish and rumble of traffic, pavement rolling beneath her. Ten minutes?

Twenty? Then a swerve as Coop apparently followed Willow into a gas station. Although her car needing gas was odd, Cate thought. She'd filled the tank only three or four days ago. How come the car was getting such poor mileage? She'd have to check—

Yeah, right. As if mileage mattered now.

The car stopped. Engine off. Radio volume turned down. Sounds of kids squealing and yelling. A playground next door? A McDonalds, maybe? She felt a huge yearning for something she'd never have again, a Big Mac. Strange. She'd never been a Big Mac fan.

And squid. She'd never had the nerve to try squid. She'd never climbed Mt. Hood or learned to scuba dive or painted her toenails blue . . .

Waiting, sounds of cars coming and going, voices. Then Coop, sounding annoyed, saying, "We didn't need to stop. The gas tank only took nine gallons."

"I guess I was looking at the wrong gauge or something. I'm dying of thirst anyway. Go inside and get me something to drink, would you? I need to walk around out here and stretch my legs a little."

"Sure Coke?"

"Yeah. Thanks."

A Coke. Suddenly there was nothing Cate had ever wanted more in her whole life than a cold Coke.

The trunk lid flew open. Cate blinked at the light. Misty here on the coast. And chilly. She flinched when she saw Willow's face looming above her.

"Don't make any noise!" Willow whispered fiercely.

In spite of the command, Cate yelped as Willow yanked the strips of masking tape off her face.

"Get out!"

"What?" Cate asked blankly. She had to struggle to make her lips move.

"Get out! Out, out, out!"

Cate struggled to fling her numb legs out of the trunk. Willow grabbed her shoulder and yanked. She heard something rip and floundered to her feet. Then she saw the knife in Willow's hand and fresh panic jabbed icicles in her veins. Was Willow going to end it right here?

Willow whipped her around and sawed at the tape with the knife. Cate's hands swung free. They felt peculiarly detached, as if they might fly off into space. Her mind felt equally unattached. Willow thrust something at her.

"Here's your purse. Run! Hide! Over behind the building. Go! Before he comes back!" She shoved Cate between the cars. "Don't call the police until I can get away from him. I'll call you. Go, go, go!"

Cate ran, dodging vehicles, stumbling, blindly heading for the back side of the building. Behind her the trunk lid slammed.

Then she spotted the door on the side of the building. Familiar stick figure with a skirt. The women's restroom! She dove inside. Two stalls. She lunged into one and slid the bolt on the door. Her face burned where Willow had ripped the tape away. The slashed tape dangled from her wrists.

The outer door opened. Coop! Frantically she leaned her weight against the door.

No, not Coop. A woman and little girl came in and used the other stall, the girl wearing red leggings and chattering about a starfish on the beach.

Cate leaned her forehead limply against the door. Shivering. Dizzy. But thankful, oh so thankful. *Lord, you did it! Thank you!*

The woman made sure the little girl washed her hands before they left.

Weakly, Cate made use of the facilities. She yanked the tape on her wrists loose and crumpled it into a ball. When she finally opened the stall door, a wild woman stared back at her from over the sink. Matted red hair, pale face crisscrossed with reddish stripes, eyes like oversized marbles.

Me, Cate realized as she blinked at the mirror. A couple of hours bound and gagged in a car trunk was not a beauty treatment.

Something clattered to the concrete floor. Cate picked it up, surprised. A paring knife, the wooden handle decorated with a red flower. Willow must have shoved it into a pocket of Cate's purse to get rid of it. It took her a moment to realize what else this meant.

Willow must have grabbed the small knife from the kitchen when she went back to change clothes.

This hadn't been an impulse rescue, a last-minute surge of conscience. The stop for gas had been a phony. Willow had agreed to help Coop with his plan to kill Cate on the coast because he'd said he'd do it without her if he had to. She'd planned all along to help Cate escape!

Maybe not the most efficient way of handling the situation. Certainly not one that had spared Cate pain and panic. But a burst of gratitude flooded through her. Blackmailer, scam artist, whatever, Willow had still come through when the chips were down.

Thank you, Lord! Thank you for doing this through Willow!

Yet what happened when Coop found out what Willow had done?

Was her life in as much danger as Cate's had been?

Cautiously she opened the outside door and peeked out.

She wasn't sure where the cars had been parked. Over there by the chain-link fence?

The space was empty now. She saw the children she'd heard laughing and yelling. Not a playground, just a ramshackle fenced yard around an old house, with three children kicking a ball in the weedy grass.

Cate closed the door and sank back against the wall. It took all her strength not to slide bonelessly to the floor. Free! Safe!

Now what? Send the police to arrest them both? Or to rescue Willow? But Willow had said not to call the authorities until she could get away from Coop. And he had that gun. Her mind felt trapped in a blender on high speed.

A name bannered across her mind. Mitch.

No, she couldn't call him. She barely knew him. He'd be full of I-told-you-so's about this latest mishap.

He was also dependable and trustworthy. Reliable as the distant boom of surf.

With shaky hands she dug in her purse and pulled out her cell phone. But she didn't have his number—

Yes, she did. She'd never put it on her contacts list, but she'd almost dialed it so many times during that week after talking to Kyle that it was tattooed on her brain. If she could just peel back the layer of fog in there. . . She squeezed her eyes shut. Yes, there it was!

Her hands shook so badly that it took three tries to get the number punched in. She waited, breath caught in her chest.

Voice mail.

She had just escaped from a killer. She was stranded in a gas station restroom somewhere on the edge of the continent. And she gets voice mail?

The wonders of technology.

She left her name, number, and a request that Mitch call her as soon as possible. "I really need your help. It's a, uh, matter of life and death," she ended. Okay, that sounded a bit melodramatic, but right now her life felt like a bad episode of *CSI*.

She went into the convenience store attached to the gas station, bought a Pepsi, and gulped it down. She surveyed the town over the cans of motor oil piled below the window. Town might be an overstatement. This place was even smaller than Murphy Bay. One motel, a touristy gift shop, a little grocery store, a couple of cafés, Mick's Kar Kare. A red Corvette decorated a wall of the building, but an actual work-in-progress was a battered pickup minus a wheel. She asked the clerk the name of the place.

"Benton's View. Beats me why it's called that." The woman folded her arms and stared glumly out the window. "Do you see a view? I don't."

Apparently not an avid Chamber of Commerce supporter of the viewless sister city of Murphy Bay.

"Is there a police station?"

"Deputy from the county sheriff's office patrols through here. Once in a while you see a state police car on the highway." She eyed the reddish marks on Cate's face. "You need someone?"

Did she? She didn't want Coop to get away. But neither did she want to endanger Willow in some way. She kept remembering that mean-looking gun. Would he take Willow hostage if the authorities tried to chase him down? Catch her in an exchange of gunfire? She spotted a display of sweatshirts and headed for them as if that had been her intention all along. "This is what I need."

She picked out the heaviest sweatshirt on the rack and

paid for it. She wasn't thrilled with the imprint on it, but she figured the fashion police weren't patrolling this area. She was just slipping the sweatshirt over her head when her cell phone rang. She stepped outside to answer it.

"Cate, I got your message. Where are you? What's wrong?"

"I-I'm here, in this little town on the coast—"

"You sound strange. Are you okay? What did you mean about a matter of life and death?"

Her bones hurt. Her muscles ached. Her face stung. Her nerves felt as raw as fresh hamburger. But she was alive. "I'm okay."

"How did you get there? Is anyone with you?"

"I'm alone."

She knew she owed him a detailed explanation. But there was so much to think about, so much to tell him, and she was suddenly so very tired, her brain a frazzle of loose wires. She slumped to the concrete walkway beside the building. "I don't have a car. I was wondering if maybe you could come get me . . . ?"

"I'll come." No hesitation, no demand for explanation, no asking how far it was. "Just tell me where you are."

"If you're busy, I can wait."

"Cate, I'm coming now. Just give me directions."

All she could tell him was that she was at a wide spot in the road called Benton's View. "I'm at the only gas station."

"I've never heard of it, but I'll be there. I'm on my way right now."

She dropped the phone back in her purse. Just a matter of hanging on now.

Mitch was coming.

She'd just sit right here, rest, calm her nerves. Everything would be all right.

Mitch was coming!

Yet something niggled at the back of her mind.

A moment later the niggle exploded into possibility. She struggled to her feet.

Coop would find out soon enough that she was missing. He'd instantly know where she'd escaped.

And he'd come back for her.

19

Cate dashed around the side of the building and lunged into the restroom again. No lock on the outside door, so she barricaded herself in a stall. Mitch couldn't get here for at least two or three hours. How long before Coop turned around and came back, with murder on his mind?

Would he ask inside if the clerk had seen her? And the clerk would say, Yeah, she was here. Acting kind of weird. I think she went around to the restroom.

Her muscles squeezed into rigid cords every time the outer door opened. Coop, barging his way in? No, a woman with perfume powerful enough to annihilate small life forms. A little girl, apparently unnoticed by the barefoot person with her, bending down to peer up at Cate from under the stall door. An older woman with matronly shoes and serious flatulence problems.

And even as she was so afraid, Cate couldn't help pondering a certain absurdity in her predicament. She'd been bound, gagged, and hijacked. A murderer was out to get her, and she was stranded. But it was no high-drama situation on the edge of a cliff. She was in a gas station restroom. With rust stains in the sink and no towels in the dispenser. In a sweatshirt bearing a picture of a cranky crab complaining about a bad claw day.

With only one place to sit, she perched on the edge of the chipped seat and wondered how the door had acquired a dent in the shape of a horseshoe. Nothing to read but a strange philosophical pronouncement inked on the wall: I am. You are. But who is they?

More restroom traffic. Speculating about what the total person looked like when all she could see were feet and a few inches of leg.

Flip-flops with green toenails and rough-skinned heels. A teenager with incipient foot problems, or an older woman trying to be cool with teenage-colored polish?

Reeboks with thick socks. Athletic young beachcomber? Older person with circulation problems?

Daisy-decorated sandals and a butterfly tattoo on the ankle. Nice. Except for an ominous-looking bruise above the tattoo.

Once she risked leaving the stall and opened the outer door to peer at the gas pumps. The misty fog had lifted. Breezy sunshine now. But too early for Mitch, and she ventured no farther out. The minutes inched by. Fifteen. Forty-five. The curve of the hard seat imprinted her anatomy. The scent of dampish concrete and disinfectant congealed in her pores. At two hours from the time she'd called Mitch, she started peeking outside every five minutes, watching for him. Another fifteen minutes went by. Twenty-five. Thirty.

And there he was! The big SUV pulling around the gas pumps loomed like a haven of safety. Cate ran to it, flung the door open even before the vehicle stopped rolling, and hurled herself into the seat.

"Thank you for coming!"

Mitch studied her face, then reached over and rubbed a

thumb across the still sensitive blotches left by the tape on her face. "What's going on? Did you and Kyle have a fight and he dumped you over here?"

"Kyle?" she repeated. Kyle seemed so long ago and far away. Another life, another universe. "You thought this had something to do with *Kyle*?"

"Well, yeah, that's what I figured when you sounded so upset. That he'd come down from Portland again and you came over here for the day and then . . . something happened."

"And you came anyway?"

"I guess I'm a sucker for a distress call from a beautiful woman."

The "beautiful" was stretching it, especially when the restroom mirror had told her she looked like something washed up on the beach. But she appreciated that he classified her call for help the way he did.

"Kyle and I decided not to have any big reunion."

He scowled. "But if it didn't have anything to do with Kyle, why are you here? Tracking down a killer again?"

"Not exactly. It's a . . . long story."

He gave her a sideways glance. "I have plenty of time."

He wheeled the SUV around the gas pumps and back to the highway, and she gave him the long story. Going to see Willow. The overheard conversation between Willow and Coop. The cat food disaster. Her car-trunk trip to the coast. Willow helping her escape. Agreeing with Willow's plea to delay contacting the police until she could escape too.

"She said she'd call me, but I haven't heard from her."

"What do you think that means?"

"Maybe she hasn't been able to get away from him yet. Maybe her life is in danger." Cate paused, swallowed, and faced an ugly possibility. "Or maybe it means she did want to save me, but she never intended to get away from him herself. And now she and Coop are headed for Mexico or somewhere together." And laughing about the whole escapade.

"Cate, you have to go to the police, and the sooner the better. If what this guy says is true, he's already killed one person, and he was planning to kill you! Your friend Willow may be his next victim."

Mitch was right, of course. She couldn't delay any longer. They went to the police station as soon as they reached Eugene. An officer took down everything, and another one questioned her further. She supplied make and license information about Willow's car that Coop was driving. Reluctantly she added information about her own car but emphasized that, even though Willow was driving that car, she hadn't really been part of the kidnapping, because she'd done it only to rescue Cate.

They seemed interested and said they'd check on the death of a farmer in California two years ago. But they obviously weren't ready to mobilize an all-out attack force of police cars and helicopters to go after Coop.

The whole thing, Cate realized as they left the police station, wasn't black-and-white plain. She was a little worse for wear, bruised, and bone-sore, but she had no proof she'd actually been kidnapped. She hadn't notified police on the coast when Willow released her, and her statement that she hadn't done so because Willow asked her not to now sounded both flimsy and peculiar. Her vague information about the old murder, and a maybe-murder of an apartment owner in the future, weren't enough to justify an arrest warrant. Coop wasn't driving a stolen car, so they couldn't even get him on that charge.

Mitch's assessment, once they were back in the SUV, agreed with hers. "I'm not sure they believed you."

"They think I'm right up there with those people who claim they've been abducted by aliens."

"Which doesn't make Coop any less dangerous. He may come after you again." After a moment, while they both considered that possibility, he asked a practical question. "I should have asked earlier, are you hungry?"

Hungry? Yes. Ravenous. Her yearning from the car trunk surfaced. "I want a Big Mac. And fries. Supersized. And a Coke." She'd adventure into squid some other time.

After a stop at McDonald's, they got back to the house about eight o'clock. That seemed strange, after all that had happened today, and it was only eight o'clock. At the door, Mitch said, "I could stay with you for a while."

"I'm going to lock all the doors, take a shower and a couple aspirin, and head for bed."

He studied her face for a moment, then leaned over and dropped a quick kiss on her cheek. Then he stepped back, a puzzled look on his face, as if he wasn't sure why he'd done that. "I'll call you tomorrow."

Inside, a note from Rebecca said she'd gone to try to talk Joe out of a grumpy I'm-tired-of-this-place-and-I'm-getting-out-of-here mood. Octavia meowed complaint about not getting enough attention and tangled herself around Cate's feet. Just a normal day. If you tuned out the middle part.

Cate locked the doors and gulped two aspirin. She stood in the shower and alternated between worry about Willow's safety—had Coop found out Cate was gone before Willow could escape from him, and turned violent?—and a sour feeling that maybe she'd been had by another of Willow's stories.

And the going-to-bed finale didn't happen.

Her cell phone rang. The screen showed the number at

Amelia's house. Would Cheryl call her? Puzzled, she answered with a wary hello.

"Cate, you made it home okay! I'm so glad." Willow sounded bright and cheerful, as if they'd inadvertently become separated on a shopping spree, and she didn't ask how Cate had done it. "I'm really sorry about, you know, everything."

"You're home too?"

"I'm at Amelia's house. I guess that's home for the moment. I need to get your car back to you."

"I'd appreciate that. Thank you. You got away from Coop okay?"

"Oh, sure. No problem."

"Willow, what about Coop? I went to the police and told them everything. I mean, he *killed* someone. He kidnapped me. And he was going to push me off a cliff! They're looking for him." Cate wasn't positive of that statement, but she hoped it was true. "Aren't you worried he'll come back here looking for you because of what you did today? For which I thank you, by the way."

"We stopped to eat. He didn't know then that you were gone. While he was in the restaurant I left a note in the car and told him our getting back together was never going to happen. He won't come back here because he'll know you've gone to the police by now."

"You should go to them too."

"Coop and I did some things we shouldn't have. But I never knew about that old farmer. I really thought he fell. Knowing he didn't made me . . . see Coop differently. And I will go to the police, but not tonight, okay? I'll bring your car over to your place—"

"You don't have to do that tonight. I can get it tomorrow."

"I want all this to be done and over with. I'll drive the car over and then you can bring me back here."

Willow's determination to return the car fortified Cate's skimpy confidence in her. Willow had definite problems in the ethics department, but she seemed to be trying to do the right thing now. And she'd definitely done right when she helped Cate escape.

"You could stay here tonight," Cate offered.

"Oh, thanks, Cate, that's sweet of you. But I'm figuring on taking off for Grandma's first thing in the morning. I have some packing to do tonight."

"You don't have a car."

"But Coop's bike is here. Under the circumstances, I figure it's a fair trade. He's got my car, I get his bike."

"You can ride it?"

"Of course I can ride it!" Willow sounded indignant. "He taught me himself. And I know where he always hides the key in a little magnetic box under the footrest."

Cate was still in her bathrobe when Willow arrived twenty minutes later, and Willow was still in the jeans and tank top she'd been wearing when she helped Cate escape. Willow gave her a big hug when Cate opened the door to let her in. Cate was surprised that instead of weariness, an air of suppressed excitement almost danced around Willow. She dropped the car keys into Cate's hand, and Cate stuffed them into the pocket of her robe.

"Would you like something to eat? Rebecca left some macaroni and cheese in the fridge."

"No, thanks anyway." Willow glanced at Uncle Joe's old grandfather clock on the far side of the room. "I'm in kind of a hurry. I'll need to do a lot of sorting when I pack because I won't be able to take much on the bike."

Cate had made a decision even before Willow arrived. She appreciated, even admired Willow for having the courage to go against Coop and rescue her. It was also conscientious of Willow to be in such a hurry to return the car. But she still didn't 100 percent trust her. Maybe the truth was something dangerously different from Willow's story about escaping Coop. Maybe they'd gotten all cozy again, and Willow was sorry she'd let Cate go, and now she was leading her into a trap where Coop could take another try at killing her.

She'd call a cab to take Willow home. She started to tell Willow that, but Willow suddenly grabbed her by the shoulders. "This will probably be the last time we see each other, won't it?"

"I guess so. But we can write."

"I'm not much of a letter writer. Look, I want to tell you something before I leave."

Uh-oh. Here comes trouble. But Cate managed to say only, "Oh?"

Willow's hands let go of Cate's shoulders, and her gaze turned away. "Beverly's ring . . . you remember Beverly's ring? I did take it." Her eyes lifted to meet Cate's again. "And I'm sorry, really, really sorry now. I'll mail it back to her before I leave."

So the ring was another of Willow's lies. Although she was trying to make amends now. But would her change of heart last until she put that ring in the mail?

"Where is it?"

"There at the house. I've got it hidden."

Cate reversed her previous decision. "Since I'm driving you over there anyway, why don't I just pick it up? I can give it to Beverly, and you won't have to bother mailing it."

Willow actually smiled, as if getting rid of the ring would be a relief. "Hey, that'd be great! Beverly will be so happy, won't she? But let's hurry, okay?"

"You got a hot date tonight?" Cate grumbled.

Willow laughed as if Cate had inadvertently said something amusing. "Not tonight."

Cate hurriedly changed into fresh jeans and a sweatshirt, and a few minutes later she parked in the driveway at Amelia's house. Coop's bike still stood in the driveway, chrome tailpipes gleaming under the streetlight, flashy helmet dangling from the handlebars. No lights shone from the house. Returning to a dark house where someone had been killed would fluster Cate, but apparently it didn't bother Willow.

"There's another reason you should go to the police before you leave," Cate said.

With one hand on the door handle, Willow gave her a wary sideways glance. "Oh?"

"Willow, you know more about Amelia's death than you told the police, don't you? More than you told me. You know it was murder. And you're blackmailing Cheryl about it."

"Blackmailing Cheryl!" Willow echoed.

"I heard you talking with Coop about it."

"Oh, Cate, you have the wildest imagination! I don't know what you thought you heard, but no, I am not blackmailing Cheryl."

"No?"

"No. And if you're going to be a PI, you shouldn't go around making outrageous accusations."

True, Cate agreed reluctantly. "But you should still go to the police."

"Sure."

It did not sound like a written-in-blood promise.

Outside the car, Cate followed Willow to the door. Willow fumbled in her purse.

"I can't believe this. Where's my key? I know I had it, because I had to have it when I locked the door when I left—"

"I have a key." Cate dug in her own purse and produced it.

"How come you have a key?"

"It belongs to a Whodunit lady. I still have to find out who and give it back."

"Okay, use that one, then. But I must have dropped mine here somewhere . . ." Willow leaned over, hands on knees, and peered around the porch and steps. "Oh, I know! I'll bet it's on the floor of your car. I tossed it on the seat when I got in and it probably fell off."

She ran back to the car. Cate already had her key in the lock and turned it. She stepped inside and fumbled for the switch to the outside light.

"Okay, stop right there," a voice commanded from the darkness. "Stretch your arms out to the side and don't move."

Cate momentarily thought, Hey, shouldn't that be "put your hands up"? But then she felt something cold and hard in the middle of her back and knew it was no time to argue semantics.

"Okay, we're going upstairs now. Nice and slow and easy. Don't try anything."

"Look, I, uh, think you've made a mistake," Cate croaked.

"The only mistake is the one you made, thinking you could get away with blackmailing me. I know our appointment was for tomorrow morning, but I decided I'd make a surprise visit and come a little early." The gun prodded her lower back. "Get moving."

The front door opened, briefly silhouetting Willow in the glow from the streetlight. "Cate, what are you doing here in the dark?" She flicked on the light in the living room.

With the distraction, Cate hastily stepped away from the

gun. Which turned them into a tableau of three surprised people staring at each other. The gun in Scott Calhoun's hand sagged only a fraction of an inch as his gaze jumped between them. Cate didn't know much about handguns, but this one had a peculiar-looking something on the barrel.

"See," Cate croaked at him again, "I told you you'd made a mistake."

Willow spun on her heel toward the open door, but a swivel of the gun cut off her escape. "Stop. Right there."

Willow crossed her arms. "You can't shoot," she scoffed with more bravado than Cate could muster. "The whole street would hear."

"You've never seen a silencer, I take it. Well, take a good look." He waved the gun like a magic wand, and Cate realized the peculiar-looking barrel must be a silencer. "I can shoot you five times and no one's going to hear. So just close the door, nice and quiet."

Willow hesitated. Scott spread his feet and added a second hand to the gun, putting him in a classic TV-shooter stance. Willow closed the door.

So, Willow had told the truth . . . in a way. She wasn't blackmailing Cheryl. She was blackmailing Cheryl's husband.

Cate's mind whipped around the revelation that this meant Scott Calhoun had killed Amelia. But he'd been out of town when Amelia fell—

Cate groaned. Some PI she was. She'd simply accepted the out-of-town story and hadn't even suspected him.

More three-way looking at each other. Whatever plans Scott had, Cate's presence obviously complicated them. Then the frown left his face, and he smiled. Not a reassuring smile.

"How ironic. The cat, the house, you. So now we have the two birds with one stone thing, if you'll pardon my cliché."

"I guess I . . . uh . . . don't get the connection," Cate mumbled.

"You don't know?" He eyed her with a tilt of head. But whatever it was she didn't know, he apparently didn't intend to enlighten her. "Okay, both of you, up the stairs. Drop the purses," he added. "I don't want you using up cell phone minutes."

Cate reluctantly dropped her purse. With a show of defiance, Willow first extracted her wallet from the purse and stuffed it in the back pocket of her jeans. "I don't trust you with my cash." In another show of defiance, she tossed the purse on a chair rather than dropping it.

They shuffled toward the stairway. Willow managed a fall on the stairs, though Cate didn't know if it was a nervous stumble or an effort to sabotage Scott's plan by tumbling into him.

If it was a plan, it didn't work. Scott adroitly sidestepped her on the wide stairs. He prodded her with his foot. Nicely clad in expensive loafer, no sock. "Keep moving. Into Amelia's room."

Willow picked herself up. In the bedroom, Scott yanked the closet door open and took a quick look around. Checking for bad guys? He didn't need to do that. The bad guy was out here. With a jerk of the gun, he motioned them inside. Cate planted her feet. The closet looked way too much like an oversized car trunk, and she'd already gone that route today.

"No," she said. "I won't—"

The bullet slammed into the carpet at her feet. The silencer didn't shut off the bang completely but did turn it into a muffled whump. It also silenced her, because the message came across loud and clear. He hadn't brought them up here to shoot them, but he would if he had to.

Which opened the obvious question. Why not shoot them? Why stuff them in the closet?

Willow, apparently with the thought that staying alive at the moment was more important than playing a quiz game, grabbed Cate's hand and yanked her into the walk-in closet. Scott shut the door, and in the darkness they heard him drag something to the door. The knob squeaked when he jammed what Cate guessed was one of the wingback chairs under it.

Then, silence. And darkness. Cate felt the room close in on her, the car trunk all over again. Panic rose like a noxious cloud, clogging her brain and senses. Fear goose-bumped her arms and jellied her knees. Beside her, Willow's breath came in heavy wheezes. The cash in her wallet wasn't going to help them here.

Determinedly Cate shook off the panic. She wasn't bound and gagged here. She could move. Speak. Yell. Not that anyone except Scott could hear. But she wasn't helpless.

Lord, guide us! What should we do?

She tentatively reached into the darkness. Her fingers touched something furry. She yelped and yanked the hand back. Then she realized the furry thing was only Amelia's fox fur jacket.

Okay, no time for over-the-top panic now. A fox fur jacket never bit anyone. They weren't in any immediate danger, even if the closet was dark and claustrophobic. "I don't get it," she whispered, wondering if Scott was lurking and listening outside the door. "What's the point in this?"

"There's a light switch in here somewhere."

An overhead light flared on. Cate blinked. Clothes surrounded them. The fur jacket. A suede jacket. Sequins glittering on a red cocktail dress. Full-length gowns. Sweatshirts. Slacks. Blouses. Sweaters. Suits. Nightgowns and robes. And scarves. Hanger after hanger of them, geometric and flowered, gauzy and woolen, long and short. Amelia must have had some sort of scarf fetish.

A mirror covered the inside of the door. With a jolt, Cate realized how sisterly she and Willow looked. Same height, same heads of wild red hair. And two sets of scared eyes staring back at her.

Shoes covered the shelf above the wooden rods holding the clothes. More shoes on the floor beneath the clothes. Tennies and boots, sandals and pumps, platforms, high heels of all colors and shapes. En masse, the shoes had a strangely disembodied look, as if they were awaiting a crowd of feet to arrive.

"Help me with the door," Willow said. "It opens out so maybe we can shove the chair or whatever it is away."

They put shoulders to the door and shoved. One, two, three grunting shoves. They shifted sides and shoved again with opposite shoulders. Which accomplished nothing more than a sharp crack that split the length of the mirror. Willow wound up the unsuccessful attack with a savage kick to the door. Which accomplished nothing except to add another crack to the mirror.

Again Cate asked, "What's the point in this? He leaves us here to give him time to . . . what? Is he planning to just walk away from his life? Disappear?" She looked at Willow. "He did push Amelia down the steps, didn't he? That's what you were blackmailing him about."

"It wasn't really blackmail," Willow protested. "It was more like a . . . business transaction. I just told him that I wouldn't go to the police with what I knew if he made it worth my while."

"What was worth your while?"

"A hundred and fifty thousand in cash."

"Willow, that's what blackmail *is*!"

Willow managed an injured look at this blunt statement.

285

"It's hardly a drop in the bucket compared to what they're getting out of Amelia's estate. There are stocks and bonds and CDs and annuities. At least a couple million dollars' worth. They could afford a few bucks for me."

"They? Cheryl was in on the murder?"

"Not to begin with. But she found out pretty quick. Scott was in real financial trouble. A while back he invested big money in some deal he thought was going to make a bundle—"

"The same deal Amelia talked the Whodunit women into investing in?"

"I think so. He must have thought it really was a great deal. He 'borrowed' a lot of money from clients' accounts so he could make a big investment for himself. When most of it went down the tubes, he was frantic to get hold of enough to pay back what he'd taken before it was discovered."

"So he decided killing Amelia was the way to get it, told Cheryl he was going out of town, and came here and pushed Amelia down the stairs instead. How'd he get her out there so he could do it?"

"I don't know. It isn't as if they gave me diagrams." Willow sounded annoyed with Cate's questions.

"What about Amelia's jewelry?"

"Getting money out of the estate would take a while, and Scott needed money right away to pay back at least some of what he'd taken. So he grabbed the jewelry and took it back up to Seattle to sell."

"And Cheryl didn't know that at first. She was howling about the jewelry being missing. Accusing you. But when she found out what her husband had done, she covered for him by saying the jewelry wasn't missing after all."

"The couple that murders together stays together," Willow muttered. "Ain't love grand?"

"What about the engagement ring? Did Scott get that too? Or," Cate said bluntly, "maybe you grabbed it?"

Willow didn't protest the accusation. "I don't know anything about that ring. I know you probably don't believe anything I say, but—"

"Can you blame me?" Cate challenged.

"I suppose not. But this is the truth. I never even saw the ring. So I have no idea whether it's Cheryl or Radford lying about it."

Willow drew an X across her heart with her finger to emphasize her truthfulness, but Cate's mind leaped over to the full saying. Cross my heart and hope to die. Which was way too close to the truth of what might happen here.

"You planned to collect the blackmail money at your meeting with Scott in the morning and then take off for Grandma's?" Which explained that earlier air of excitement about Willow. Anticipation of a big blackmail payoff would do that.

"I didn't see any point in sticking around here."

"Or maybe you had some clever plan to sneak off and join Coop somewhere. You could live it up for a while on a hundred and fifty thou."

Willow didn't bother with an injured look. "I'm scared of Coop." She wrapped her arms around her body in a protective gesture that made Cate think this was definitely the truth.

"Apparently Scott doesn't see any point in paying you off when he can kill you and get you out of the way permanently."

And me too, Cate added glumly to herself. Although the man seemed to have an unwarranted personal hostility directed specifically at her. He'd seemed quite pleased to include her in tonight's plan. Although sticking them here in the closet did seem an inefficient method of murder. It would take a while for them to starve to death. Perhaps he just intended it as enough time to allow him to disappear? But that would mean walking away with nothing, and a no-payoff ending seemed unlikely for a man willing to push an old woman down the stairs.

Willow didn't comment, and Cate asked another question. "How'd you find out about all this?"

"That day I found out Radford had come here about the engagement ring, I overheard all this other stuff too. Cheryl and Scott were in Amelia's office, arguing and blaming each other. I heard enough to tell me what was going on, and then I guessed the rest of it."

"You guessed close enough to make a strong case for black-mail."

Willow didn't protest the word this time. "I don't suppose blackmailing a killer is a real smart idea," she muttered.

"You think?" Cate muttered back.

"But he hasn't killed us," Willow pointed out. "We're here. Someone will come and let us out sooner or later."

Cate grabbed an armload of clothes and piled them into a cushion to sit on. But before she could plop down on the pile, an acrid scent stopped her. Something burning on the stove in the kitchen? Barbecuing?

Scott was taking a leisurely moment to cook up a snack?

Then the meaning of the scent hit her.

◆ 20 ◆

Cate froze halfway to the floor. "Do you smell that?"

Willow was trying on the fox fur jacket. A gorgeous jacket, but several foxes too large for Willow. The cracked mirror had shifted and split her reflection, so one side of her face and body drooped in a psycho sag.

She eyed herself critically, as if she were contemplating a purchase. "I think wearing the skin of some dead animal is really gross, don't you?" She tossed the expensive jacket aside, then lifted her head, apparently getting a whiff of what Cate smelled. "What is that?"

"Smoke," Cate said.

"Smoke?"

"He's started a fire."

"A fire? What does he want with a fire?"

"I think he's figuring on burning down the house. With us in it."

"But that's crazy!" Willow cried. "Cheryl's inheriting the house. He wouldn't burn down his own house!"

"Why not? No doubt plenty of insurance. And getting rid of both of us saves him a hundred and fifty thou in blackmail money and does away with whatever we know. Permanently."

No wonder he hadn't wanted to shoot them! He was

planning to make the fire look like an accident, and bodies with bullets in them wouldn't fit that scenario. Bodies, according to Uncle Joe's book on arson, had an annoying tendency—at least annoying from the arsonist's point of view—not to burn up completely in a fire. Bodies trapped in a closet might still raise questions, but Scott no doubt had an alibi for himself already figured out. His car hadn't been in the driveway.

Willow took a three-step run at the door. She thudded into it. A shard of mirror crashed to the floor, but the door stood as solid as a rock wall.

The smell of smoke intensified. A wisp drifted up from the crack at the bottom of the door. Cate snatched a dress off the rack and jammed it against the crack. Smoke insidiously sifted higher, around the sides of the door, the wisps multiplying like unfriendly ghosts. Willow coughed. Cate grabbed a hanger to stuff fabric into the narrow cracks around the door.

Where was the smoke coming from? She couldn't hear any crackle of flames. Had he set the fire downstairs?

Then . . . foom! Whoosh! The explosion whammed the door.

A memory from long ago: a neighbor, impatient with a slow-burning debris fire, tossing gasoline into the lethargic flames. With exactly the same foom and whoosh of explosion. Plus a loss of eyebrows for the neighbor.

Now she could even smell the gasoline. No Boy Scout campfire methods for Scott. He was all speed and efficiency.

"He's trying to kill us!" Willow gasped, as if that truth only now fully penetrated. She pounded the door with her fists. More falling shards of mirror.

Now a close-up crackle of fire, then another whoosh. The canopy on the bed going up in flames? Smoke thickened in the claustrophobic closet.

Yet even as Cate stood there feeling both a cold chill and a hot sweat of fear, an irrelevant thought tromped around in her head. Uncle Joe had assured her: no excitement, no danger with the PI assignment. Oh? Then how come her life was on the line for the second time this day? Double jeopardy. Unfair! She was supposed to be just dipping her toe in the PI business, trying it out, thinking it over. Instead, here she was, up to her armpits in killers.

Although there was the fact Uncle Joe had also told her to stay out of Amelia's murder . . .

"We have to get out!" Willow cried. She twisted the doorknob frantically. Except, with something braced under the knob on the outside, the movement was useless as wheels spinning in mud. She whirled to stare at Cate. "How can you be so calm! We have to do something!"

Calm? Cate might not be ramming the walls in panic, but she was hardly calm. Thudding heartbeat, slick palms, one terrified eye staring back at her from what was left of the mirror. A thread of prayer looped endlessly in her mind. *Lord, help me to think! Help us to get out of here!*

A steady haze of smoke oozed around the door, Cate's barrier of fabric useless against the assault. Louder crackles from outside the door. Willow battered at the broken mirror, then whirled to look at Cate again.

"Wouldn't this be a good time to do the prayer thing? Throw out a Bible verse or something?"

Cate grabbed Willow's hand and squeezed her eyes shut. "Lord, I know you've already answered my prayers for help once today, and I thank you for that. But we're in a bad situation here, so could you do it again? Bring us some help, or show us a way out? Something! We ask it in the name of Jesus."

Willow clutched Cate's hand, eyes closed and breath held as if expecting to find herself miraculously whisked to a place of safety or drenched in a fire-extinguishing downpour. When nothing happened, she opened her eyes and looked at Cate accusingly.

"That's it? Can't you do something more?"

"I guess I could do cartwheels while I pray, but God doesn't need that. No theatrics necessary."

"Something is necessary. Because nothing's happening!"

Cate threaded her fingers together. Think. Think! Unlike most closets built in modern homes, the closet in this old house had been added to the interior of a bedroom that didn't have one. Maybe there was a weakness in a corner joint, a place where they could break out?

She yanked clothes aside, trampling them as she clambered to a corner. She pounded the walls on both sides of the corner, hammered until her fists ached, but no crack or weakness appeared. She finally stepped back and rubbed her throbbing hands.

Blue-gray smoke hazed the room in an acrid veil. Willow coughed again, and smoke burned Cate's throat until a spasm of coughing shook her too. She grabbed a sweater to cover her mouth and nose, but it was like trying to hold back Niagara with a sieve.

"Get down close to the floor. The smoke isn't as thick down low." Cate took her own advice and dropped to her knees on the floor.

Willow tumbled to her knees beside Cate, her shoulders hunched. But over her shoulder Cate spotted something. She dropped the sweater from her mouth and jumped to her feet. The fallen clothes and hangers revealed a different-looking area on the outside wall. An odd-looking square, like a frame.

Then Cate realized what it was. One of those strange, oddly placed windows visible from outside. And it hadn't been boarded up when the closet was built. It had simply been painted over!

She grabbed a high-heeled shoe and hammered. Glass shattered. Cate stuck her nose to the ragged opening and sucked in a sweet gulp of fresh air. Willow scrambled to her feet and elbowed Cate at the opening.

"We can jump!" Willow cried.

She grabbed another shoe and together they smashed more glass. A shard slashed Willow's hand, but she didn't stop hammering even as blood trickled down her arm. Frantically Cate pounded to smooth the bottom edge of the frame. They'd have to crawl out over it in order to jump.

Then Willow croaked, "Look."

Cate pushed her face through the opening. They were on the second floor of the house here. She'd never been around on this far side of the building. And what she saw was no easy drop to freedom. The lot sloped away steeply under this side of the house, falling away to a street she'd never driven on far below.

If they jumped, they'd hit the slope and keep going, right on down to the hard pavement.

So they could cower in the closet and burn. Barbecued redheads. Or jump and wind up like smashed tomatoes down there on the street.

Cate stood and stretched as far out the window as possible without losing the clamp of toes to the floor. Smoke poured from around a first-floor window in the tower section. A tongue of flame broke through and licked up the corner of the house. He'd set fires on the first floor too, probably even before he'd set the one outside their closet door. Up here, the fresh air from the broken window acted like a draft, and the fire beyond the door rose to a menacing roar. And the temperature in the closet climbed ominously.

Willow suddenly thrust Cate aside and leaned out the window herself. "Hey, isn't anybody out there? Fire! Fire!" She grabbed hold of the window frame and shook and pushed, like Samson bringing down the pillars of the Philistine temple.

The window frame, unlike Samson's pillars, did not collapse. Willow slumped backward, face buried in her hands. Cate stepped up and looked out . . . and down . . . again. *Lord, even if it looks like we'd be jumping to our deaths, should we try it?*

Prisoners tied sheets together to break out of jail. Classic escape system. Amelia, however, hadn't stored a helpful supply of sheets in the closet.

But she did have a boutique of scarves!

Cate grabbed a handful of them, but her moment of enthusiasm fizzled as she stared at them. They were made for decorative purposes, not strength. Knotted together, how many would it take? How long to tie them together? And how strong would the result be?

Is this the way to do it, Lord?

No answer in words from the Lord, but a crash from the bedroom galvanized Cate into yanking more scarves from hangers. Silky scarves, wooly scarves . . . Cate didn't try to choose. She just knelt and tied, one frantic knot after another.

Willow huddled on the floor, head down, hands clasped behind her neck. Cate kicked her in the hip.

"Help me!"

Willow looked up, eyes bleary and puffed from smoke. She rubbed them and blinked. "What are you doing?"

"I'm making a way out of here! Grab some scarves and help me tie them together."

Willow floundered to her knees. She stared at the clumps of tied-together scarves in Cate's hands. "It'll never work. We'd get halfway down and they'd come apart or break."

"Fine. You stay here and turn into a crispy critter." A gross but descriptive term Cate had read in Uncle Joe's book on arson. "I'm climbing down with this."

After a long scowl, Willow apparently decided she'd rather try even a questionable escape method than become a crispy critter. She grabbed scarves and started tying.

"Why not use dresses?" she asked. "They're longer."

"Okay! Anything. Just tie something to something, okay?"

They tied in frantic silence for several minutes. When the tangle of tied garments circled them several times, Cate paused for an inspection. Black cocktail dress knotted with wool plaid scarf. Orchid nightgown tied between black linen slacks and gold-threaded black shawl.

It looked like the work of two children who were going to be in big trouble for playing with Mommy's good clothes. Or the work of a couple of madwomen.

So what? They could create an artistic masterpiece some other time. Right now, all that mattered was would it hold together? Cate didn't know much about knots, and she suspected Willow knew even less.

"Here, grab one end and let's test how strong it is." Cate held out an end to Willow. They scrambled to opposite sides of the closet.

One knot instantly pulled loose, thumping Cate back against a wall. She retied it. They scrunched low and moved on down the line of knots, testing them. Two more came loose and had to be redone.

Whatever government agency oversaw safety in the workplace would never approve this as an escape system.

"What'll we tie it to in here?" Willow asked. "It has to be anchored somewhere."

"I don't know . . . look around!"

Which suddenly became more difficult because the room went black.

"What happened?" Willow cried.

"The fire must have burned through the electric wires somewhere."

A faint light from the starry sky glimmered through the now glass-less window. Flames from the first floor added a more ominous flicker of light.

"How long does this thing need to be?" Willow asked as she peered at it in the faint light. Before Cate could answer, Willow jumped to the window. "I hear something! I think it's a siren."

Cate lifted her head. Yes! A siren. Help was on the way! A second thought slammed into the moment of triumph.

Even if help was on the way, how long before firefighters found two women trapped upstairs in a closet? They wouldn't know anyone was in the house—

All they'd find would be two very crispy critters.

Willow apparently realized that too. She repeated her question. "How long does this thing have to be?"

"I don't know. But we're out of time. This will have to do. We've got to get out of here now."

With shaking hands Cate looped the makeshift rope around the bracket that supported the shelf of shoes, and tied one more knot. The most important knot of all. She flung the other end out the window. They watched it drop to within a couple feet of the ground.

"You go first," Cate said.

"Oh, great. You want me to be the test subject. Then if it comes apart, you'll know not to try it."

Cate ignored the grumble and boosted Willow to the window. She managed to scoot around and sit with her feet hanging out the window.

"Am I supposed to do a Tarzan yell when I do this?" Willow asked.

"Whatever."

Willow grabbed the makeshift rope dangling from the shelf bracket and swung out into empty space. Cate leaned out to watch Willow slither and slide down the makeshift rope. She was going to make it!

But a few feet from the end, a scarf ripped. Willow screamed as she slammed to the ground, torn end of the makeshift rope still clutched in her hands.

But she hit so close to the house that she didn't tumble and roll down the slope to the street below. She jumped up on the uneven ground and waved the tied scarves victoriously. "I made it! C'mon. Do it!"

Behind Cate the closet lit up as a tongue of flame ate through the wall. The escape rope was shorter now, farther for Cate to fall. Which made tumbling on down the slope more likely.

With no one to give her a boost, Cate shoved clothes and fur jacket under the window, then clambered atop them. She spotted where a section of the rope had almost torn in two, cut by a shard of glass clinging to the window frame. She climbed down, grabbed a high heel, hammered the spot smooth, and replaced the torn scarf with a long black skirt. Smoke poured out around her. Sirens wailed closer. But not close enough for rescue. The fire would engulf the closet first.

She scrambled back to the window, legs dangling over the

edge. Then hand over hand, feet dangling, body swaying, she skidded downward. Her hands hung up on the knots. Flames shooting from the first floor grabbed for her. Smoke billowed, enveloping her in an acrid cloud that choked her lungs. She hung on grimly. Only a few feet more . . .

A knot gave way. Cate felt it slipping loose. Going, going . . . gone! Falling. Dizziness swept through her. She'd hit and go right down that slope, right onto hard pavement . . .

Her falling body hit something softer than dirt. Something that crashed beneath her to the ground and tangled around her. Sirens were right out front now.

Hands shoved at Cate. "Get off me," Willow snapped.

Cate scrambled away, grabbing at dirt, weeds, anything to keep from tumbling down the slope, astonished as she realized what Willow had done. "You broke my fall! You stood right under me and caught me."

"You need to go on a diet." Willow stood and shook herself. "You practically squashed me."

Cate still felt amazed. Again, when the chips were down, Willow had come through. Under the force of Cate's fall, they could easily have both tumbled down the slope. But she'd put her own safety on the line for Cate.

Above them, flames shot out their escape window. More flames fully engulfed the tower now. Glass exploded as a lower-story window burst from heat and pressure.

"You rescued me twice today," Cate marveled.

"So I win my hero badge. You can pin it on later. Let's get out of here! The whole house may collapse."

They scrambled through weeds and blackberry vines toward the corner of the house. Heat radiated off the old boards. Flames and smoke poured through ragged holes. Sparks and ash fell around them. Cate slapped away a hot spot in her hair. A section of roof collapsed with a whoosh, and a galaxy of sparks filled the sky overhead.

Scott must have set half a dozen fires, maybe a dozen! Flames danced inside every window.

And where was Scott? Long gone. Figuring they were dead by now. Busy establishing his alibi, if he even needed one. Tallying his fire insurance payoff.

They finally rounded the corner of the house, into the unkempt grass of the backyard. Flames hadn't reached this back side of the house yet, but windows glowed like red devil eyes hungry for victims. A riot of sirens now. Yells. A tangle of boards littered the old rock garden below the stairs. Except there was no stairway now. Only a lone broken board dangled below the open doorway.

Firemen dragging a hose burst around the other corner of the house just as flames erupted through the third-floor doorway. Their sloping yellow hats gleamed in the flame light. They aimed a blast of water upward. One of them spotted Cate and Willow.

"Anyone inside?" he yelled over the roar of the fire.

"There was a man inside earlier," Cate yelled back. "I think he got away!"

"Get back, farther back!"

Cate and Willow, staying well back, circled around to the front of the house. Fire trucks, police cars, and an ambulance overflowed the driveway. Onlookers filled the sidewalk and street.

"Let's find a police officer," Cate said. "We have to tell them what happened."

"You know what Scott's going to tell them, don't you? He's going to blame *us*! Guess who they'll believe. I want to get out of here!"

Willow looked as if she might take off at a run. Cate grabbed her arm and dragged her over to a police car, where an officer was talking on his radio. Still holding on to Willow, Cate told the surprised officer a jumble of information about Scott Calhoun locking them in the closet and setting fire to the house. He didn't sound skeptical, but he asked the obvious question: why? Then Willow finally started talking too, about embezzlement, missing jewelry, murder, and blackmail.

Willow lifted her hand to motion at the now-missing upper level of the house, and the officer spotted the blood running down her arm.

"We can finish your statement later. Right now, you let the EMTs take care of that hand."

Cate jumped when a voice barked from the radio. "We've found somebody back here! Can't tell if the person's alive!"

The officer took off at a run around the flaming house.

"You go over and get that cut looked at!" Cate yelled and took off for the backyard herself, but Willow was right behind her.

Flames blazed up the back side of the house now. Firemen and officers together, working dangerously close to the burning house, were frantically throwing boards out of the tangled pile of the fallen stairway as if they were toothpicks. Two EMTs hovered over something under the pile. A minute later they loaded a motionless form on a stretcher. Cate saw a leg. A loafer. No socks. A moment later the back wall of the house collapsed, burying what was left of the stairway.

The EMTs ran with the body on the stretcher. And Cate knew it was a body, not a living man, as they passed by her. Twisted arm, oddly bent leg . . . and the grisly sight of the broken antler from that old metal statue sticking out the side of his head. The officer following was carrying something else he'd found in the pile. The gun.

Scott had planned the stairs as his escape route after setting the bedroom fire. But his weight, or perhaps the force of his dash down the stairs, had brought them down.

He'd used the word *ironic* earlier. Cate still didn't know what he'd meant then, but she saw the irony here. Scott had used the stairway to kill Amelia. Now the stairway had killed him.

Cate and Willow went back to the front of the house. "Let's get an EMT to look at your arm."

"I just want to get out of here."

"We'll go to my house. You can stay there tonight. We'll go to the police again tomorrow morning. You have to tell them about Coop too."

But they couldn't leave in the car, Cate realized when she reached the street. Fire trucks and police vehicles with lights flashing still surrounded the car.

"We'll have to wait—"

Willow wasn't waiting. She broke away from Cate and ran for Coop's bike. She fumbled with the footrest and threw a leg over the big machine. A moment later it roared to life, and Willow proved she did indeed know how to handle the bike as it wove through the vehicles. Coop's helmet swung wildly from the handlebars.

Cate couldn't see her and the bike once they were out on the street, but she heard the departing roar of its engine even over the roar of the flames behind her. The sound echoed with an odd finality.

Cate just stood there, dismay flooding through her. Where was Willow going, roaring off into the night? A suspicion washed through her. Coop.

And Cate? Déjà vu. Stranded again.

◆ 21 ◆

Cate looked at her watch. She couldn't do this again. She just couldn't.

But she took another look at her trapped car, felt the aching muscles in every part of her body, picked out a guy with a cell phone clipped to his belt, and asked if she could borrow the phone. He took one look at her bedraggled appearance and handed it over. She glanced at her watch again, groaned when she saw the time, but punched in the numbers.

A sleepy, "Hello?"

"Hi. It's, uh, me. Cate. Do you suppose you could come get me again?"

Mitch let out a big sigh, but he asked for no explanation, just directions.

She was waiting halfway down the street when he stepped out of the SUV a few minutes later. He stared at what was left of the house for a moment, but then, looking for her, his gaze roamed vehicles and people. She stepped out of the lingering crowd. "I'm, uh, sorry to bother you again."

"I wasn't doing anything except sleeping. Did you have anything to do with this?" He jerked his head toward the house. Firefighters had tamed the blaze from a roaring inferno to occasional flares, but only the garage, a ragged section of the kitchen side of the house, and the fireplace and gaunt chimney remained standing.

"You mean, did I start it?"

"The thought occurred to me."

"No, I did not start it. Someone tried to kill me. And Willow."

He nodded as if that didn't surprise him. "The same guy as before?"

"No, this was a different one."

"What do you do, give out numbers so they can get in line?"

"I'm thinking about it."

"Where's Willow?"

"Good question."

Cate and Mitch were heading back to the SUV when a car cautiously crept around the corner. A silver BMW. The driver started to drive on by them, then spotted Cate and stopped short.

Cheryl jumped out of the car. "Why are *you* here?" she demanded. "Where's Scott?"

"You'd better talk to the police."

She ran up to Cate and grabbed the neck opening of the sweatshirt with both hands. Her face twisted in panic. "Something's happened to Scott! He was supposed to meet me after—" She broke off without saying after what. She shook Cate with hysterical strength. "What have you done to Scott?"

An interesting take on the situation, considering the circumstances. And no questions about Willow or the burning house.

Mitch stepped up and broke Cheryl's grip. "Talk to the officers."

Cheryl suddenly went from edge-of-hysterical to limp as she stared at what was left of the house. "I told him this was a bad idea. I told him, I told him!" Then she fisted her hands and glared at Cate. "So, what do you think of the house you stole from us now?"

"I didn't steal your house," Cate said, bewildered by the venom in Cheryl's peculiar question. "Scott burned it down."

"You don't even know, do you?"

The same puzzling words Scott had used. Cate shook her head.

Mitch took Cheryl by the arm. "C'mon. I'll take you to talk to an officer."

Cheryl suddenly thought better of being here and resisted with tiger ferocity, but Mitch marched her up to an officer and left her.

The eastern horizon was paling by the time Mitch parked the SUV in front of Uncle Joe's house. In astonishment, Cate spotted the big bike in the driveway. The front door flew open. "I heard you drive up—"

Rebecca stopped short when she saw that Cate wasn't alone. Willow's head appeared behind Rebecca.

"What are you doing here?" Cate demanded.

"You said I could stay here tonight. I was just going to leave on the bike . . . but then I didn't."

"Willow has been telling me what happened, but she didn't mention Mitch," Rebecca said.

"He came to rescue me." Again.

Rather than demanding instant details, ever-practical Rebecca said, "Sounds to me as if Mitch deserves breakfast." She stood back from the door. "But ssshh, so we won't wake Joe."

"He's home?"

Rebecca rolled her eyes. "It was either bring him home or have him out there on the street thumbing for a ride."

Cate headed for the bathroom attached to her room. Rebecca showed Mitch to the other bathroom. By the time she got back to the kitchen, both Mitch and Uncle Joe were sitting at the table getting ready to dig into the pancakes Willow was piling on their plates. Cate noted that Willow's cut hand was already neatly bandaged.

"Joe decided he wanted breakfast at dawn," Rebecca said by way of explanation for Uncle Joe's presence.

"Which you sure can't get at that place," he grumbled.

Over breakfast, Cate and Willow told the full story of Kidnapping by Coop and Fire by Scott. Rebecca made occasional murmurs of dismay, but Uncle Joe just sat there listening.

"So you not only located Willow, you also solved the mystery of Amelia's death."

"Blundered into it," Cate admitted.

Uncle Joe stabbed at a pancake. "And now you've broken my record."

"Your record?"

"I've never had more than one attempt on my life in a single day." Uncle Joe sounded undecided whether to chastise or commend her. "How do you feel about being a private investigator now?"

"The way things have been going, I'm not sure how long I'd survive."

Uncle Joe nodded. "I'll expect a complete report on the Amelia Robinson case for the files."

"Yes, sir."

◆ ◆ ◆

Cate and Willow went to the police station and filled in details about Scott and the fire. Willow, though she looked uncomfortable doing it, told them about Coop, the dairy farmer's fall, and her escape from him after Cate's kidnapping. As soon as they got back to the house, Willow said she was leaving. Cate brought up arguments. The police might need to talk to her again. She had no clothes or other belongings. She had no title to the bike.

"I'll manage," Willow said stubbornly. "I've got my wallet and my driver's license and a little money."

Cate filled a sack with clothes from her own closet, and they stuffed it in a saddlebag on the bike. Rebecca loaned her some more money. Although Cate suspected she'd better consider it a gift.

Willow buckled Coop's flashy helmet on her head. As she sat there astride the bike, she said, "Tell Beverly I'm really sorry about her ring."

"Where had you hidden it?"

"In a little metal box in the medicine cabinet in my bathroom. I'll call you when I get . . . somewhere."

Yeah, sure you will. But all Cate said was, "I'll look forward to hearing from you."

"And maybe sometime, when you think of it, you could do the prayer thing for me?"

Cate nodded. She waved as Willow zoomed off, red hair flying out from under the helmet. God worked in mysterious ways. Maybe he was working on Willow.

◆◆◆

Cate saw Mitch every day or two. They hiked along the river. They helped with a Feed the Hungry rally. They went to church services on Sunday. They barbecued ribs in the backyard. They drove by Amelia's house once. It was surrounded by yellow crime scene tape and a lingering odor of watersoaked, burned debris. The police interviewed her twice more. She read more of Uncle Joe's books on crime. Remembering her regret over things undone in her life, she and Mitch went to a Chinese restaurant that served squid. Not bad! She painted her toenails blue and surveyed the results. Like ten little unseeing eyes staring up from her feet.

Not everything undone in life needed to be done.

She wrote up a report on her investigation into Amelia Robinson's death, with full information about Scott Calhoun's method and motive for murder, for the files.

She could tie up most of the loose ends in the case. Newspaper reports said Cheryl was facing various serious charges. Other details came from Doris McClelland. Texie had returned to her home. The key, which was now buried in the ashes of a house that no longer existed, had belonged to Hannah. Krystal was suing someone over her investment loss, although Doris wasn't sure who. Doris herself, although the news was not relevant to the case, had just found a lovely purple lace blouse at Goodwill. One loose end couldn't be tied up. Radford Longstreet, when Cate inquired at the address Mitch had found for him, had moved out, no forwarding address. Had that engagement ring ever existed? She'd never know.

Uncle Joe read the report one evening. "Very thorough," he commented. "Although I believe I did tell you not to get involved."

"Yes, you did." She waited, but Uncle Joe simply closed the file. He didn't bring up the subject of further assignments.

With considerable reluctance, Uncle Joe finally admitted he needed more physical therapy than he could get at home, and returned to the rehabilitation center. Cate started job hunting again. She read local newspaper ads and made phone calls. She searched online and sent emails.

Then she received two phone calls. The first came before she was even out of bed one morning. She answered with a groggy hello.

"Hi, Cate, it's me, Willow!"

"Well, it's, uh, good to hear from you." Cate blinked at the clock.

"Did I wake you up? I keep forgetting. There's all that time difference between here and there!"

"Where's 'here'?"

"Grandma's, of course. In Florida! Though I won't be here long. I've got a job! I just wanted Rebecca to know I'll be sending her the money I borrowed as soon as I get my first paycheck."

"A job," Cate repeated.

"It's with these people who're doing a research project in the Okefenokee Swamp! Three months at least. I met them when I went through Georgia on my way down here."

"But don't you have to . . . I don't know . . . have a degree or something to be on a research team?"

"I'm going to be their cook! Don't you just love that name? Okefenokee, Okefenokee," Willow bubbled the string of syllables. Cate winced. Bubbles hurt her head so early in the morning.

"What about Coop?"

"Coop is a monument to all the mistakes in my life." Willow had sobered now. No bubbles. "Mistakes I've learned enough not to repeat."

"I'm doing the prayer thing for you," Cate said.

"Keep up the good work! I'll call you again. And give Octavia a big hug for me too, okay?"

◆◆◆

The next call came that afternoon. Cate stiffened when she heard the name. Roger Ledbetter, Amelia's lawyer. "You're working for Cheryl now?" she asked warily.

"No. I'm not the kind of lawyer Mrs. Calhoun needs at the moment," he said in that smooth lawyer way that warned her that even if Cheryl wasn't his client, he wasn't about to supply confidential information. "This call is about you and the cat. Octavia, I believe it is."

Octavia was at that moment curled around Cate's neck. Cate gave her fluffy tail a stroke. "Octavia is fine, thank you. Have you decided on a price for her?"

"The probating of Amelia's will won't be complete for some time yet, and recent events add new complications. But I thought I should talk to you now. As you know, I am executor of the will. And the will makes specific provisions for Octavia."

He explained that Amelia's will gave him the task of finding a caring, responsible owner for the cat. In doing this, he had considered what Cate had done in providing a home for Octavia when the cat's welfare was threatened, and how she'd offered to purchase the cat. Plus there were the satisfactory results of an investigation into her character and personal life.

The word *investigation* clicked in Cate's head. "You mean *you* sent that guy around asking the neighbors nosy questions about me?"

"I believe that was part of the private investigator's procedure, yes," the lawyer agreed without apology. "So I've concluded that you do meet Amelia's qualifications for ownership of her beloved companion. I'll issue a transfer of ownership to you."

"I don't have to post bond? Furnish fingerprints? Pass a written exam?" Okay, snide, she admitted. But this was the guy who had someone poking into her trash.

"The will didn't make those stipulations." He sounded as

if he took her facetious questions seriously, although he did add, his tone still businesslike, "Although you might have to sing something from that *Cats* musical."

"Okay. I'll start practicing."

Octavia now decided the back of Cate's ear needed a good tongue washing. Ah, the joys of cat ownership.

"There is an additional provision in the will. It says that whoever qualifies for ownership of the cat also, in order to provide a suitable environment for her, acquires the house, along with—"

"The house? You're saying the *house* comes with Octavia?"

"That's what the will specifies, yes. Along with funds for home upkeep, cat food, et cetera."

Now Cate understood Cheryl and Scott Calhoun's desperation to get Octavia back. They apparently hadn't known at first what the will said about Octavia. When they found out, they were frantic to get her back so they could also get ownership of the house. Which also explained Scott's comment about the ironic situation with her, the house, and the cat. And why he was quite pleased to include her in his murderous plans for Willow and burning the house.

"There are some provisions, but nothing you'll find onerous, I believe." While Cate was still working on *onerous*, the lawyer added, "Of course, there is the complication with the house itself."

"Toast."

Small silence as he apparently digested the word. "Well, yes, an apt description. Toast. But there is adequate insurance, and we can work together on the rebuilding. Something that will be suitable for Octavia. And you, of course," he added, as if her wants were a minor afterthought. "I'll be in touch to discuss this."

"A house," Cate said to Octavia after the phone call ended. "You and me, we'll have a house."

Mrrow.

◆▶◆

Cate went back to job hunting, but it was a halfhearted effort. Because she knew now what she wanted to do with her life. She went to Uncle Joe in the rehabilitation center. He'd just returned to his room from a physical therapy session, and he was not in a good mood.

"They give you a new hip, and then the first thing they do is try to wear it out," he grumbled.

"Uncle Joe, I want to be a private investigator. Full-time. Permanently."

Uncle Joe inspected her thoughtfully. "You can't get a PI license until you have, I think the requirement now is 1,500 hours of investigative experience working under a licensed private investigator, and also meet various other requirements. Until then, you need an interim license."

"I want to do that. Whatever it takes."

"I was beginning to think you were never going to ask."

She blinked. "You were waiting?"

"I figured it was a decision you had to make on your own."

"What do I do now?"

"Look at the files in my desk drawer. We'll talk about your next assignment."

"But you're retiring—"

He finally smiled. And gave her a wink. "That's just what Rebecca thinks. Welcome aboard."

◆▶◆

Cate and Mitch drove to the burned house that evening. She'd told him about the lawyer's call concerning the house and Octavia. She hadn't yet told him about her conversation with Uncle Joe. The yellow crime scene tape was gone, but the scent of burned wood and soggy ashes remained. The chimney stood like a lonely sentinel in the midst of the destruction. Would a proper feng shui arrangement have avoided this? Cate doubted it. Not unless Scott Calhoun had stumbled over a properly placed chair and hit his head on the mantel before he set the house on fire.

This visit to the house had a purpose, although Cate had little hope of success. They clambered through the debris to where two walls of Willow's bedroom remained. And yes . . . a corner of a warped medicine cabinet clung to one wall. It wouldn't open, but Mitch yanked it free and smashed it with a stomp of foot. Inside, a metal box, misshapen with heat. Mitch had to stomp it too, to get it open.

Inside, the contents were unidentifiable crumbles. But within the crumbles . . . a ring! A wedding band, two rows of diamonds, four stones in each row. Still bravely glittering.

They took the ring to Beverly that same evening. Cate offered Willow's apologies, which Beverly chose to believe meant Willow had taken the ring accidentally, and Cate didn't try to argue her out of the belief. "I do miss that girl's meat loaf" was Beverly's final declaration.

Mitch took Cate home. At the door she turned to him. "There's something I guess I should tell you. I'm going to start working full-time for Uncle Joe. I want to be a private investigator. A real one."

"I thought you might."

"But you don't approve?"

"Wait here. I have something for you." He ran back to the

SUV, dug in the glove compartment, and returned with an oblong box and handed it to her.

She opened the box. A pen resting on white velvet lay inside. "That's nice, Mitch. Really nice." She was pleased but puzzled. It was a lovely blue pen, but she had a pen. Everybody had pens.

Mitch picked it out of the box. "It's a special pen. With video and audio. I thought it might come in handy."

A spy pen! "How does it work?"

"Beats me. But we'll figure it out." He touched her cheek. "I admit it. I don't necessarily approve of the whole PI thing. But I can live with it."

Cate stretched up and kissed him. "Just what every PI needs."

"The video pen?"

"I was thinking of a guy always ready to gallop to the rescue."

"Anytime."

Lorena McCourtney is the award-winning author of dozens of novels, including *Invisible* (which won the Daphne du Maurier Award from Romance Writers of America), *In Plain Sight*, *On the Run*, and *Stranded*. She resides in Grants Pass, Oregon.

Don't Miss the
Ivy Malone Series
in Ebook

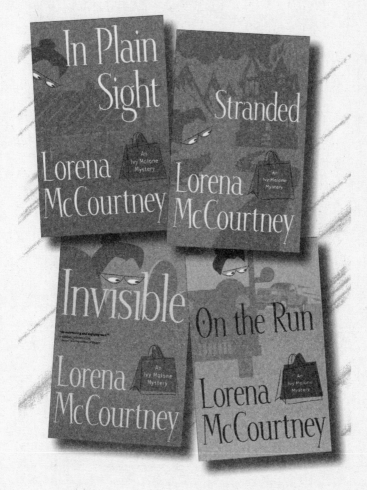

Available Wherever Ebooks Are Sold

Revell

a division of Baker Publishing Group

www.RevellBooks.com